To Linda
with best wishes
31st July 1997

Peter.

A
Monster
Unto Many

A
Monster
Unto Many

Peter Giles

FREDERICK MULLER LIMITED
LONDON

First published in Great Britain 1980 by
Frederick Muller Limited, London, NW2 6LE

Copyright © 1980 by Peter Giles

British Library Cataloguing in Publication Data

Giles, Peter
 A monster unto many.
 I. Title
 823'.9'1F   PR6057.I53/
 ISBN 0-584-31094-3

Typeset By Computacomp (UK) Ltd, Fort William, Scotland
Printed in Great Britain by Biddles Ltd, Guildford, Surrey

To F.B.
without whom, nothing worthwhile.

To E.
without whom, chaos.

To one other,
without whom.

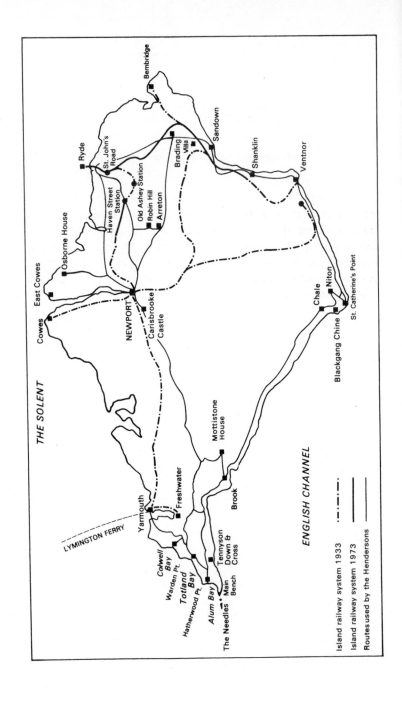

DISAVOWAL

All the characters in this book are fictitious characters. If by some accident they bear names already in use or happen to follow professions that living people follow, or live in houses like real existing houses, or play or work very much as actual persons do, that is so because fiction cannot but recall realities if it is to deal with life.

H. G. Wells,
'Brynhild',
1937.

[from 'How Dear are Thy Counsels'
– Dr. William Crotch]

LOOK WELL, LOOK WELL IF THERE BE AN – Y WAY OF

WICK– ED–NESS AN – Y WAY OF WICK-ED-NESS IN ME

'When I was a child, I spake as a child, I understood as a child, I thought as a child: but when I became a man, I put away childish things.
For now we see through a glass, darkly; but then face to face: now I know in part; but then shall I know even as also I am known.'

'O where shall wisdom be found, and where is the place of understanding? Man knoweth not the price thereof, neither is it found in the land of the living. The depth saith it is not in me, and the sea saith it is not in me.'

'Glorious and powerful God, we understand Thy dwelling is on high, above the starry sky. Thou dwellst not in stone temples made with hand, but in the flesh hearts of the sons of men, to dwell is Thy delight, near hand, though out of sight.'

'I know where I'm going, and I know who's going with me.'

The pier is only a short one. The same tides have crept up the heavy timbers and down again for one hundred years. The same salt sea has eaten and corroded the hard wood and metal to suffer a sea change.

The lift of the tide causes, apparently, the movement of seaweed. It floats, seemingly dead, suspended on the salt mirror. It would seem always to have floated languidly on the surface, up and down with the ocean. But it hasn't. Helped by the swell, it has swum up from the depth, a ganglion of green arteries rising purposefully, its many eyes bulbous and cold, its cancer choosing a few luckless stones so far.

For though we shall all be changed, not all will wait for the last trumpet. Some emerge considerably earlier than at Tuba Mirabilis.

BEFORE

The sun was tinted with the red dust screen of the industrial Midlands as Derek entered the library. It was like a pompous mausoleum, in its ordure-coloured stone and dulled umber brick.

The thick-legged owlish librarianette seemed purposely slow. Derek was sorry it wasn't the girl he fancied.

Time ticked on, crowded by books and polished library sound. The queue shuffled forward slowly. He found that wherever he stood, the rich spires of the sandstone cathedral would not fit equally into the neo-classical library windows after all. But this whispered reverence would fit the cathedral.

At last, the librarianette produced his reserved volume on the Isle of Wight. Derek watched as she stamped it dismissively. It didn't look the lively photo-filled reference book he'd hoped for, but he hadn't courage enough to refuse it. Barbara had chosen the Isle of Wight, and this was the only book available at present. It would have to do. It was heavy and warm, as if from a shelf by a radiator, or fresh from a hot hand not attached to the cold librarianette.

Published in 1933, the first smudged date on the cluttered sheet could have been May of the same year. The grey numbers blurred and ran over, almost onto the hairy end paper. The last stamping was illegible. He carried his parcel of 1933 out into the freckled 1973 Midland sun.

The cathedral's sensuous body beckoned as he came back into the Precincts, and her many eyes followed him from the West Front. Resisting her temptation, he turned left up to Vicars' Close. All but two eyes lost interest as the echo of the low brick tunnel swallowed him.

Highways, Bridlepaths and Resorts of Wight lay incongruously on the suave modern coffee table. Derek was aware of a strange ascetic smell. Had the cat peed in the corner again?

The book possessed a pathos, an innocence in its 1933 photographs and the coy ink sketches. It attracted him. He unfolded the battered map in the back end-paper. His eyes were drawn to West Wight, the left point of the diamond land.

Then his gaze travelled across to Osborne. Queen Victoria's grey Osborne. He recalled that large purple tome kept in the book-case in his unlamented parents' holy front room. Something about seventy momentous years, filled with monochromatic significance, stiffly posed Royals and statesmen.

There was always that one photograph. A laden ship, heavy with death and black smoke, leaving East Cowes with a cold empress, iced permanently inside flags and oak. Muffled guns, barked orders. Salutes as stiff as her reign. The lowering sky, the sepia gloom. He had returned to the picture endlessly, and the heavy volume had borne testimony to it, falling open at the page automatically.

Wight. The schizoid isle. The land of holidays and sepia past. Derek had not the slightest wish ever to go there, but Barbara had. They would therefore go. It was important this year.

Because Henderson life was so complicated, holidays always seemed distantly unreal. The world could have altered by August. Yet other people were ironing the tent in February. Husbands belonging to Barbara's neat friends seemed to lead a machine-like life, but they did organize superb holidays. Derek always left booking grievously late, if he did it at all.

'No panic yet,' he'd smile. 'No panic.' But there always was in the end.

Barbara hated the heated discussions on the subject. Indecision maddened her. He had therefore moved precipitously this year, to please her. He would arrange it faultlessly, then she would not believe that rumour.

So, not due at college today, he had revisited the public library. Perhaps the Isle of Wight book had arrived at last from Timbuctoo, or wherever it was loaned from. It had, but from Shepherds Bush Borough library, London. Nearer, but just as exotic these days, Derek thought, though initially the book looked dull and cold.

Yet, even now it still felt oddly warm, as if just put down by someone with a fever. The past stared up from coarsely screened photographs of nearly empty roads. There was the usual figure accusing the camera, directly confronting the lens with a challenge, leaving the rest of life blurred and caught forever in some marvellous position. But in one street it was reversed: everything clear except one rushing man. A panicking pickpocket, maybe?

The tall black cars were so few that each hinted significance. Though hazed by dots, the photographs seemed strangely sharp, stark, three-dimensional: Derek was drawn right into their world, frozen since the shutter clicked.

That boy standing alone on a pier, staring hypnotically out of 1933. Derek felt the power of confrontation. It was move or be sealed behind the half-tone screen of grey. Shifting his eyes at last, Derek turned the page quickly. The pointing shadows of the cathedral spires, reflected through the window, distorted over the new rosebud on the sill, hit the floor and fingered his deckled pages. 'Person', the fat ginger Henderson cat, still regarded him plumply with one eye from his nest in the other armchair.

Minutes later, before Evensong, Rupson-Fortson, the dusty-fronted travel agents in Deacon Street, supplied a modern guide to accommodation in the Isle of Wight.

Derek seldom made mistakes, yet today he'd made several in a simple anthem by Dr William Crotch. It was really odd. Not especially difficult, the piece was so ordinary it had not been even rehearsed. Yet right from the opening bars the four-square harmony possessed an added dimension, even an extra voice part: there seemed to be two treble lines. The high one was apparently solo. But nobody was singing it.

They came to 'Look well, look well, and see if there be any way of wickedness, any way of wickedness in me.' The phrase always had a strange translucent chromaticism, sliding through several keys in several bars, but this time the repeated words were disturbing. This time he was aware of a nakedness inside him, an unsuspected vulnerability, and something else.

Dr Andrew Denning coupled the reeds and opened the swell box while slowly adding weight to the pedal organ. There was a corresponding shudder from carved, candled stalls and quire canopies as the sixteen-foot open wood tone rumbled through.

The rich crescendo, crowned with voices like cream on rich cake, took them all to a climax on the phrase 'look well'. During this, something made Derek look up.

A small boy was sneering at him through the tomb of Bishop de Mandeville near the High Altar. Even from that distance, Derek knew it was he who was being watched, he who was the object of those eyes. Wondering why was enough to make him lose his place, and several chords held tenor notes not in Crotch's score. Derek sensed Dr Denning's ire emanating from the high organ loft.

The senior chorister completed Derek's discomfiture by half turning as the anthem's final echo winged into the vault. Sometimes Derek hated Baker's sheer superiority in all things.

Derek hurried back to Vicars' Close. He was glad to miss the probable liquid post-mortem on the anthem, led by Saville, senior counter tenor, in the Angel Croft Bar.

Derek entered, through the low tunnel, into the little quadrangle of medieval half-timbered houses which had caused many an automatic American hand to pass to an automatic Japanese camera. He noticed for the first time how the grass, surrounded by the small houses, itself embraced a cartoon isle of irregular paving slabs. In the centre of it grew a single flowering tree.

The little black front door firmly shut in the faces of the Close, the world of Wight lay ancient as before on the coffee table. Beside it, Barbara had placed, tactfully, a pencil and paper, Tio Pepe and glass, to which Derek now added the accommodation guide.

There were endless and varied hotels in Freshwater and Totland alone. Reaching for his sherry, his fingers flipped 'Highways' accidentally, nearly causing catastrophe. The orange spotted back flyleaf was revealed for the first time. That odd tang was stronger and it certainly came from the book.

But there was writing in pencil. Faded, yet clear enough, were somebody's holiday notes. His attention was seized by the words 'Arr. Totland' at the top. Under it lay a detailed plan of a week dated from Sunday 30th July based on West Wight. Here and there a planned excursion had been altered, and 'too tiring for lad' was inserted on one heavy day.

Sunday 30th July — Totland Bay Hotel
arr. Totland via Yarmouth (Freshwater Station)
lunch.
Explore Totland Bay and pier.

Monday 31st
Early at Totland Beach
The Needles and Alum Bay A.M. (Chair Lift!)
Tennyson Down — no
Blackgang Chine P.M (Whitwell Sta.) Totland in evening

Tuesday 1st August.
Haven Street Station
Arreton Manor (Merstone Sta.) Totland in evening.

Wednesday 2nd.
Colwell Bay early
Osborne House (Whippingham Sta.)
Ryde late afternoon (Ryde Esplanade Sta.)

Thursday 3rd
Carisbrooke Castle (Carisbrooke Sta.)
Newport Carnival (Newport Sta.)
Tennyson Down and Cliff Walk (too tiring for lad) Evening?

Friday 4th.
Robin Hill Park
Brading Roman Villa (Brading Sta.) Yarmouth Castle? too much
Totland Bay in evening.

Saturday 5th
Sandown (Sandown Sta.)
Totland Beach later.

Sunday — Church?
Totland for swim
Yarmouth town (explore) Freshwater Sta. Yarmouth Sta.
depart 1.15 ferry.

5

Next to almost every place visited was written the nearest station. Ironically, they had stayed in Totland Bay, one of the few places not actually on the railway. Freshwater station looked a bus ride away.

The handbook for 1973. Here was a different story. The planning wizards had closed all but a short length on the east coast, and this was served by electric trains. Ironically, as British Rail was trying to pull out of the island altogether, a private company had begun to run steam trains based on the old Haven Street Station, now left isolated with a mile or two of track.

Derek made a mental note to take James, and thought abruptly of a childhood ride in the old corridorless green coaches. Browned advertisments for an Edwardian Harrods looked forever behind glass above the smoky seats.

But he'd never been to the Isle of Wight. Still, he supposed all branch line coaches were similar; some of his boyhood was spent near the Canterbury-Folkestone line, now also a ghost, the track a green lane through the valley. A hidden path to a destiny by the sea.

What if they not only stayed at Totland Bay Hotel, but actually used the itinerary? The Henderson holiday settled in one stroke? The idea excited him. Follow a path planned, lived out, by who? Each documented day would echo somebody else's experience.

It was like cathedral music: knowing that each day was part of an enormous scheme lived out through long centuries. It moved him that what he sang now had been sung here in these stalls by men and boys perhaps since first written.

It moved him especially on Martyrdom Day, when lined before the shrine fragments, the Foundation sang the plainchant 'De Profundis' for St. Linc, murdered by the Normans in his cell on Moat Lake Island.

But Derek actually dreaded singing *When David Heard that Absalom Was Slain* when they commemorated Michael Este, its composer and Cathedral Organist well before the Civil War. Derek's tears sprang up so easily. The piece built slowly with poignant word-painting, until Saville's liquid voice took the leap of a fourth at the phrase 'He went up to his chamber and wept'. It always began the magic.

This anthem always achieved what the other lay vicars called

Derek's wet dream face. He could not help himself: the music, the words, were all a tunnel into other people. The knowing smirks from Cantoris embarrassed him, but only afterwards. Luckily his singing did not blur as did his glasses, eyes and the centuries behind them.

So here in this evocative book was escape into more time already lived. Barbara and James need never know. He suddenly realized why he never planned holidays in time: he had to act on the spur of the moment. A ten-month countdown was just impossible.

Barbara would certainly not sympathize with his plan. She was not a spontaneous person, but thought she was. Thus she would reject any secondhand itinerary. But not if she didn't know.

Derek lifted the telephone.

'We three are booked in to a splendid hotel overlooking the sea,' Derek said happily as Barbara entered the low-beamed room. 'Then here's a reward, from Jamie and me,' she smiled, thrusting an irregular brown paper parcel into his hands. 'Be careful opening it.'

It was a spouted, white onion-shaped pot. Inserted in the top was a large cork pierced by an angled glass tube. On the side, in large Victorian lettering, was 'Dr Nelson's Improved Inhaler', and directions for use.

Derek was ecstatic. The cure for his bloody catarrh throats. Barbara certainly didn't seem off him now. Knowing he was planning the holiday had banished the rumour. Perhaps he was safe. 'Saw it in Lincoln's, only £1 because of Friars' Balsam caked inside,' she said, removing the cork, 'but caustic soda should shift that, and hey presto!'

Derek examined it lovingly, and watched Barbara as she began to dust the sideboard. The curve of those calves still excited him, as did the delicate but almost sturdy feet. The buttocks were perhaps too big now, but the thighs still held promise. She still retained a firm flat width across the stomach, hip to hip, something he always needed in a woman. He'd hated his mother's figure, and still remembered it too clearly.

Barbara had a small head, fine bone structure, and her brown hair flicked across her half-open mouth with each movement of the duster. He loved her lips, for all the world like ...

Derek found himself admiring her full but still perky breasts moving in restricted orbit under the blouse. Yes, she was sexually attractive. And so was Hazel. Dr Nelson's Improved Inhaler was oddly voluptuous too. He would use it daily, a heavy breathing kit. He bore it to the kitchen for cleaning. Barbara went to the window.

'Oh no, Derek, the bud has opened but it's dead already. Why? It was so lovely.'

'Nipped in the bud,' came Derek's voice, uninterested, from the kitchen. 'Must've been dying as it opened.'

Barbara grieved over dead young things. For this was like a child dying, and she thought of her poor wet, shrivelled embryo eleven years ago last month. She still mourned that lost boy. 'Coincidence, that library book coming from Shepherds Bush,' she said.

But Derek didn't hear her.

Derek and Barbara were almost the opposite to each other in their basic outlook on life. The resulting cross was more a kiss than a crucifix. Barbara's no-nonsense mathematical brain had been a real relief to him when faced with income-tax forms. She was secretly proud of his over-imaginative mind; and her life with Derek had been an exciting one in many ways, part of the world of the arts, though securely based in a medieval cathedral close.

The world in which she had been raised was conventional: a Tudorbethan 'semi' off the Watford Bypass. A father and mother neat and stereotyped as the puppets in 'Camberwick Green': he a minor accountant and she working in an undistinguished office behind Harrods. In 1930, just before a nice wedding, she had left for ever, without regret, ready to make a warm home and Ovaltine for Ovaltineys.

Derek's childhood had been devoid of the cosy quality of Barbara's. His parents, middle-aged when he was born in 1938, had always inhabited a sober world of their own. Derek could still recall intercepting their strange glances, and hating their whispering.

Their world, he was sure, had not been disturbed unduly by his removal to Kent during the Blitz. So their sudden deaths within a few months of each other had not been the shock expected for an only child of ten.

Derek had been with his grandmother when his mother had finally succumbed to her cancer, and there again when his father keeled onto the carpet, his tea reaching the ceiling. Derek watched him rushed to Canterbury Hospital, never to return. It therefore seemed appropriate that Derek should live with his grandmother. In any case, there was hardly anyone else.

He was not sorry to leave number twenty-two, Poplar Grove, Shepherds Bush. It had been a strange house for its time. Apart from the hand-coloured wedding photographs of his parents in the front room, there were no family photographs anywhere; no albums of clipped-in snapshots.

Derek's father, a tall forbidding man, had kept a newsagent's in the Uxbridge Road near the Metropolitan Underground Station. When there, Derek would experience the regular rumble and roar of hidden red dragons at unchanging intervals. How keen he was to spend a day with someone and sandwiches, exploring the London Underground system. It never happened.

The terraced Victorian house had always felt tidied up after something. The dark-smelling hallway had always seemed ready to lead him somewhere exciting, a potential tunnel of discovery, though never of love. But it led only to cold rooms.

All heat and light seemed banished from the house, and his parents appeared almost disappointed in him, even when, aged ten, he'd sung his first solo in St. Luke's choir. His father arrived late, and sat at the back amongst old hymn books and brooms. Mother never attended, ever, though he sometimes sensed that both had once been active members.

About this, as about so much, there was a roomful of heavy silence. Almost a resentment. He wasn't a wanted child; he'd decided this in adult retrospection. Derek always regretted they'd never lived to see him enter Trinity College of Music. That would have shown them.

When his aged grandmother had died, kindly cousin Jean had taken him in just in time for his traumatic adolescence. Southwood, Middlesex, still felt like home, though Jean and Ray had moved. Three distinctly different houses, all childless except for himself; two years' National Service, then digs as a student in Notting Hill Gate, beginning the break from Southwood's obstinate charisma. All this time, contact had been discouraged with rumoured Hendersons scattered round the country.

Swallowfield Cathedral Choir was advertising for a tenor just when Derek obtained his Fellowship. Accommodation was offered. Just a year or two, he'd thought privately, then St. George's Chapel, Windsor.

Vacated positively by the death of an inevitable old lady, a pleasant house in Vicars' Close, Swallowfield Precincts, was being quietly retained for his mother by the Chapter Clerk. When Derek was given tenancy by the Dean and Chapter, the rent was mysteriously higher, and the Chapter Clerk never spoke to Derek afterwards unless he had to.

So Barbara and Derek hurriedly married. For financial reasons Barbara remained Assistant Bursar at Trinity for a further term. Her weekends in the Midlands caused many rich rumours round the unpermissive Precincts, as Derek had purposely not broadcast the marriage. Surreptitious curtains moved slightly for months.

Part-time teaching at Wellingham School of Music came his way almost immediately via the abrupt departure of the cathedral assistant organist under a cloud lined with little boys. Outside singing engagements built up quickly. But it was Swallowfield itself which held him. It quickly became magic, usurping Southwood at last and banishing Windsor for good.

Derek would gaze from the back-landing window at the noble multi-sculptured west front of the red sandstone cathedral, the stiff figures of saints and kings in their individual niches. Each one to him represented one of the Precincts community: all of them had their place in God the Father.

It was amusing to identify the Dean with the Christ in Glory over the main west door, the Bishop with St. Peter above it, and the Chapter with the other disciples. The Honorary Canons were represented by the male saints; lay vicars and minor canons by the minor male saints. St. Nicholas seemed appropriate for Selwyn Moresby, the former assistant organist.

Various female saints took care of the assorted Close ladies, but it seemed especially blasphemous to associate anyone with the beautiful, wan Blessed Virgin.

Sometimes he would play the dilettante, changing the affiliations about, but he never changed his mind about Henry Dixon, Chapter Clerk. He remained always the ugliest, largest gargoyle, from whose mouth, in wet weather, there vomited a fair mix of pigeon droppings and water.

High on the gable was St. Christopher carrying a little boy on his back. From a distance, Derek always thought, secretly, the face had a look of his own. But the face of the boy he could never focus, even using the telescope, though he liked to imagine it was Jamie.

There was one sculpture which defied all attempts to characterize, an especially worn Victorian Trinity at the gable point. Even through field glasses, the Holy Ghost appeared almost to be attacking the Father and the Son.

SUNDAY

The ancient Morris Minor Traveller, with its half-wooden body, creaked shabbily off the Lymington-Yarmouth ferry. Derek lavished no love on the car, but they had to use it to keep with the itinerary, now copied on old School of Music notepaper.

James sat happily in the back, hemmed in by luggage. He'd always liked the idea of a hotel: the sort friends stayed in. He was a day-boy at the choir school, which crowded the Vicars' Close houses. Tight proximity gave residents the feeling that they lived in the playground. Especially when boys would flatten their faces like carved medieval grotesques, masks against the glass of kitchen windows overlooking the yard.

The other day-boys went home after Evensong each evening, their polite choristers' pace changing abruptly to normal boy gait once outside the Precincts into Deacon Street. They waited until safely past Garrick House, where Dr Andrew Denning and the vivacious Sally lived surrounded by daughters, music and railwayana.

The daily schedule of a cathedral chorister is crowded, but Jamie felt strangely singled out as neither boarder nor day-boy.

Derek had explained to him how he could never have a brother or sister, but not that it involved rhesus sensitivity and if Barbara did conceive a child it would probably be still-born. But they had told him of the endless blood tests and eventual transfusions he'd had on birth.

Barbara would not consider adoption. They could not agree on this: Derek remembered vividly his only childhood.

Anyway, his son was safe and sound. A son whose head was

always wrong in the driving mirror. It was wrong now, though Derek suppressed his temper. They were on holiday, but still in hot Yarmouth Harbour. The Morris Traveller nosed towards the irritable holiday queue waiting to cross the metal bridge spanning the water. Once over it, and through the masts, Barbara struggled as usual to read the map.

As usual she noticed the correct turning as they passed it. As usual it ended in Derek stopping the car to read the map himself.

Finally, on the A3054, the car climbed up from Yarmouth. Behind them, masts and sails were all that was visible of the crowded harbour except the strange church tower near it. 'Cowes Week' thought Derek automatically, but from here it suggested a flooded Kentish hopfield.

Small-scale landscape. Snatches of twinkling ocean. Soon after the signpost to Warden Point, Derek felt himself turn the wheel, tacky in the southern heat, to sweep them positively right into the Avenue. The tree-lined street, its smug guest-houses to the left, its heavy green beeches the seaward side, drove them down.

Derek glanced in the rear mirror. The road behind was advancing not retreating, but only in the mirror. It was all wrong. There was no sound anywhere, not even from the Morris. Neither seemed there any vibration.

Later, Derek looked back to the odd impression that the flickering trees and gateposts were a huge silent film flashing past, black and white on each side, and that the car stood still in the middle.

Each flicker was an element or unit of time. No other vehicles. No other movement. Just the silent racing behind the glass. But surely the car windows had been down?

Now there was a slowing. The Morris stopped with still frame on each side. Totland Bay Hotel was a castle with red-tiled roofs and turrets. Was it just the bright sea which dazzled his eyes so intensely? That jumping and shining from silver water under the sun? Jewels from a million crowns.

That reminded him. The King and Queen were at Osborne this afternoon, and going on to visit Princess Beatrice for tea in her castle at Carisbrooke.

Their first hotel lunch was over. James could not wait to get wet. He was already hot in trunks under his trousers, and as Barbara was not happy for him to go alone, they agreed to split up. They would meet later by the little pier.

Derek, secretly pleased, Godspeeded them. The migraine had faded just before lunch, but he'd declined to accompany them. He wanted to think, not talk. For he knew all this by heart. Not just from photographs. He walked out through a side door into the grounds as if meeting an old friend. Or was it a former friend?

The hotel expressed 1875 in red brick, stone, timber details and an array of turrets, one especially large like a Victorian rocket. There were balconies and myriad windows. It dominated Totland Bay, which the hotel company owned even now.

From wooded Hampshire far across the water, past Hurst Castle and West Battery, the hotel must once have appeared, at night in clear weather, to be a liner which never moved. But by 1973 the blaze of lights had diminished. The liner was shrunk and even then at sea only in season.

Though it was still the quiet end of the island, other lights crowded round like thriving Arab dhows or busy begging boats. The little pier no longer received several crowded paddle steamers per day. These were once met by carriage or taxi either depositing the wealthy from, or bearing them to the hotel via the curving private drive. How the horses had hated the steep climb, under the iron bridge connecting Turf Walk with the grounds, and up to the beached ark.

No longer on summer evenings was the hotel hemmed in by elegant penguins escorting beautiful wraith-like figures round the gardens, or sitting on benches surveying the dancing sea and the future.

For the future was nearly at an end for Totland Bay Hotel. An old surviving paddle-steamer called twice on Sunday and a few times weekly with trippers, and guests arrived mostly by Beetle or Mini. Some stayed in the plebian accommodation: two or three six-year-old Mondrian-like small blocks, already shabby, standing by the main building.

More expensive rooms were available in the original building, and Derek had felt compelled to book two of these. It seemed oddly right. Although desperately 'modernized', they still

14

retained a shadow of their old comfort. But the grounds wore a neglect which merely hinted at last rites.

Derek felt instantly familiar here, almost part of this haunted place. Like the totally unexpected recurrence of a forgotten dream, or resuming an old love affair. Like starting again with Hazel. Or with ... But there could be no comparison with Swallowfield, his real mistress. His purest love. Why then such a feeling for this place with no real past? There seemed no answer.

He came round a corner to the conservatory, which stood on squat stilts, then entered the main foyer, wide and spacious with a fine polished wooden floor. The heavy revolving door was dark too, but the rest of the decor was white and gold. Somebody had decided that the original wainscoting should be lightened in a curiously dark white, chipped here and there, giving the effect of chocolate flicked about discreetly.

The receptionist's desk was empty, except for piles of brochures. That ancient hall porter with wire-framed glasses completed the furnishings. Derek had caught him gazing at them oddly as he helped Jamie with his case on arrival.

The lobby was tall and long, with a heavy white cornice under a dark blue-painted ceiling which raised instead of reduced the apparent height.

Looking up, there seemed to be no ceiling; it was a dim but starless universe or perhaps a gargantuan vault, the top of which was obscured by shadow. It occurred to Derek automatically that when white it had been less worrying to the eye.

The imposing sweep of the stairs descended importantly at the lounge end of the lobby, and old comfortable easy chairs and sofas arranged in squared groups stood on the enormous Persian carpet. Small tables were spread about with periodicals and top newspapers. Off the old cigar-smelling lounge was a large old cigar-smelling billiard room.

The bar, all Threadneedle Street and Grinling Gibbons, was in a large alcove, under and beyond the stairs and landing. Its enormous carved length was only half-used now, except at Christmas, and when the Isle of Wight Independence Committee booked the whole hotel for a weekend conference in 1972.

The ballroom was now accommodation, and the spacious restaurant split into two: formal, or plastic self-service. The former still led out to the comfortable conservatory of light wood and glass, with elegant cast-metal columns which recalled Paxton. Here indeed still stood tubs of huge ferns, and, between them, light cane furniture echoing Imperial Airways.

All so different from the rest of the building, anxious to be modern but only achieving Festival of Britain spindle, Scandinavian sterility and sociological County Council welfare.

Derek wished it had been left as it was, except that air conditioning would have been an advantage now. It felt so stuffy, yet windows were open. There was that same smell he'd noticed from the old book: an off, vinegary, almost fishy tang, mixed with ammonia.

And it was so hot. The sweat ran down his chest. His buttocks felt moist. The hotel could do with a deodorant too, Derek moved forward, his senses picking up the past like antennae: the Indian Army colonel and family, the bank manager and family, the bishop, the techy elderly spinsters, the lonely small boy wandering about, catechized into 'Thou Shalt Not'.

Derek remembered discreet maids, gliding footmen, rich guests anxious about the Depression and whether another bank crisis would occur in 1934. He could see in situ heavy furniture comfortable in its appointed place for all time, a dimension which knew nothing of social equality and G-plan.

Then the heat hit harder. There was James looking at him intently through the far window on the seaward side of the restaurant. He did not return Derek's wave.

It was like the night before the holiday. Derek had woken abruptly, very hot, to see a pink James standing quite still, gazing at him through the bedroom door. But the glass made James oddly blue, cold, and surely his hair was wet?

A passing waitress, lips pursed and white cap useless in the sea of tumbling dark hair, obscured his view fleetingly. When she had passed, cruiser-like, towards the dockyard of the kitchen doors, the boyish figure had gone. All Derek could see were the grounds, bushes, and, far off, the small pier end.

It was then that he experienced the first pang of fear.

Barbara and James stood waiting outside the pier shop.

Through the turnstile, the perspective of thin wooden slats sped off to their destination a mere four hundred yards away. Some planks were split. Why unmended? The iron seating, which was part of the rail on both sides, was peeling its pale blue paint. It revealed a dark green underneath, like a butterfly turning into a chrysalis.

Anglers stood hopefully, at intervals, surrounded by cherished tackle and gear. At the end of the pier was a hut-like building with large overlapping roof eaves, a hum of activity, and snatches of pop music about it. Over the top stood a short empty flag pole, and what looked like a wireless aerial.

Barbara and James still waited in the hot sun. Barbara wasn't surprised. She'd had to endure irritating delay all her married life. Derek never reached anywhere without being sidetracked. He had been warned for unpunctuality at the School of Music, and by the Dean; but was never consistently late enough for serious trouble.

Yet he wasn't entirely without system. A strange mixture; perhaps owing to his Gemini birthday, Derek was epitomized by railway Bradshaws and years of cathedral music lists, not one missing but none in the correct sequence.

Barbara loved him, despite his untidiness and Hilary's jealous stories about him. She endured his irritating foibles and infuriating remarks, particularly his usual phrase to excuse lateness: 'Wist ye not that I must be about my Father's business?' when he finally appeared.

'Couldn't we go on the pier, Mum?' said James suddenly, longing to run down its slatted length to discover the little building.

'Not yet, Jamie,' Barbara replied, peering up the drive towards the hotel, expecting to see Derek's stocky tenor figure, as she had done for the previous twenty minutes of any moments, 'Dad will be here soon.'

She squarely blocked the pornographic paperbacks in the wire-strung racks by the pier shop, causing real hardship to a soft-eyed man, in late middle age, who pretended to be choosing a real life romance. The things they allowed these days, thought Barbara, no subtleties. Outright pornography, brazenly displayed. She worried about James.

'Child corruption, and the law encourages it,' she would maintain.

But Derek seemed almost to encourage it.

'We live in liberal times,' he'd reply wearily, 'they get it from school, from other boys, newspapers, television. We're in a permissive society.'

'Permissive! I should say! What's it all doing to young people's minds? You should know — you meet students most days. And cathedral choristers.'

'Lay vicars don't talk much to the boys.'

'Including James, your own son,' she said, landing neatly onto a point of contention, 'because you're always late in. What you find to talk about I don't know.'

And now she waited yet again, but less irritably than usual, for there was undeniable tranquillity here. She had already noticed a slight change in Derek since their arrival. Perhaps coming here would help him relax. Perhaps it would change lots of things — even persuade him of the value of logical organization. So many of his ventures had foundered for lack of it. She thought of the defunct Midlands Soloists Ensemble and Rent-A-Choir.

But he seemed different about this holiday, overseeing it single-mindedly to the smallest detail. A strong word, but it almost amounted to obsession. She realized, thinking it over, that the change in Derek had taken place before they came here.

And now, just as James was about to explode with impatience, and the man to pluck up courage to request her to move, Derek appeared from round the distant bend under the bridge, walking slowly, and with a boy beside him.

As Jamie ran away to meet his father, the soft-eyed man finally pushed forward to the pornobacks, where he settled, engrossed apparently in 'Stella's Holiday Love'. Barbara considered a Telegraph Crossword Book for the beach. Or would she prefer a novel?

Then the man slipped a book into his pocket. Barbara wondered which was worse, bought or stolen porn? How the man stinks. She looked up. Derek was almost with her, Jamie now by his side, clearly requesting cash for the pier.

'That boy you were with—' asked Barbara, 'who was he?'

'Boy?'

'The one walking with you just now.'

'Which boy? I've been on my own.'

'Never mind. I just thought. ....'

Then Derek said, irritably, 'Talking of boys, thanks for sending Jamie up to collect me. Charming. Surely there's no hurry on holiday.'

'He only wanted his pocket money.'

'No, at the hotel. I saw him through the window. His hair was wet.'

'But he's been with me all the time, haven't you Jamie?'

She looked down at her son's dry head.

'Yes,' said Jamie, excitedly. 'Now can we *please* go on the pier? I wish to peer at the pier. Get it?' His unconcern dismissed the incident effectively.

Barbara led the way through the turnstile, glad to escape that stubborn smell of urine. She already had tickets from an ancient machine evoking 'Tomorrow's World, 1910.'

Once through the complication of metal, and out from under the station-like canopy, they moved into a new, open world, James flying forward at last, causing anglers to turn and frown.

The ocean stretched away on three sides. Slightly to the right, just visible, lay West Battery and Hurst Castle seemingly marooned at the entrance to the Solent. Warden Point hid Colwell Bay along the coast on the right, while to the left Hatherwood Point masked the Needles.

The sea was as blue as ordinance survey, and several yachts veered over to a wind picked up in mid-channel. There was no movement on the pier, except for the Hendersons in simultaneous two-speed: James and the adults. The anglers stood statuesque, like surrealist figures.

Derek and Barbara stopped spontaneously in a gap to watch a yacht negotiate Elbow Buoy in the distance. James jumped happily on down the pier, to the anglers' annoyance.

Derek stared back at the shore, conscious of action re-play flickering again, conscious of the cathedral tower that day he'd first reserved *Highways*.

Barbara seemed silent, still following the curve of the yacht. She might have been talking for all Derek knew. He heard nothing from her, or from anything inside this great amphitheatre. All sound was stifled as if by blanket fog.

The cries of the distant beach, of gulls, James's galloping feet, music and babble from the pier end: all this was missing, but not gone. Derek just knew instinctively that it was he who couldn't hear them, only he was affected. Was he ill? In a moment, would he look down and see himself borne on a stretcher towards a waiting ambulance? Would Barbara and James worry round the premature cortège, while curious onlookers parted reluctantly? Fascinating, but unlikely.

No question of it. He was meant to remember that day he'd played Nelson from the cathedral tower.

It had been like being living sculpture, standing amidst the canopied niches and pinnacles which clustered round the base of the cathedral south-west spire, level with the lead roof. The ancient stone figures which had looked so sharp, so complete from below, were really roughened and craggy, without detail. The most weathered of all had a mummified appearance, as if from tight bandages and the fetid air of an Egyptian burial chamber. Or the running of restless salt tides, thought Derek.

He had moved round his curious windy room. The spire shot up above him, a medley of stone geometry crossed by huge timbers which obscured the point.

Derek peered over, but it was impossible to see anything of the west front. He turned. The great central spire loomed over its offspring, the two western steeples. Derek was surrounded by cathedral. The air sang through the sprockets; the sculptures hummed through their shrouds; there was an almost continous low chord of E major.

He set Jamie's telescope up to view across the nearby theological college roof, on which stood frozen clergy of brick, and over Moat Lake at its back. Beyond this lay the little city.

Derek's over-rich imagination had always blurred the line between reality and dream. It worried Barbara sometimes.

It always intrigued him to look through the wrong end of the telescope, because it changed apparent truth. By projecting what you saw much farther away, it added to the scale of everything, though conversely all was made so much smaller. Thus, Minster Park round Moat Lake now looked enormous, pushing the city away contemptuously.

Now Derek reversed the telescope and shot instantly into the world of models, near at hand. Perhaps to be closer was most artificial of all. God's-eye view from the tower.

Dam Street. Wedge House. Through the telescope, it didn't seem so incredible, that musket shot from this tower, the ball that had killed Sir Astley Wedge, General of the Puritan army. It was on the second of March, 1643, St. Linc's day.

Derek reached Moat Lake again, swinging down dizzily to the island. The telescope had more spectrum tones than usual. Everything wore an intense individual aura: violet, red, white; blurred like seeing through holy water imprisoned in the brilliant glass.

There was a clawed wood finger in the murky municipal water. The little green off-shore island from which it jutted was diamond-shaped. Reduced by the hot spring drought, the surface was turgid and lazy. There was no dancing sparkle, no holy water there, as the superb large-scale paddle steamer, metallic and polished, thrashed slowly towards Lilliput.

Derek saw the distant boy apparently radio the boat against the miniature pier in a professional way. A stillness for the model passengers to embark or disembark, while the liquid radiation of khaki water spread towards the bank, then the steamer inched away from the driftwood. Its paddle-wheels churned green into yellow-white, as it steamed heavily off towards the farthest shore, overhung by an out-of-scale weeping willow. The distant figure followed the little ship round. Both were absorbed by long fronds which would not be penetrated by Derek's lens.

The boy had had a look of Jamie.

Something caused Derek to swivel the telescope back onto Dam Street. He could almost see the Market Place but for the bend by Littlejohn's bookshop. Then, as if walking, he followed Sir Astley's last steps in this world back up the narrow street.

He had no model ship with him now, the boy who stood staring up from outside Wedge House, almost shimmering in lens light. Then he bent slowly and gathered something from the pavement, something horrid, on the end of a wide stick. Turning, he pushed it through the polished letter flap of the gleaming white door of Wedge House. Then he gazed slowly up to the tower, as if knowing he was watched.

The Wight sun illuminated the sea without help from any lens. Derek stood not on a tower but on the small pier, jutting from the island. There was the great shape of the hotel with its cathedral spires. He stood between pier end and hotel, between past and future. But, as always, the present was already the past.

Having reached the little building, James was looking back, and Derek recalled the boy so like him, who gazed through the hotel windows, but who did not wave.

'We could explore more later this evening,' Barbara was saying enthusiastically, at the end of some minutes' monologue. He had the gist of it, but ignored her. There was pressure as if something had cut into his thought. Or somebody.

They walked past the anglers and their trailing wires. The hut building turned out to be an amusement arcade, larger than expected. James was wandering round, hoping that the machines would work without coins. An attendant watched him, catlike, from his cubicle.

Beyond the amusement hut was a small landing stage on two levels. Wide steps led down to the lower stage under the pier, like a medieval high altar above the glittering shrine of a saint.

But there was no shrine, and the whole structure of timber and metal suggested a stage set of massive construction, mummified by the sea salt and honed by the wind and tides.

A simple but rusty lighting system existed to warn approaching ships. Derek could see no obvious reason for the presence of the wireless or television aerial on the hut roof. The water round the pier timbers was mirror-clear and blue-green. Through this looking-glass was the world of another pier, and in its structure shoals of small fish could be seen at varying depths fighting over something deep, something dead.

Here on the lower level it felt appreciably hotter, and Derek was glad to climb the stairs again to escape the intensity of baking timbers and rotting marine life.

Having squandered some pennies on a few slot machines to Jamie's satisfaction, they set off back for a cup of tea, helped by old enamel advertisements outside the clicking, whirring amusement hut. One proclaimed 'Mazawattee Tea' in white against rich blue. A slightly myopic-looking woman with nineteen-thirties teeth between nineteen-thirties lips was about to absorb rich brown liquid from a pearl-white cup.

Standing conveniently near an old 'Five Boys' chocolate advertisement, the man from the bookstall was pretending to watch the steamer distantly approaching the Pier end.

Derek never saw the steamer arrive. He and James had already started off back along the slatted pier. The turnstiles were like the London underground. Cockfosters Station first opened today, thought Derek, oddly, knowing perfectly well he was forty years late. He ran his hand along the hot tubes of metal as he passed through.

Barbara caught Derek and James up only when they had turned right onto the beach. Underneath the pier was a striped cool world leading to the water. The sand was harder and dirtier. They reached the line of weed on the edge. The sea came in along shadow bars, the creamy breakers gleaming and tumbling, lit by thin strips through the slats above.

There was a massive broken jellyfish, the size of a small table top, decaying on the water's edge. It was very dead, corrupting almost as they watched. Pieces had ripped away and flapped with the movement of the waves. There was a drift of seaweed in the large putrid gash in the middle. An aura of corruption spread from the perimeter of the body.

'It came up from under the pier,' said Jamie, but Barbara turned him firmly away before he could throw the stone.

'What if it hadn't died?' muttered Derek, noticing the steamer half-way now to the headland.

MONDAY

Derek dreamed obscenely about a Cockfosters tube station enveloped in the corpse of the giant jellyfish. It took him several minutes to recover, lying quite still, clammy beside the sleeping Barbara.

The morning of their first full holy day, before breakfast. In through the open sash came the burst of breakers on the beach. The sands could be theirs alone perhaps for one hour.

They explored the immediate hotel area, and walked along the shore past the disused lifeboat station towards Hatherwood Point. The catarrh which plagued Derek's singing life would surely clear on this crisp sea morning. The salt would cut in and leave him free and clean for ever. More effective even than the inhaler back in the hotel room.

But only James and Barbara swam. Derek now just sat on the shingle and watched them fight to avoid being the first under. Standing on the brink in bathing trunks, he'd looked at the ocean rolling to him, but couldn't dredge up any enthusiasm. It was already hot, almost stifling, and the water was warm and sensuous.

He had watched his feet sink into the miniature Goodwins of the water's edge. The sucking sand clung to him. He moved as if to step back, but it let go only reluctantly. He saw the casts his feet made flooding over, the particles spinning round in bewilderment, the water rushing greedily in to take complete possession. He watched helpless as both prints were filled, and the spell broken. Soon they lay destroyed under the swirling salt and he was free.

Slowly, he had returned to his clothes, and here he was

dressed, looking out to sea instead of waving back to land. He'd swim later. Time twinkled by.

'Thought you loved swimming,' Barbara shouted, returning, and dripped all over his dry clothes as she burrowed for the towel's sanctuary.

Then she went through a tremendous routine to convince the few others on the beach that she did not possess what all women possess. James was still romping in the distance with a friend found in the water.

Derek's eyes returned to Barbara. She moved under the desperate bath-towel like a trapped bird, head pecking down nervously as she hurried to dry herself. He held the towel, and laughed at her feverish activity under it. This irritated her and increased her speed, until she regained safety and composure inside clothes.

Derek looked down towards the water's edge. James had found a large piece of driftwood and was attempting to convert it to a raft. The friend had disappeared. An amateur athlete jogged by in his privately Olympic world, dreading return to Manchester insurance. A terrier wagged its way about the beach in a series of zig-zags, pausing to pee at strategic points. Just one cloud was poised over the pier.

'I'll go down and get Jamie,' Derek said suddenly, thinking of breakfast.

His son was strangely cold, despite the early heat. Quickly dressed, they walked him back up the hill to the hotel.

Later, pushing aside her empty plate, Barbara opened the modern handbook. Luckily she seemed uninterested in the older one. 'Who lives in Carisbrooke Castle?' She spoke suddenly, sipping coffee.

'Princess Beatrice,' Derek replied automatically, without knowing why, but it satisfied Barbara.

Her pleasure at his knowledge, his organization, pleased Derek. In fact, it was beginning to seem all his own programme and he congratulated himself. He thought again of that faded writing. The hand was not unlike his.

Monday. 'The Needles and Alum Bay A.M. (chairlift!) Blackgang Chine P.M. Totland Bay evening.' he read from his own shrewd copy. He'd had to consult the modern handbook for details of the Chine. 'Blackgang Chine's an odd name,' said

Barbara after an interval.

'Something to do with smugglers. It's a kids' paradise. The setting's magnificent. There's an incredible chair-lift at Alum Bay, too,' he pointed at the handbook, 'plenty for this morning.'

He played the keen family man, but privately longed to walk alone along the soft Totland beach. Stand undisturbed on the pier. Gaze into the sea. To climb to the hotel up the unkept rocky hill, once so carefully tended. He wanted new insight into this place, fluttering like an old heart, ready any moment to fade from the photograph. And he must think about last night. He had that mirror on his mind this morning.

It had happened while undressing for bed, anticipating the luxury of sheets laundered well. Barbara had been down the corridor in the bathroom.

So hot, he'd thrown the windows open, but the intense temperature grew worse. Moths came in at him. He'd never sleep in this tropical atmosphere. The old book at the bedside exuded that same smell, but stronger now, like an overfull chamber pot.

His eye caught a fleeting movement across the winged mirror. It was curiously dark glass. His naked image stood thrice frozen, eye to eye with him. There could be no movement away until his image had looked him over thoroughly, because suddenly he knew there was a contest here. Dark though the glass was, the figure glowed with light.

His feet unable to move, his eyes were pulled deep into the mirror, almost through it. The image surveyed him coolly. It saw his almost hairless body, legs a trifle too short, head slightly too large. It observed the practical hands, the large sensitive blue eyes through hated spectacles. It glanced quickly and appreciatively over broad shoulders and strong neck, disparagingly over the high forehead, at neat hair, now brown not fair.

The three-dimensional glass figure was able to see clearly the small ears, heavy nose and thickish lips.

Derek's legs refused to carry him from this confrontation. His eyes burned back at him through the glass. There was a sneer in his double's expression, more powerful each second. Derek could not pull his eyes away. The double put its hand on its groin, and smiled suddenly, and Derek found he had done the same. He tried to snatch his fingers away but failed. It seemed to him that the image imitated the jerk a split second later. He tried again, but found it changed to a slow caress. He stiffened with pleasure.

'I am in control of me. I *can* take my eyes away.' He muttered the words slowly, and felt strengthened.

But the image grew stronger too, and he could not stop his hand. As he stared, his double looked younger, age fell away and for an instant he saw himself a boy. An aroused, naked boy. But there was a difference. It concerned the expression.

There was an alien facet, a coldness which was never him. A coldness which contrasted with the dripping heat. He closed his eyes at last, shutting it all out and away. He felt his other hand searching the dressing table for something heavy. It was automatic, he could not help himself. The one movement he now could make, shutting his eyes, had made possible the next.

The heavy metal-backed hairbrush crashed into the dark in front of his still closed eyes. The mirror split and exploded in great jagged chunks and fell like thousands of bells onto the polished wood of the dresser. Derek experienced an end to the tension, a freedom almost post-coital.

His eyes opened. There was no image, no haunting in the glass, for the glass was gone. But even as he exulted over it, he knew there would be no peace until that image was reassembled and reckoned with. Or was in not smashed but freed? Had he freed it, breaking the seal? Had he been taunted into it? Shards of bright glass lay everywhere. Not one of them showed a fragment of human image, as he'd hoped they would. So the figure had burst out. He had not destroyed it.

His pale thighs were warm and wet. He thought it might be blood from a cut until he saw it.

Derek had just managed to drag on his pyjama trousers before Barbara ran in. She had not seen his condition. He had refused to discuss the broken mirror except to say it was an accident. Luckily, Barbara had just fussed him for possible cuts.

Alum Bay lay a mile or so to the south of Totland, and was

reached through rolling downs culminating in white cliff faces. The famous multi-toned sands came from a section of cliff born of another geological age.

They reached it after a full breakfast. To his surprise, Derek had found himself able to cope with food very well, despite the bad experience the night before and troubled sleep afterwards. This morning his mouth had felt like a parrot's cage. He hoped he was not sleeping with it open again. The inhaler should prevent that. He had managed to pacify the hotel manager with a cheque for the broken mirror, but Barbara was still ruffled and puzzled.

Here at Alum cliff top it was clear, fresh and a different world. After examining the Marconi memorial, they turned their attention to the chair-lift near it. Its intricacies suggested the original heavy wireless telegraph equipment commemorated on the obelisk.

There was a continuous cable with huge supports at regular intervals, each one getting higher as the cliff edge was neared. The double seats dangled from it, and on the cliff edge one extra tall gantry coped with the rambling drop into Alum Bay. It was a high but gradual cliff, half collapsed into gentler moulds long since grassed over, like a mammoth graveyard tumbled centuries ago into the sea.

The operators helped people on and off, so movement was never interrupted. It resembled scoop systems he had seen round Midland collieries.

There was a small crowd in the tiny booking office, a toy station with clerk framed by a Norman window. Two holes in the glass: a way in and a way out. A break in the barrier.

Once airborne and dangling, Derek decided Magritte would have loved these slow swinging chairs as they swayed off into the sky. Derek and James moved off together, side by side, while Barbara followed. They clung tightly to the thin bar in front – all that prevented them tumbling into the foliage far below.

Soaring slowly, there was a moment when each chair unit reached its zenith at the high gantry before the breathless descent towards the beach. The translucent ocean was rich blue against yellows and browns on each side, and the towering white of the cliffs from Tennyson Down stretched to the jagged Needles on the extreme end: a triad frozen in the swelling mirror.

Reaching the highest point, Derek felt the jerk and change of direction and they started down. Immediately, the heat built up very rapidly. He began to sweat. There was no going back, no way of stepping off. He was powerless and manipulated, a doll, like one of Jamie's 'action men'. A hollowness of body. Only when he could manage it did he glance round at Barbara.

She was clinging to the bar, about three chairs back. He was astounded, for Jamie sat with her, very pale, Jamie? Automatically, he glanced at his son, solid next to him, fair hair blowing flat back in Thirties style.

He looked back again to Barbara. The seat next to her was empty, and her frightened figure was above him in the air. He felt disturbed, disorientated.

He was beginning to see boys where none existed. Selwyn Moresby would welcome this phenomenon. It occurred to him why Selwyn was attracted to them: their clean-limbed bodies, almost feminine voices and features, their availability, their smooth skin and short trousers.

The suspicion threshold was much higher with boys than with girls, and Selwyn had so much opportunity. At Swallowfield, the sub-organist always took the morning rehearsal with the choristers.

Even today, other adults were inclined not to notice a casual arm round the shoulder,a playful slap on the knee. So he supposed. Unless you were stupid enough to be obvious, which Selwyn had been once too often.

Boys were simpler creatures than women. Most had a quite clear prurient interest divorced almost entirely from emotion. They welcomed experiment with those friendly but single-minded little beings who shared the same clothes, those jealous brothers craving attention out of all proportion to their size. It was like carrying with you an alternative personality, a rigid but red-blooded ghost. Derek remembered boyhood dealings with Mr Hyde.

Yes, boyhood was a strange time, and boys odd beings, and becoming odder. That pale intense face through the hotel window. The boy in the chair-lift. They were the same: it was Jamie's face. However imaginative, he could not accept haunting by a living son sitting next to him. Was this the stuff of which nervous breakdowns are made?

They had reached beach level now, and crashed their way through the deep pebbles. The cliffs beckoned. They spent some time filling a phallic test tube with sand which seemed to represent all earth colours and their amalgams.

Barbara wanted to buy the sands from the stall, which offered them in tubs, each fitted with a chained scoop; but James insisted on gathering his own with a plastic icecream spoon, so it all took much longer. Barbara trailed after him to help.

Derek sat on the shingle beach and gazed at the sea. It was more of a bottomless turquoise lake in a huge chalk quarry, he decided, the translucence of the water like a rare blue wine. The open sea beyond the bay was another world away from the gentle wave-flops, as they overturned in a desultory fashion on the gleaming stones and sand.

Because it was still early, few people had yet arrived, but each cable-chair deposited more figures at the far end.

Derek's mind drifted onto the strange itinerary and its original author. For whom was it intended? He wanted to imagine them, but found he couldn't. They would not be conjured up. He was forced to try reason. It seemed somehow masculine, methodical writing. Had the author planned for a family? Was he the father? There must be a child and if just one, it must be a boy. Something about 'too tiring for the lad'.

Quiet was needed to investigate the many further clues on the pencilled plan. Barbara was the obvious person to consult, but how could he now confess it wasn't his? Anyway, she'd not believe his fantasy.

He was glad of her unimaginative nature at the moment. He'd finished with Hazel a few months before, after being seen with her, in London, by the Dean. What bloody luck, he'd thought. But it was just as well. Barbara and he had been becalmed in a cool phase, his feelings for Hazel had deepened. There had been many despairing conversations in corners of obscure pubs, much agonized hand-holding in Paddington Station buffet.

The crisis had come and gone on grass near Marble Arch. They had discussed divorce and remarriage, and it had nearly happened. 'It's Jamie,' Derek had mourned. 'Barbara could manage, but he could not.'

'Children adjust,' Hazel had murmured into his ear.

'Not well. Jamie's an only child. Remember you have two. Could you really leave *them*? Anyway, I'd never get another cathedral job – guilty party in a divorce.' Hazel was not convinced.

Then they'd encountered the Dean in Harrods with the Archdeacon of Westminster. The Dean, a notorious gossip and unliberal in the extreme, might mention it to Barbara. And Derek was supposed to be researching 17th century solo song alone in the British Museum.

So the affair was doomed. They saw each other just once again. Then, no more did Derek attend courses in London, and Hazel visit a succession of seminars on concert management.

For a few weeks Derek had avoided conversation with the Dean. He'd thought he'd detected changes in Barbara's attitude to him, as if she'd heard something. It was always after her friend Hilary had been in the house.

Or could it have come via Alan, Hazel's husband?

'I'll tell him,' she'd threatened on that last ever meeting in the County Hotel, Wellingham. 'If you finish with me, I'll have to tell him.'

He hadn't believed her. Perhaps he should have done. Since then, he had found a genuine rekindling of love for Barbara.

Anyway, he still had his affair – the most important of all. His affair with the cathedral. Every morning he would burst slowly through the brick tunnel from Vicars' Close and there, spread before his loving eyes, would be the spectacular west front, pinky-brown with almost purple intensity in the shadows.

Contrasting this pinnacled richness with its soaring spires, he would savour the cool smooth grass, gently sculpted, flowing in liquid shapes over countless buried forgotten foundations and unmarked stoneless graves, tumbled deep under the thick even pile of the grass.

It always suggested Henry Moore-like reclining figures covered with a gigantic carpet, or some Midland Pompeii awaiting discovery. Or a Stanley Spencer Resurrection. He wondered which would happen first.

Sometimes he would fuse the two visions, producing a mental picture of grottos of half-sleeping figures waiting on one elbow. Some resembled the bandaged ones in the niches high above.

31

Yes, one bright morning, the carpet would roll back to the sound of the stone trumpet at the lips of the angel on the west front gable. And he would see it. He would hear Tuba Mirabilis.

But on every ordinary morning his eye would drink in hungrily the sensous curves of the gothic as he walked down the Close. The road sank deep into the green, giving apparent extra height to the cathedral's proportions, suggesting almost Chartres or Cologne. Once out of the south east gate into Dam Street, the road fell away more as he reached the stone yard where the freelance garages stood, not far from Wedge House.

The cathedral was a woman, and beautiful. Even God was in love with her, and had come to live within her exclusively, for Derek now felt His presence nowhere except inside her.

The last clear glimpse of his elegant love was through the rear window of the Morris, as he passed under the confident metal railway bridge near the ancient Hospice of St. John Without the City. Here the chapel incense replaced that railway smoke with which it once mingled. Derek longed for his love to use perfume.

Later each day, when returning, he would catch his first thrilling sight of her three spires from just past Stratton. The Ladies of the Vale. He never knew; was it a woman with three lovely heads, or three beautiful women?

He looked at the Needles, their three chalk spires and buttresses like a bleached cathedral from prehistory. God formed them long before inspiring William Waryck to build Swallowfield.

A stir of air flickered the itinerary page. The pencil writing stared up at him. There was a question mark or two, suggesting some doubt about certain places, and possible alternatives were either ticked or crossed through.

Was one of the group old? Or ill? Were the two or three downland walks too much for them, causing a change to be written retrospectively? This demonstrated a tidy mind. It seemed the list was intended to help others. Was he the first to use it since 1933?

Barbara and James came down from sand mining, delighted with the now striped test tube, still phallic but pyjama'd. It stood on his hand, gleaming and shining.

'It's like a condomed beacon,' Derek said.

'And now our sandwiches call,' said Barbara smiling brightly, and diving as deep now into the airline bag as she had dug into the cliff a moment before.

'Sandwiches were *invented* for the beach,' said James loudly. 'It's obvious from the name. Sand which is on the sea shore! Get it?'

They were both pleased that James had begun to use word-play.

'I must go down to the sea again,' said James, and Derek automatically added: 'to the lonely sea and sky.'

When James reached the water he flinched at the sudden chill after the baked stones and sand. There was the sound of someone eating giant cornflakes, as a heavy plodding woman lurched solidly by in the shingle. Behind her the relentless chair-lift deposited more humans than it scooped up.

'Dad!'

To Barbara's regular embarrassment, James seemed to shout more than other boys. He was waving back to them. His voice penetrated all other sounds.

'THAT BUOY, DAD, LOOK, THAT BUOY.'

Derek, misunderstanding, found himself shaking slightly. He stared out wildly. James stood alone.

'Which boy? What do you mean?' he managed at last.

Barbara was diverted from Agatha Christie. She glanced quizzically at Derek. James waved and pointed to nothing that Derek could see straight away.

'The buoy, Dad, that boat has hit it – it's sinking.'

He understood at last. A tiny dinghy had really collided with a buoy out in the middle distance. He stumbled forward in the deep shingle down towards Jamie.

'Yes, I see. Anybody in the water?' He had reached James, by now extremely cold, yet there were plenty of happy bathers further down.

'It's sinking, Dad,' said James again, excitedly. 'Think we ought to do something?'

Caught somehow under the rim of the buoy, the dinghy began to sink. As it filled, a little figure wrestled windmill-like with the oars.

The boat floundered as they watched, and a soaking child climbed akwardly onto the now frantic righted buoy, and clung to it, curled embryonically round the cage.

Derek wondered if anybody would rescue the marooned figure, or if he himself would have to get involved. He hoped not. He looked round. Nobody seemed to have noticed the drama.

He was therefore greatly relieved when a fast launch speared round from Hatherwood Point, abruptly altered course, and snatched the child deftly off the buoy. This bobbed wildly for a few moments as if angry to have lost the only inhabitant it had ever sheltered in its lonely life. The launch swept back the way it had come.

Derek and James stood together in silence in the shallow water, the sand dissolving and reforming round their toes. That wet figure on the buoy brought back that lost son. Derek saw again the pathetic pink embryo wrapped in a towel and Barbara's silent face against the white pillow. James broke into his thought, and said slowly, 'That boy could have drowned.'

'Boy?' (Derek had still half hoped it had been a girl in shorts.) 'Unlikely, Jamie. He wouldn't have drowned, he had the buoy to cling to.'

'Two boys together in the water, Dad!'

Derek heard himself laughing at the joke, but could not laugh in himself. The sea felt suddenly very cold and dark and it penetrated him, changing his blood to ice water. He thought of the cold empress inside leaden oak, borne across the bleak Solent.

Then there were two boys in his mind, struggling in vain in dark, heavy salt water. For a moment both faces were visible, mouths open, eyes open, like marble, before they sank downwards for ever, amidst bubbles.

Both faces were his own.

The road from West Wight to Blackgang curved and wound sinuously and gently along superb cliffs and downs.

A child's game, thought Derek, a game involving elastic. The car was not free. It felt as if it were on the 'Scalectric' lay-out in the attic. But it was made of elastic. He sat behind the wheel, almost not needing to steer at all.

'Let's have a look at Mottistone House,' said Barbara suddenly, 'it's more or less on the way.'

They turned off the coast road near Brook. Mottistone House lay a mile or two beyond.

As they strayed farther from the road to Blackgang, Derek began to experience difficulty in going on. At first he put it down the heat and assumed it was the start of a migraine.

He noticed his reactions becoming progressively sluggish and his speech vague. At last, having seen the car overtaken by a fat district nurse on an ancient cycle, James, showing an uncanny aptness, almost startled Derek into an accident:

'Really think we'll make it, Dad?' He laughed sarcastically, watching the car's speed drop to an all-time low. 'Need some new elastic?'

Derek managed not to snap back. The Morris crept to a halt on grass near Mottistone, releasing a long line of impatient traffic. Barbara and Jamie got out just as impatiently. Derek was slower, convinced that when he got out the car would spring back to the Blackgang road.

Annoyingly, they found the superb honey-stoned fifteenth-century house closed, even to National Trust members. Secretly relieved, Derek began to stride back to the corner where they had left the hot Morris. The tension was almost unbearable. He must get back to the main road, get on to Blackgang. But Barbara was already sitting on the grass, and Jamie wandering off with a stick.

'Don't you even want to take any slides of it?' called Barbara, puzzled again, gazing towards the Tudor gatehouse.

'I'll get a postcard from a shop somewhere.'

'But that magnificent—'

'I've *told* you no, I'm not interested. We'll save the slides.'

Barbara jumped to her feet and strode towards him.

'More than one of us can take a photograph,' she said, taking the camera and deliberately spending some minutes adjusting it. Derek sat fuming in the car with the engine running. She was slow on purpose.

He felt better when the car regained the main road, and the remaining tension dissipated as they neared Blackgang. He said 'Blackgang Chine' several times to himself, savouring the sound, enjoying the resonance.

Barbara glanced at him quickly. Derek was an odd man.

Chale was a small village with a grey church which looked

Cornish; its heavy tower a beacon by the road, isolated, lonely near the sea. The Chine lay beyond.

It began on a height overlooking the huge whalebone sweep of the coast, and plunged down into deep woodland. It was 'Alice' land. Here anything was possible in a kingdom of make-believe, a world in which scale was upset, in which Toyland was real and all else a dream once dreamt. But when? Time was of no consequence, held no sway.

Blackgang was cheap, superficial, commercial and at times beautiful. But in it adults could slide comfortably back to a childhood which never was, children could dream of a world which had never been, or perhaps been only once. Either was an escape. Another existence.

They stood before a large chart of the Chine. Jamie hopped excitedly about, first stabbing at this, now that. Derek's eyes glazed before the list. Unusually, Barbara had to organize the route.

It was a roasting sun. Tilted towards it, the Chine seemed to attract more heat and light than its due. There was a blaze of holiday clothes, Disney-red roofs, exotic plants, startling greens: unexpected flashes of powerful pigment from every direction except the sky. And there it was all white light.

Derek knew that the elastic had indeed stretched from here. No question of it, for him Blackgang Chine was anything but family amusement. He had been brought here for a purpose.

The terraces slipped gradually away downhill like a dream. The paths became even steeper, lined with exotic plants, shrubs and sculptured trees. The result was an irregular maze on a steep hill: because of the incredible pitch you couldn't move directly downwards, but had to edge laterally along the ridges. Nothing was direct.

Obscured, until you were on them, were huge monsters from prehistory, situated carefully at intervals. Jamie insisted on being photographed with his head inside a Stegosaurus's mouth. Barbara was more concerned with scrupulously catalogued flora than with ancient fauna. Derek's mind worked differently. The ground levelled out towards the bottom of the Chine and broadened into dark forests. The journey down felt absurdly easy, easy to walk from fantasy through prehistory, then forest into the sea. The looking-glass world could reverse Darwin.

Oddly out of sequence, yet fully appropriate to a dream, was the Wild West town, a lifelike collection of timber buildings which lay past the dinosaurs and into the woods. Children lurched by, clasping the all-American shoulder, gasping 'Yuh gaat me,' and collapsing in agonized death, only to rise, miraculously, a minute later, with the words: '*Now* I go for your gun.'

The covered wagon was full of several independent games taking place simultaneously. A stylised shoot-out was taking place in each section of the street, and the saloon doors burst open continuously to eject gamblers, who would draw imaginary six- shooters and re-enter to avenge themselves.

Boys crouched behind barrels, or edged round wooded corners. Balcony rails should have collapsed but didn't. Each building was in convincing three-quarter-scale, and you could explore inside them all to re-enact your favourite Western film. Many an outwardly plump and mild accountant had become lean, mean, and Gary Cooper.

They walked real easy, yet maintained a faintly amused smile for their wives benefit. Their sons were not so hypocritical: they admitted to being Butch Cassidy and the Sundance Kid.

Like most mothers, Barbara stood happily watching her offspring at play. Derek found himself actually wanting to join Jamie and a group of boys who poured out of the Marshall's office in a posse. They sprang on horses, leaning hard back on the reins. It was a genuine effort of will not to scamper after them to the show-down. They whooped their way into the woods, towards the totem pole. Barbara wandered into the saloon.

Derek wondered was there a lavatory here? There had to be, said his body. Oh, to be young and unselfconscious again. Those perfect woods. See how high you could piss. So much else you could do in them.

There was a momentary lull, and the real dust settled a little. Through it, into the sun, the grainy light was like an over-enlarged print. Some molecules penetrated Derek's sinuses, building towards an enormous sneeze. The peppery pressure increased unbearably, his mouth opened in spasm, eyes distorting. The last thing he saw before they closed for a powerful ecstatic climax was the small figure on a nearby balcony. The sneeze exploded, leaving him momentarily dazed.

Were those millions of light particles, in swirling miniature colour, merely dust? Or were they fragments of him, molecules burst and freed to fix on someone else?

He felt damp, uncomfortable and weakened. He investigated. The power of the sneeze, unbelieveably, had caused him to loose some control of his bladder. Luckily the picnic bag would cover the embarrassing patch whilst it dried.

The boy. Who was he? Looking like Jamie, looking like Derek. A real, unreal boy. One who could appear when he wished, seemingly where he wished. Was he a sort of succubus, dreamed up by Derek's vivid imagination? Or was he a guilt figure, the boy who never was — Barbara's poor embryo son?

He thought of the boy staring from behind the tomb during Crotch's anthem. The same, except that the lad on the balcony, like all the boys here, had two close fingers extended, his hand an imaginary gun. As if shooting Sir Astley Wedge from the cathedral.

Or was it accusation, remembering the first boy of all, the telescope on the tower. And St. Christopher high on the West Front. A corrupt blessing or a sly, obscene gesture?

The two close fingers.

You don't need lavatories in make-believe land, but the owners had kindly provided a few. The nearest one was a long tortured walk. More than once, Derek had been tempted to find a quiet bush, but there were so many visitors. Just when he'd reached the stage of not caring, even welcoming an audience to share his relief and prowess, he espied the sign 'Conveniences'. A queue of restless women jigged before the 'Ladies' entrance. He strode past them and burst into the other doorway. The stalls were crowded but a cubicle door was open.

There never had been joy like this. He stood for an eternity, reading the surprisingly few graffiti messages and hearing others arrive and leave round him. Still he went on like a fire hose. At last it wavered and stopped, though he had to look to know, so sensitive was his abdomen. Leaving, he felt the attendant watching him admiringly. He was surprised to find this pleasurable.

Blackgang had given up most of its secrets by mid-afternoon. They had eaten a chips-with-everything lunch, except that they were called French Fries and more expensive. The land of fantasy served the most unfantastic food.

'We haven't been to Hell's Mouth,' grumbled Jamie, still resentful over the lack of second helpings.

'All right, don't get your knickers in a twist,' said Derek, 'we'll see it before we go. And the model village.'

They enjoyed being Gullivers in Lilliput. Derek thought secretly: the little streets stretch out like London from the attic window, and I can see into bedrooms.

Jamie wished he owned it all. What he would do, what he would play! Was the scale so ridiculous for his own model railway? Yes. Could get a scale 1 layout, though. He'd have to arrange steam to come up from the funnels, up over the rooftops.

'Let's see Hell's Mouth, then go back to Totland,' said Barbara. 'I've had enough now.'

'Let's get the Hell out of here! I'd go through Hell to reach the hotel!' said Derek, laughing. Jamie glanced at him condescendingly.

They found Hell's Mouth in a flat clearing in the bushes off one of the terrace paths. It was deserted, a rare thing at Blackgang in August. The large head had apparently burst from the earth like a stalkless mushroom or something out of Bosch, with open mouth and eyes. The expression was ferocious. Over the gaping jaws were the words 'The Mouth of Hell'. You could go into the dark and up steps to peer through the eyes.

'Looks like fibreglass,' observed Barbara. 'Go on, Jamie, get into an eye. Derek, you stand in the mouth. It'll make a good photo.'

She settled to adjust the camera, then backed away on to the path, finally squatting on haunches to obtain dramatic effect. Then, just at the point of making the shot, she noticed movement in the other eye. It resolved itself into a child's head wearing a cheeky smile.

Nuisance. He must have been on the inside platform all along. But she wanted just James and Derek, not this strange boy. He would spoil the exclusive Henderson occupation of Hell. Captured by the lens he would intrude on their world for ever.

Noticing Barbara's gaze, Derek peered up, and seemed to start slightly at the sight of a third head. She heard him explain. Obligingly, the lad disappeared backwards into the black, and Barbara captured a strange slide which one day she would burn.

Then, Hell's Mouth vomited, and three living beings returned from temporary death. The boy from the other eye ran to a large family which now appeared in the clearing. One girl carried a large new kite.

'C'mon Catherine, 's my turn for the kite.'

'No.'

'Catherine, it's time Geoffrey took over,' said a parental voice. It resonated unexpectedly in the dry clearing.

Derek stood very still. *Geoffrey took over. GEOFFREY TOOK OVER.* He felt himself go cold, even in the heat. That phrase. Why did it stick so behind his eyes? Geoffrey took over. ... Nausea flooded his stomach. There wasn't much time. A vomiter's instinct got him back to the right place, and passing the queue of jigging women he lurched into the urine-smelling echo marked 'Men'.

He just made it into the cubicle. The smell of the place nauseated him. He retched time after time. The vomiting was only partly caused by the abhorrent stench of rotten fish. Did they *ever* clean the place? Yet it was all right before.

He knelt before the cold white W.C. basin. Scribbled in wild pencil amongst the obscenities was: 'See you on Sunday for special fun – Geoffrey.'

ECHO

This is written in a big diary, but it is a letter to you. It's so you'll know all about me when you come to me. It's in my best writing.

Mother and Father. Sometimes I really hate them. It's not fair, why can't I have a brother to play with? The other boys, they have brothers and sisters, but I have nobody. They don't let me play in the street, but other boys play there. Then I see them at school, they won't let me join in, so I don't have any playmates.

Sometimes Mother lets me go to another boy's house to play, but not very often. Course, when I'm there we can play in the road if it's not near our house. But they don't really ask me again. Why? I'm on my own again and that's it. I pay them back though. When they do things they shouldn't, I tell on them. I go secretly to the teacher after school, and she gets them the next day. That way they don't know who's told. Sometimes I put dog shit through their letter boxes. That's a laugh! Uhr!

I'm ten. I've been old enough to play in the road for ages, and I thought I was old enough when I was about eight. Don't see any reason why I can't now. I'd be really careful about motors and not be run over. Anyway, they don't drive that fast. Not like Brooklands or Malcolm Campbell, or those new Hydroplane boats. I've got the set of 'Speed' in my cigarette cards.

Living in London's all right, but there aren't so many secret places. In the country you can find places for camps — just right for jumping out at people, really making them scared. Old tin coal bunkers are good fun for making camps. I sort of collect secret places and imagine myself in the bitter cold night there, curled up, safe against the wolves, or hunters.

We go to Kent on holidays. That's country. Mostly I go alone, but sometimes Mother and Father come. We stay with Grandma and

Granddad. Playing on my own there is better than the same in London. In London it's all streets and the parks are too open. I go to Ravenscourt Park sometimes, but it's better on Wormwood Scrubs. I like Kensal Green cemetery to play in best, but I tell them I'm going somewhere else.

When I build a camp, I imagine there's a gang against me, and I have my own gang and we have battles. We invent catapults and traps. I make masks. They hide your face. And your spots. You're not watched much when you stay with Grandma. It's nothing to how it is in Shepherds Bush. I have great fun. There is only one problem, y'see, when Grandma keeps telling me watch out for the charabancs. They go too fast in the lanes, taking people round on trips.

And there are single decker buses — not like London ones. London Transport buses have two sort of peaks on the front like caps, one at the top, one half way down above the driver.

Grandma once had a dog which was run over by a charabanc. The driver tried to stop, but the dog was dead all right. His head was squashed. Some old ladies were sick at the horrible sight. Poor old Sandy, his head was twice as wide as before. Looked as if he was smiling.

We sometimes go out on daytrips on a Sunday. The train from Westbourne Park Station soon reaches the country. But you've got Mother there and you can't do anything secret because she's always watching you, saying don't. Father doesn't come with us often. He's no fun.

We go on the G.W.R. Everything is brown on the G.W.R., like shit. We go through places like South Ruislip. And Denham. I'm always thinking what I'll do when we get there. On the way back I do engine numbers in my notebook. I love trains. My Hornby set is quite big, and it's in the attic. It's G.W.R. too. You wait until you see it.

We always go on a little train called the 'Push-and-Pull'. That's really good, a Pannier 0-6-0 engine. Strange. All it has to do is go backwards instead of turning on a turntable. The engine is in between the two carriages. Once we came back home a different way, back through Hanwell and into Ealing Broadway. Then we caught a tram.

It was a slow branch line, kind of squeaky, but I quite liked it. The stations weren't real stations — they had chinese-looking huts, all corrugated iron, on the platforms.

We went past Cuckoo Hill, where there is a big orphanage school. Father said Charlie Chaplin went there, and he has marvellous films. I really like them. I like the way he walks as well. Almost as if he's messed himself.

His eyes I think are very strange 'cause they're all black on the edges, so I have the feeling they're some kind of make-up. Like railway smoke.

The carriages on that line are really like one long compartment. Most of the seats are in rows on the two sides, and down the middle are long thick wood lines all close together like lots of nails. At each end there are pictures round the door, which slides.

What really is odd is there are all these different pictures of different places, but surely you can't get to them by train? It doesn't go very far, only about ten miles I think, and so really I don't know why they put them up when the train doesn't go there. Perhaps it's to brighten the coach up. Symonds Yat's a funny name.

There are all old lamps, a glass bowl stuck to the ceiling, and one side you pull one of the chains and you light the lamp, and it catches with a pop. When you want to stop it you just pull the other chain. Like a lavvy, but with two chains.

There are lamps like them at Sunday school. They make a kind of funny noise, all bubbly, but they are gas, 'cause Mrs Spencer has to turn them on, standing on a chair. They hiss like anything. Her legs are fat, all the way up I bet. Right into her knickers.

The seats in those carriages are all soft with fat carved legs, like Mrs Spencer's. They're all kinds of brown patterns, and they joggle about when you're on them. You're legs itch like anything.

The carriages joggle too. They seem to be bowing, and sort of nodding, and what's funny is that the trees round the fields nod back, telling something. Wonder what? They're like ships in my history books, Nelson's fleet.

We live near the London Underground. I'd like to go on it and explore every tunnel, I really would. With you. I'd do the Metropolitan and you'd do the Central Line.

We'd meet on some faraway station, getting there by completely different routes, in the right time. I can't do it until you come. Other boys won't go with me, they just won't, even if we were allowed.

Those mysterious bits you can see on the end of the platform, they are all kind of spooky. It suddenly goes all black past the narrow platform. Howling noises come out like ghosts.

I don't like the Underground when it goes above the ground too much, like the Metropolitan. But it's good where they have these high

43

brick walls with little arches set in. You can look up and see sky. I'd still rather go on the other ones because they are like tombs.

On the Circle Line it goes above ground too, and all these houses stare down at you from ever so high, as if they'll jump on you any second. It all looks ruined by bombardment like the Great War.

When you come we could go down the canal, and make rafts. If you were at my school it'd be good, because then I'd make more friends. I'd have twice the chance of getting friends. I'm bigger than the others and forward for my age. That's what I've been told. I might be going up two standards in September.

Our house is terraced. It's got very secret places where you can build a den. Like the cellar. It's very dark, so's the hall. But that's not so dusty and damp-smelling. The attic is even better— you can just see out of the small window, they don't go up there much.

The garden's long and thin. The front garden is very small with a brick wall. It's the same as all the others, really, with a patterned tiled path, all zig-zag.

All the houses look the same at first, but are different in some ways from next door. Ours is a different house.

Mother was very ill once. The doctor came and was talking to Father, all quiet, and when he'd finished talking he came out with a serious face. Before he went out to his motor, which is a Rover, he said to my Father: 'She was very lucky.' They were in the hall and I was in the front room behind the door.

What did he mean, lucky?

This was when she was going to have you. But something happened, I don't really understand it, but suddenly I just knew that you weren't coming, and I found that you weren't born.

I don't see why she was lucky, losing you, and it was her fault. It was her fault, must've been. Other boys' mothers have lots of babies, and so I can't see why she could lose my brother, and I really blame it all on her.

When I'm supposed to be in bed I sometimes sit on the stairs and listen to Mother and Father when they don't know. I found out they didn't want me when I was born. They wanted a girl. That's all Mother thinks of even now. 'Can't go through it again – all that trouble when he was born.' The only things Father thinks of are his shop, The British Legion and his garden.

He is very tall and bald, and older than other boys' fathers. Always wears a white collar with round edges and the same green tie.

I've just remembered that he also likes the church, that's another thing, he's a churchwarden at St. Luke's, down the road. He has a drink at the 'British Prince' on the way home every Sunday. He was in the Great War, something called an Old Contemptible. Every year on Armistice Day he parades with medals on. He won't talk about it. Just says 'I went over the top at the Somme. My friends didn't come back. They drowned in filth.'

Wish he'd tell me about it. I've seen his eyes all watery on Armistice Day. But he's not soft. He beats me if I have an accident in the night, I do try. I do. I do. And I have tried not to pick my spots.

I'm in St. Luke's choir, but Mother doesn't really go to church because of the dinner. But all the other Mothers go and they have Sunday dinner to make. They can't all have cooks.

The only times she goes are about Harvest, Easter and Christmas. That's the only time she goes. She's not very pretty, my Mother, and wears glasses. And she's fat with thin legs and red blotches on them like beetroot stains.

We've got a pond in our back garden. I wish I had some terrapins. Pity that tortoise drowned. I've got a couple of super floating warship models. I'd like to join the Navy, and be captain of a battleship or even the Hood. I've seen it on the cigarette cards. It's exciting, a great big battle cruiser … no-one can sink her. Biggest in the world.

I put a picture of the Hood on my bedroom wall once, from my Boys' Own Paper, but Father wasn't very pleased. He wanted to keep the magazines to bind into a book. He's never pleased, ever.

Those G.W.R. carriages have notices in ever so old black printing, and I always read them. When you look, each word is in different writing. Some are big and heavy and some are little. I know what they say by heart:

'PASSENGERS on RAIL MOTOR CARS are REQUESTED NOT to CROSS the LINE except by the BRIDGE or TUNNEL BENEATH at STATIONS.' Sounds like our Vicar! If you say it as you go along it fits the train wheels over points at a junction.

There's an island in our pond. I'd like to have a real one, just small, and have a yacht to get back to England. One like the King's — the one he races in.

You'd live with me and no-one would be allowed on our island except if we said yes. We'd have a speed boat as well, with an aero-engine in it, and we'd have a Schneider plane with floats, like the Supermarine. That's on cigarette cards too.

There'd be lots of bushes and trees on the island, and little beaches. And free sweets and ice-creams everywhere.

Sometimes I sing solos in the choir, because I've got a good voice. The organist sometimes plays us records of Ernest Lough, on his portable gramophone, at choir practice. He's a bit cissy but he can sing, Ernest Lough. Bet he's got a big one.

We all sang better after hearing those records. (Nobody shouted any more. I don't like it when they shout.) We didn't like his kind of wobbly voice though.

I heard some choirmen say that bringing the records was the first good idea Mr Hopkins has had. I bet they liked Mr Smart better then him. Mr Smart who dropped dead. He really knew about music, but we could lark about more, especially his favourites.

Mr Smart died playing the organ on Armistice Day. His foot jammed in the pedals, and he fell on the manuals making a terrific row. Father helped get him out. Said Mr Smart's heart had stopped. That pedal trombone has ciphered ever since. His shiny shoe got stuck that day. I hate that noise. My ears hurt.

Mr Hopkins takes me for piano every week, and just sometimes helps me with the organ. My legs are long enough, but they say I'm too young to start properly. I'm just allowed to play the organ after school.

It's a Harrison, and it's got three manuals with loads of different stops. Loads. You can make super trumpet sounds. And there's a stop called tremulant makes it go all like that organ in the cinema nearest us – the Pavilion. The Silver Cinema's got an organ like a human voice, some German name. Could be Werlittsen. Can't spell it.

When I'm there on a winter evening, the church has gone all dark, With just the organ light on it's ghostly. I don't like it very much, because at the end I have to switch off the organ light and get across the chancel in the black.

It's not a very old building, built in about 1873. Frightening though, on your own in there. But you're not really alone. I'm not allowed to use the pedal trombone in case it jams on again. While I can't use it at least I know I'm safe from Mr Smart. If I did use it, and it jammed, it would open the door for him. He'd get in to me. Don't know why he'd harm me, but I'm really scared. That huge reed would get stuck down by his shiny shoe, just as when he died.

He'd be next to me at the organ, his thin face looking from that little brass plate to his memory. It's kept shiny by Mrs Smart. He was different to Mr Hopkins. Mr Hopkins is fatter and taller, with straight *black hair stuck down with grease, parted in the middle.*

On those winter evenings I creep out slowly in the dark, all scared, hoping that I won't stir up anything to get me in the back, inch by inch until I reach the vestry door and light switch. Sometimes I'm all tingles when I reach it.

Once I got lost in the stone corner leading to the pulpit. Horrible. If it hadn't been for Alec Turton coming and putting the lights on, Smartie'd have got me even without the trombone to call him. Alec saved me.

Mr Smart would have taken me away, that first night, gripping me with those soft hands, but all cold and dead. When he was organist he used to take boys off on their own sometimes.

Mr and Mrs Runciman made a stink about an organ lesson of Smartie's which took two and a half hours one evening. Mrs Smart was out at the Womens' Institute annual general meeting with refreshments after. It was all smoothed over, but Lionel Runciman left the choir. Why such a fuss I don't know, don't expect Lionel minded it. Smartie died soon after.

Alec was senior chorister. He took organ lessons with Smartie. I heard that when he played a wrong note Smartie would move his hand further up from Alec's knee. Bet Alec didn't mind. He was the first one to call Mr Smart 'Smartie'. Alec is a good organist. He just made mistakes on purpose. More and more of them.

Anyway, Alec is still like that himself. He says he likes a boy to help him with his organ practice, to point out his mistakes. He is fifteen now with a moustache, and assistant organist with Mr Hopkins. He's going in for music.

Mother and Father aren't keen on organ lessons for me because of all that. It isn't fair. Mr Hopkins is quite different, he really is. Wouldn't have mattered if he wasn't. He comes to our house for my lesson. Mother and Father say our piano's better. But the vestry one's a Broadwood, given by a rich lady, so that's wrong for a start.

That brass plate to Smartie. I've read it so often on Sundays: *In Affectionate Memory of Albert Smart, A.R.C.O., 1880–1932, Organist of this Church for Twenty Years. A Gifted Musician and Teacher, He Loved his Choir and his Organ. This is Erected in Memory of Him. 'For I Will Consider Thy Heavens, and the Work of Thy Fingers'.* I think that's right. Some of the choirmen thought it was very funny.

I cover the plate with large music when I practise, to stop Smartie *looking out at me. He left some money to buy new choir clothes each year for one boy, and I was the first to get one. My old cassock was rotten. The new one feels like his hands moving over you. Like being taken over by a dead man. Uhr.*

I'm different from the others. I'm sort of apart, chosen. Smartie wanted me to go on a paddle steamer with him down the Thames once, to Southend on a day trip. They never had children. Mother and Father didn't let me go though.

If you were here now, Smartie wouldn't ever be able to come back to me. He only touches boys like that when they are alone, and his wife isn't near. I'm alone all the time, that's the trouble. I don't want him back dead.

Y'know, one day I'll get Mother for losing you. Pay her back for you. A slow painful curse on her.

TUESDAY

Dr Nelson's Improved Inhaler, plus sea air, were proving a match for Derek's catarrh. He could read while inhaling, except that the pungent fumes made his eyes drip tears over the itinerary.

It commanded the Hendersons to Haven Street Station and Arreton Manor today. He hoped the Bank Holiday crowds wouldn't prove infuriating. Surely it *was* Bank Holiday today? The first of August?

At first, he'd been delighted with the Tuesday entry, but not now. It wasn't the Manor, but the railway. Why not by-pass it and go straight to Arreton? He told himself that Jamie would be mortified. But the truth was he dare not try. The strangeness of yesterday frightened him, and it had to do with this railway.

They parked the Morris in a field near the station. An old Rover stood near, smelling of craftsmanship. Lesser vehicles stood guard, in British regulation line abreast. Somebody's car radio was donating the Rolling Stones, unasked, to the innocent island air.

The grass was browned by sun, oil, and the pulping of tourist tyres over the season. Plump hands, on green boards, pointed visitors importantly to the station down a rail-cinder lane bordered by darkly hollow bushes.

Haven Street was of yellow and red brick. Entering it was to step into the pages of 'Highways', but coloured in three dimensions. There was one platform, double-sided, but with no canopy, reached by barge boards over hot metals, silver and brown. Between them, ancient oil and cinders lay like flat, regulated Pompeii.

On each side of the two main tracks were railway buildings on the small Wight scale. The station-master's house, converted to an overcrowded railway museum, stood near the level-crossing gates. These moved only to admit engines to two hundred yards of remaining track. On it stood rolling stock in various stages of restoration. Then sad wilderness began behind a wire fence.

The station ticket office had become a crowded bookstall, as popular as the trains themselves. The waiting room beyond was now a small cafeteria which spread onto grass next to it. Wood and metal chairs, with circular metal tables, stood like railway-green toadstools.

A smell of acrid creosote rose as Derek, Barbara and Jamie crossed the track. The platform was crowded with excitement. Cameras waited in itchy hands, as parents prepared to photograph offspring next to the train. Despite earlier misgivings, Derek looked forward to the mile and three-quarters up the single track to nowhere now, and back.

'I think I'll give it a miss,' said Barbara suddenly. 'I'd prefer a coffee.'

But Derek was adamant.

'You must come with us.'

'But seventy pence! And I don't even like trains very much!'

'We've already paid. You must come. Please.'

So she did.

Derek covered his ears as the little 0-4-4 engine clanked importantly by, bursting steam. 'Calbourne,' Jamie read out loud. Excitedly they positioned themselves where they hoped a carriage door would occur. The coaches squeaked to an agonized stop, and everybody fought to open the doors first amidst flaring steam. Like a first world war gas attack, thought Derek, automatically. 'Let 'em orf first … let 'em orf first.' The guard and porter shouted happily, as they played real life trains with flags, whistles and watch-chains.

Derek climbed into the dusty compartment last. It smelled of ancient Gold Flake and stale Edwardian steam; sitting on it, the deep seat felt like almost sharp carpet pile, as if grown brittle from years of passengers standing to see out.

Another group took the remaining seats, with two excited boys, one about twelve, the other a toddler. There was a sour granny. The weary parents obviously had the eternal problem of calming the boys down, and perking granny up.

Through thick partitions came bumps and yells as other youngsters tried the seats as trampolines. The coaches filled; slamming of heavy doors sounded the length of the patient train.

Then it was the turn of the narrow windows. They slid vertically via ancient straps with the incised railway crest on a fossilized roll near the end. Out came the heads: toffee apples in bunches.

Derek found his eye drawn to the two boys. Jamie and his older brother would have had similar age differences. Two boys, preferably nearer in age to each other. That would have been just right. Barbara hadn't borne a grudge about their first son, but Derek bore a guilt, for the miscarriage had been his fault. She *had* known best, yet he had cajoled her into the car.

Jamie had taken up with the elder boy, the younger was now on his mother's lap. Barbara was watching his antics, and her face betrayed her. As usual, it was a matter of time before she was drawn into conversation. Odd in one so shy, but strangers always talked to her. Granny and the father were talking about the price of the tickets and the delay in starting.

Derek looked again at the brothers. He thought again. Was this boy he kept seeing his *idea* of his first son? Some projection of his guilty mind? It would explain the resemblance to Jamie.

It was at least possible, and sounded psychologically fitting. But why now? Why had it chosen to come out now? As if hoping to suppress the answer, he thought of the ceiling. Without raising his eyes he suddenly knew that originally the compartment was lit with a large half-globe fitted flush to the ceiling. It had a see-saw and chains.

When he finally managed to look up, there were newer electric light bulbs on either side. The old fitting brooded down like Big Brother's eye. Everything was reflected in miniature, distorted round the smooth glass bowl. Nothing was spared, nothing missed, and all was in some way distorted by the eye into its will. Derek noticed how both he and James were pulled into the centre, their heads large and bent and nearest the pupil, and their bodies stretched like water weeds over a waterfall.

The eye burned down onto Derek's head. He could feel it through the thin Copperfield cap he'd bought for the holiday. He was relieved when a cooler breeze blew in, dispersing dead air as the train lurched off.

Granny sat disapproving the view from her window seat, and all three boys were hanging through the opposite open window, rather dangerously, he began to think.

This thought was cancelled abruptly. He was acutely aware of each small detail of the faded photographs and map in flat glass panels above the seats. They would not be ignored. They would not leave him alone.

Trying to remember afterwards, he would be certain that to start with they were Island Views. He would remember one of Carisbrooke Castle. That would be tomorrow. But, astonishingly, today they were scenes from the old G.W.R. carriages which he remembered as a small boy, and then from Southwood days. Symonds Yat, Land's End and Worcester Cathedral peered across at him, dark and brown-grey.

Behind him, Newbury Town Square, a view of the Malverns and Tom Quad, Oxford, were trapped by the barrier of glass. But in that barrier he sensed a compulsive invitation.

Was it his own or James' head which looked back at him, mingled with browned Malverns? Neither. It was the mirror image lurking, smirking insolently, waiting to resurrect through the frame. Derek knew that his eyes were looking into yesterday. This was no boy of 1973.

His stomach in spasm, he managed this time to edge himself out of the side of the glass, thereby sliding the image out too. As he did so, he found himself enveloped physically by yesterday in the round, seeing right through compartment walls like tinted perspex to the coach end.

The seating was somehow rearranged. The once holiday crowd, which had bundled so joyously onto the train, now sat quietly behind newspapers and shopping bags. Nobody was without their hat. A little girl studied *Sunny Stories*. There were boys in black boots and short trousers, and now, through the larger windows, were great flat fields with ship-like elms in line abreast.

But now was the present of the sepia photo views inside. This train was the old Push-and-Pull on the Greenford-Ruislip suburban line. He knew it, but couldn't prevent it, like being awake during one's own operation. Outside was all colour, for they jogged through a Middlesex innocent and green, big brother to the sepia views behind glass, down there round the sliding door. He seemed to remember a car approaching a hotel, and flickering film behind the car windows. But when was that?

There were his favourite notices in authoritative Great Westernese: PASSENGERS on RAIL MOTOR CARS are REQUESTED NOT to CROSS the LINE except by the BRIDGE or TUNNEL BENEATH at STATIONS. He said it out loud to himself, fitting it to the rhythm of the wheel clicks, as he used to. The carriage blacked out abruptly as they passed under a deep bridge. When the light shot in, the Push-and-Pull was gone, so was Middlesex. Suddenly he was with his mother in a crowded compartment on their holiday.

He sat swinging his legs, his short grey trousers ended too early, and the tickly cushion-covering made his thighs itch. His mother always said that other boys looked sloppy with trousers too long. Rough boys who played in the road.

There were boys having a fine time at the window, and he jumped up to join them. One, brushing against him, pushed his cap off. It fell on the grey floor.

'Pick up my bloody cap, you sod!' shouted Derek, stamping his foot. The astonished boy made no move. There was a silence broken only by the clack-clack of train wheels counting out the seconds. But before Mrs Henderson had managed any words, Derek seized the boy's jaunty holiday cap and whirled it hard and true, high through the window. It swooped down onto a passing single decker Vectis bus, and was borne away for ever. The boy turned on him instinctively. Derek felt himself astonished at his own enormous strength.

James stood open-mouthed as adults dragged his father away. The other boy had retreated, crying, to the opposite window and had trodden on Granny's feet.

Mrs Henderson gave her son a restrained dressing down, while the boy's parents, embarrassed and incredulous, comforted theirs.

'What's the matter with you, Derek? Have you gone mad?'

'He did it to me so I did it to him,' Derek retorted indignantly. 'He threw ... my cap on the floor. How was I to know his'd go through the window? Not fair just blaming me.'

His voice had become shrill. 'Derek! It's not funny any

more,' Mrs Henderson whispered savagely in a hiss meant for his ear only. It could not mask her red embarrassment. Derek showed no remorse.

'I just paid him back. Why don't you ever let me play in the road?' He saw his mother turn to the open-mouthed parents.

'I'm *so* sorry, I can't *think* what ...'

'You're lucky — Peter's all right,' the woman said angrily, 'but just get your husband to a doctor.'

'Touch Peter again, and I'll touch you,' said the husband to Derek, 'Mental case or not.'

All the boys were placed firmly back in their seats. Silence. Derek couldn't understand it. He'd only paid the boy back, after all. Other boys did far worse ...

He sat down, swinging his legs idly, looking at the bushes brushing past the window. That's a good tree to climb. He noticed several promising clumps where a camp could be made. He could have taken that Dawn Rollings from Mafeking Road there with no problem.

His mind played over numerous secret games with little girls of about his age, games fixed mainly below the waist. It was surprising how many little girls shared his interest.

There was a shudder as the train jerked still. The boys sprang up to peer through the fierce steam escaping up the side of the coach. A smell of hot oily water. He could just see through some hawthorns into the grounds of a large house where some girls practised show-jumping. He gazed at them silently, the leather roll pressed against him, low down. Their plump thighs were astride, emphasized by the jodhpurs, and he found himself thoughtfully watching the spread legs over the fat little ponies.

'Can we get out here?' said James.

'No, there's no station. We just reverse,' explained the man irritably.

'I'm getting out—' said Derek, trying to open the door. 'Let's jump down to the track. Bags I first.' Mrs Henderson gripped him hard by the arm in a way she reserved for James.

'Sit down,' she said, summoning all the firmness she could.

He obeyed reluctantly. She stared hard at him, her body shaking with anger and miserable embarrassment. How *could* this happen? And in front of strangers in a public place. He'd flipped, without warning; it dawned on her that various odd things said recently by Derek may have all pointed to this moment. How could she face her friends at home?

('I'm *not* surprised— *I* couldn't live with him— All that mess, never knowing when he'll be in, no proper holidays. And that old car. You have a *right* to nice things.')

How could she face Maureen and Peter? Or Sarah and Nigel? It went through her mind, automatically and she hated herself for putting it before anything else.

But what of *now*? This nightmare. How could she get them off this cursed train? What if he became violent? And why was he behaving as if in a subnormal boyhood? She'd had to order him about as if she were his mother.

The train jerked and began imperceptibly to move backwards, slow squeaks and heavy clicks which assumed the familiar pattern of wheels on rails as the speed built up.

As the rhythm grew fast, Derek became more excited again. He stood up, abruptly like a puppet. He scuffed his shoes on the gritty floor, then stood on the seat, his hands grasping the pole and mesh luggage rack. The other boys watched as he swung his weight on the rack and tried to climb into it with no success. By fortune or good craftsmanship the groaning rack did not collapse.

'For God's sake get down, Derek!' Mrs Henderson said desperately, her face stressed white.

He appeared not to hear her until she repeated it. Then came a puzzled expression.

'Why do you keep calling me Derek?' He laughed again oddly. 'Couldn't do this in Mr Smartie's cassock! Alec Turton likes me best in short trousers. He'd have helped me up all right!' He giggled.

Everybody stared at him, James looking ready to burst with tears. His eyes said 'my father is insane.'

Derek looked down at them from his height, his feet plunged deep into ancient cushion. As he stood, swaying slightly, he felt elated and very special.

They looked so small and unimportant. Father was not with them again. Never has time. Today's antics in this train would undoubtedly bring a punishment when he got back to Shepherds Bush, but meantime it was worth it. Here he was a giant. Same as when he looked through his bedroom window.

Derek turned again to the rack. Putting one foot on the window sill, he managed to hurl himself more or less onto the rack, which bowed in the middle. The brackets looked ready to burst out of their fixings. The string mesh squeaked and bulged but did not tear. High in his perch, he resembled some animal deposited by flood water in a tree.

'I've damn well had enough of this,' the other man stood up at last.

'Come down or I'll pull you down. Bloody fool. What do you think you are doing? What an example to the children.' He stood trembling angrily, his wife open-mouthed and embarrassed at his outburst.

Barbara collapsed on the opposite seat. It *was* all over. He *had* flipped. She should have seen it coming. Trust Derek to spoil their one decent holiday in years. She began to cry, her tears bursting silently out, her shoulders shaking as if in a miserable orgasm. James stood with his back to her, pointedly staring through the window.

Then Derek got down quietly and red-faced from the rack.

'What must you think of me,' he said, trying to smile lightly.

'Just that you're a looney,' grunted the Granny, glaring hard, thin lips pressing and unpressing.

Derek felt ridiculous. What *had* he been doing? He remembered little of anything after his accidental glance into the mirror between the photo views, and before Barbara had begun to cry. Everyone's eyes were on him, except Barbara's. She had turned and was trying to wipe her tears away.

'I do apologize, everybody,' said Derek, attempting a smile of assurance. 'I must need this holiday! Been overdoing it lately.' He turned awkwardly towards the other boy's father, now seated, flushed and self-conscious.

'Disgraceful behaviour,' replied the man stiffly.

'It *was* only a joke,' said Derek. 'You let your hair down on holiday, don't you! Got a bit carried away!'

'That's one way of putting it,' said the mother, unsmiling 'you ought to be taken away.'

Derek resisted the temptation to agree. It would sound impertinent or pathetic, and wouldn't solve anything. He wished himself anywhere.

'Just a little holiday *joke*,' he said again lamely.

'I suppose my boy's cap was also a joke,' accused the man. 'You see a doctor, that's all. You're lucky the rack wasn't damaged. You'd have had to pay for it.' He examined it in the public interest.

Silence. Derek sat down. The boys stood together in an embarrassed group, looking out of the window. The train began to slow for Haven Street, and Barbara stood, relieved, pretending self-assurance, normality. But what of Derek? She glanced at him doubtfully. He certainly did not have that leering expression now, or that objectionable cocky look.

Everyone else stood, also relieved, disguising any last embarrassment with their shuffling.

'He was only joking, I do *hope* you understand,' Barbara said to the woman. 'Please let us pay for the cap.'

The woman stared at Derek momentarily.

'Just get him to a psychiatrist.'

The train shuddered still and they stepped out through rising steam reminiscent of a Baker Street fog. The other family collected itself hastily.

'Escaped lunatic,' came Granny's gutteral voice as they walked quickly away. 'Somebody ought to phone the asylum.'

The Hendersons stood silent while the excited passengers chattered past. The train moved slowly out onto a siding, to make steam noises. The fireman clambered down, watched from a distance by envious boys. When the last passenger had left the platform, James turned hesitatingly to Derek, who had dreaded it. The boy's face was white, his voice prematurely adolescent, his eyes wet.

'Dad, what's the matter? Were you really joking?'

'What do you think? Talk about holiday spirit! Everyone takes everything so damn seriously!' Derek tried to laugh. 'Po-faced lot!'

Barbara was not smiling.

'Jamie, see if there's anything you'd like in the shop.'

She pushed some coins into his hand, and he set off eagerly towards the throng of people buying things they'd hardly look at again. She waited until James had disappeared, then turned angrily on Derek.

'Christ, Derek. What the hell were you playing at? Are you ill? That was no joke. You didn't know who you were, did you?'

57

She leaned forward accusingly, but concerned too. Derek said nothing but walked slowly forward to peer down at the heat-crinkled track.

'I'm going off the rails,' he said feebly.

'But what's the *matter*? Are you worried about something? You were acting as if you were a kid. You must see ... a doctor.'

More like see a priest, Derek thought, but what's the good? He turned. 'I'm all right now, but don't fuss. Please. I just had a weird experience. Been feeling odd on this holiday. Can't describe it, it's ridiculous, must be imagining things, but—' he broke off. Should he confess the truth about their itinerary, the boy he kept seeing who looked like James?

Should he burble out, irresponsibly, fears only half formed? Like his growing fear of hearing the name Geoffrey? Could he ever utter the name? How could he say any of this without appearing to be unhinged?

'Who's Mr Smartie?' Barbara broke in. 'You mentioned Mr Smartie in the train, when you were ... something about a cassock. And about somebody else too. Turton? Allan Turton?'

Derek ignored this. 'Don't know a Smartie.' He stopped. 'Yes, wait a minute, a Mr Smart was once organist of St. Luke's, where I sang as a boy. I think they called him Smartie. Well before my time. There was a brass plate about him on the organ. Could be him. Albert, Arthur ... Alfred ... Albert I think.'

His words flowed, chased one another like eager jigsaw pieces. 'Yes. He died suddenly while playing the organ. Left money for a new boy's cassock every year. Or was that at Southwood? No, I remember the brass plate. There *was* something about that first boy. What was it? Too long ago. Anyway, it was all kept very quiet. Apparently, the solicitor messed things up, and the funds fizzled out. No more cassocks.'

'Who's Alan Turton then?'

'Alec, not Alan. A raving queer. Now Music Prof. at some northern university. And a well-known organ recitalist.'

He paused. Time ticked by. Barbara waited.

'In fact ...' Derek puzzled, 'Turton was a choirboy at St. Luke's and learned the organ with Mr Smart, and I *remember* him then. But how? This is crazy. He was years before me! Queer right from the start – he actually liked Mr Smart interfering with him. And Alec tried it on with various boys, once with me when I was very frightened of the dark. I couldn't find my way out after organ practice. It's really vivid, even now. Dead Smartie had almost got me, then Alec came, switched the light on and saved me. Then ...'

'But, Derek, you've always said you only began organ lessons at thirteen, in Southwood.'

'Yes. No.' Derek was white, shook slightly as he looked away towards a fussy engine shunting trucks. 'I don't know. I remember clearly just taking *piano* lessons from the church organist, but at home. My parents wouldn't allow me to learn on the vestry Broadwood. It was a Mr Hopkins. He always seemed slightly afraid of me. Guarded, almost. He certainly wasn't strict, as with the other boys.'

Barbara stood silent. Derek continued almost as if she were not there.

'No, I never learned the *organ* at Shepherds Bush, they wouldn't hear of it. Wouldn't even let me sit on the stool. 'Spose I was a bit young. But I remember reaching the pedals, my legs were long enough. Yet that's impossible – I was always small for my age and had trouble when I first started learning in Southwood with Duncan Jackson. But I still honestly remember playing before, in Shepherds Bush! It was always after school. In winter, when I'd finished practising, the console light was the only one in the church, except for the Tabernacle. They wouldn't let me use any others because of the expense. It wasn't a rich church.'

His voice was higher pitched than usual. He shook slightly, like a desperate smoker suffering symptoms of withdrawal.

Barbara thought the Gemini twins are splitting; he's utterly confused, undergoing a nervous breakdown. She could tell them nervous breakdown. It sounded better than mental disorder. Perhaps she'd nurse him at home. The college might pay his salary for a while. The cathedral probably would too. Trembling slightly, she began to plan it out.

'I need a drink,' said Derek suddenly, 'a double. Where's the nearest pub?' He surveyed the surrounding landscape from the vantage point of the dry cracked platform. Heat crinkled from the brown metals. A pleasant smell of hot soft tarmac mingled with the creosote, almost like incense.

'Nothing very near,' said Barbara, 'I'd better drive.'

'Drive me to drink!' Derek began to feel more normal. He could joke. He had explained something of his worry, the tip of submerged volcano. Talking of it, admitting it, even the train experience, had taken some pressure away.

He had openly admitted to Barbara that he was going through some sort of paranormal experience. Though she was worried, he felt she was prepared for the inevitable next development.

It was a drama, opened in Swallowfield, but when had the plot begun? He must think it out, Assemble the fragments of mirror glass, into the oval frame, thereby assembling himself.

He'd had his chance on the train, but thrust it away. Trains were obviously important to Geoffrey. Derek sensed his own journey was one way in a corridorless coach. Steam obscured the view from sealed windows. He was a prisoner. The mirror glass must be restored before the journey ended.

At the platform end they met Jamie carrying a huge railway poster of a train, like the one in which they had just ridden. It was a blown up black and white photograph of 1930s vintage. The old locomotive and coaches approached a station platform unrecognizable to Derek. He promised himself a closer look through the comfortable glass of a drink.

Fifteen minutes later, in the beer garden of 'The Volunteer', they unrolled the poster. It resisted with spirit, being content to remain rolled up like Jamie's telescope.

Derek, half-way through his second whisky-mac, had begun to get over the morning's experience, and was looking ahead to Arreton Manor. He was also enjoying the pie and pickled onion snack. Numerous birds pecked at the crisp crumbs from James's precious bag while Barbara tried to forget her morning with a ham sandwich.

He looked again at the poster. James and Barbara were guessing the characters of the passengers in the photograph. It was a seaside station, and there was a pier in the distance, with a steamer caught forever approaching its end. It wasn't Totland.

The train had just reached the end of the platform, and just one opening door had disturbed the smoothness of the coaches' sides for somebody's quick getaway. Gusting steam obscured detail, but through it a fair-haired boy was clearly trying to open the door to be first out. The window was down and his hand gripped the outside handle. His face was eager as it looked toward the camera and directly at Derek. There was something about the set of the head and neck.

'That boy's trying to get to us,' remarked Jamie, 'and that other head is his Dad's.'

'That's just a blur,' Barbara said. 'He went on the wrong train – he's trying to get back. Those are his parents.' She pointed to some more blurred figures on the platform.

'I'm looking forward to Arreton Manor,' said Derek desperately, taking a large mouthful of whisky-mac, 'but first we're going back to Haven Street shop. A surprise for you Jamie.'

Barbara was also surprised. Perhaps Derek wanted to get him a book or something.

Silence. The birds grew brave, until a distant shriek of whistle shocked them away. On a quiet day before the war the whole island must have sounded like a marshalling yard.

'We're surely not going back *there*!' she said at last. But they were.

The shop had cleared because the next train was due to leave. Barbara looked round nervously. What if they met those people from the compartment? Where *would* she put herself? Her stomach turned over at the thought of it, but Derek seemed completely unaware of the possibility.

It was an Aladdin's cave for rail addicts. Barbara expected Derek to stop before a case with 0-0 gauge engines in it, or technical books, but he strode to a huge yellow signal-arm in the corned behind piled sleeper bolts. Marked at fifteen pounds, it was expensive even for 1973. Barbara was amazed when she heard Derek discussing it excitedly with James aghast when she saw his cheque-book in hand, and an eager assistant heaving the metal arm from the corner.

'What are you doing? You're *not* buying *that*, surely?' But he was.

'We like it, don't we Jamie? Just right for the wall above our model railway.' He turned defensively to her, his tone curiously juvenile again.

'It's stupid, Derek, we just can't afford that,' Barbara hissed, hoping the assistant could not hear. 'What do we need it for? It weighs a ton.'

But Derek turned away and wrote the cheque. Short of tearing the pen from his hand there was nothing she could do.

Soon they were driving on to Arreton Manor, the signal-arm lodged at an angle suggesting a railway guillotine. Jamie was forced to sit right behind Derek's head in the mirror, a position which Derek would not normally tolerate. Also lodged in the car was an angular atmosphere, and a chill which Jamie was trying to break with bright conversation.

The atmosphere softened the farther they got from the railway. Barbara had just begun to speak again as the Morris lurched dustily into the chalk-white lane to the house. The green bushes were blanched, spattered with dust as if never disturbed.

The car came to a jagged halt in a chalk cloud which drifted round it like in a Western. The small wooden-bodied station wagon was not, after all, so very different from a prairie schooner.

The unambitious car park was a few minutes' walk from the house, so they began to pick their way with wobbly steps down the lumpy lane. Derek ran back to lock the back doors of the car, leaning his elbow on the wood to shut them properly as always.

'Waste of time,' said Barbara, sniffily. 'No-one's going to pinch that signal.'

Derek ignored this, checking each door and window, then rejoined them, running hard, and hopping from the firmer peaks of the miniature Himalayas which the track resembled. Just as he did in Kent when a boy, he resolved only to tread on the very highest mountains. He felt like a giant in ten-league boots, but one mistake would cause the boots to vanish.

Barbara looked at him curiously. Everything Derek did now was significant.

'Hey, hope it's open today – Bank Holiday!' He stopped, suddenly. 'Still, Haven Street was.'

'Bank Holiday? – You're out of date! Been changed to the end of August for years,' Barbara replied. Jamie laughed.

The manor was set in between gentle hills at the foot of the

Arreton Downs, and occupied a small valley of luxurious trees, rich soil and chalky walls with creepers. Admission was through the inevitable gift shop. To Barbara's disappointment they negotiated it safely, without paying for anything except three tickets.

Piqued about the signal, she had spied a set of attractive placemats which would look well in a certain Vicars' Close dining room. A jam and Jerusalem lady, in hat and frock, sat in an honorary position behind the counter.

Up on the gravel plateau in front of the house itself, the warmth of the silver stone with its streaks of pink and ochre attracted visitors towards the main door. This was flanked by two realistic sculptured guard-dogs at the foot of the steps.

Jamie, like every other child, and his father, couldn't resist putting his hand in the nearest open stone mouth, daring the animal to bite. But it didn't, its petrified head and blank eyes waited instead for the ball which never came; or perhaps had come and gone. A ball thrown by the Gorgon?

There were other visitors that hot day in that last summer, but by chance the Hendersons were able to explore almost alone. They had arrived early in the afternoon, and the human flow which both kept the house in existence, and also blighted that existence, had not yet built up after lunch.

Arreton. Derek felt long love present here, not just of this cherished place, but the continuing human love he'd never had as a child. It was never far from his thoughts. Was he the loving father he should be? His own split personality as musician and parent always grated.

To walk here was to know security and warmth. The polished timber shone family pride, worlds away from identical screens, furniture, wainscoting, in many another house now catalogued as a museum.

They were even welcomed individually, if briefly, by an upper-crust lady, and Derek looked automatically at the hands which, he suspected, persuaded jewels out of Elizabethan oak.

It was really all a jewel. The colours were as rich and as deep as the years. Derek found himself wanting total silence to dispel any tourist air left here, to let Arreton come into him as he had entered. And it did come in the form of a series of gentle shocks, occuring at almost regular intervals.

They stood before some Charles the Martyr relics. Charles was remembered particularly in the hall. Derek found the permanently lit candle in its seventeenth-century candlestick especially moving. Charles was still on the island.

It was a sanctuary light, though the flame did not float in oil. It was disembodied: a presence, a visible spirit. One lit candle is always more evocative than a score: the poignancy of ego sum, the frail dance of life. That flame is life's fragility. Exhausted, or extinguished, it becomes a blue spiral up, home to heaven. But, smashed down in excommunication, does the wraith sink, despairing? He wondered, thinking there had been no candles in Swallowfield Cathedral during Cromwell's reign. There had been grass in the desecrated sanctuary. There had been horses in the aisles. His lady was violated. Humiliated. The great organ case was torn from the screen, its huge eyes blinded. God was gone.

Michael Este had premonition, so Derek liked to imagine, when he composed *Peccavi* for the viols. A penance in advance, Este taking on, like an atonement, that greatest sin: the violation of God. For Derek had convinced himself it was written in and for his holy city, later burned and smashed by Parliamentarian cannon.

Because of *Peccavi*, their sin was become Este's. Swallowfield and he were both scarred for ever. Living there had burned Derek, too, like an ancient radiation. Derek thought of it often, but most of all on St. Linc's day. Peccavi.

Este had died in 1648, still nominally cathedral organist, never to know God back in His Sanctuary.

Because of the cruel cannonades, the red brick Precincts houses are, in reality, medieval underneath seventeenth century clothes. Derek had never been in most of them, but imagined what they were like under their dresses, their secret places.

You would never suspect their humiliation now. But hate does not always heal inside, and perhaps it burnt others like Derek, that radiation of guilt.

There was one ancient ex-lay vicar who lived in Vicars' Close, who refused ever to allow the installation of electricity or gas. His house was built over and round the brick tunnel entrance to the Close, but there were never any visitors. The old man kept himself, candles burning, in vigil for the past as the old

64

do. His house was lantern to himself, to the dark close nights under the quiet stars and the black bulk of the cathedral.

So the vigil of Charles's candle in Arreton found an immediate response in Derek. Its flame warmed the corners of the wooden room. James considered it briefly, then wandered off. Barbara was fascinated by an ancient inventory book, its ink the hue of many a faded candle flame.

The house opened itself to them with a smile and feminine softness. They walked in the perfume of old wood, each rich room leading to a richer, like a transformation scene. It was tactile music, reminding Derek of that wet Friday before the holiday, when they'd sung the Crotch anthem, so aptly named, with the chromatic passage. He heard again that musical transformation, composed and sung in mellow candle-light.

Ancient wood is often like iron, but the light in this house fell on no hardness; the oak had lost its edges. It was rounded, almost pliant. Arreton was an old lady who'd had within her so many lovers.

The oldest and roughest timber was on the attic stairway rising to the 'Echoes of Childhood' Museum. Both Barbara and James were keen to see it. They went ahead eagerly. Derek found himself alone on the stairs, his hand resting and feeling the texture of the banisters.

Above him were James's excited feet, resonant through ancient attic oak, then Barbara's. He examined the hollowed treads under his own, and enjoyed the pitted timber of the balustrade in detail. There was something about the phrase 'echoes of childhood' which echoed in his own mind. Echoes of a child. No echo is ever lost, but this one is special. Which child? Childhood echo … it was an emotive phrase.

The hard dry banister wood looked at him, carved by countless penknives over Island years. He thought of the back of the organ in the gallery of Southwood Church. There, generations of blower boys had left scarcely any of the original wood surface without a literary texture. More figures than a ledger. Dry echoes, scratched names in the acetate stone, wood and plaster on the green hill.

Why is it that ancient graffiti is moving, yet modern graffiti is vandalism? Perhaps because time itself imbues poignancy. Or is it that even the very letters, scratches from the past, have a control, a dignity unknown today? In the past, the idiot could not write. Now he can.

One name took his attention, standing forward more than most. 'Geoffrey' it said, in large capital letters. *That* name again. It should have been unremarkable: there were so many names. John, Peter, a lone Alfred. Even a council-house Kevin in ballpoint. There were crosses and places where knives had been sharpened; but his eye always returned to Geoffrey, incised in a businesslike way. It almost seemed to have eaten itself in after the cut, like acid in an etching plate. That timber would hold it until Doomsday.

He moved up the stairway to the landing. An ancient simple door of planks set in a crude frame was on the left, and the museum lay behind. He stopped. That third pair of trailing feet; they had a softer sound, a hesitant padding, gingerly following the positive Hendersons.

His hand touched the door several times before he managed will-power enough to open it. James was at the far end. On the other side was Barbara, admiring an intricate eighteenth-century doll's dress. But he himself was the third person.

He knew now. It was just time before Barbara and James became fully implicated, drawn in to the confrontation – indeed it had started. All he could do was contain, absorb the development as long as he could. Or perhaps the only answer was to get them off the island. Was it even possible? He remembered the rushing man in *Highways*, his apparent panic.

Derek strode into the room and went straight to James standing before a panorama of Redcoats in an unfashionably brave British square, which unfashionable Derek so admired. But Geoffrey stood in the front rank of his mind. Would he *allow* them to escape the island?

Barbara was still in the doll collection, James inspecting a Pollock toy theatre, and Derek stood by the low dormer overlooking the front of the house, guidebook in hand. Two lads had quarrelled and fought a duel on December 28th, 1540. Thomas and James Leigh. Large house, estate, companionship, yet they killed each other. Madness.

An idea struck him and he walked quickly back to the stairs, perhaps their names were there; preserved in the house they both coveted. But no, only Geoffrey stared at him.

66

It was a confident style of lettering, not one of your furtive scratches, your ashamed graffiti. It was proud, yet there was a secretive curl in certain of the letter forms. Exploring the texture of the letters, he recalled Barbara's graphology look. Something made him press hard onto the wood. The name lay reversed, deep, Geoffrey in the mirror, the mirror formed of his flesh.

James and Barbara came out of the attic.

'Jamie, it says here that two boys fought a duel where we're standing. Back in the sixteenth century. Killed each other with swords. Nice juicy bit of history.' He showed them the entry.

'*Both* killed?' puzzled Jamie. 'How?'

He stood on the top step and surveyed the landing. 'You'd think one would have won, would have one ... Get it?'

'Could happen,' Barbara broke in, interested in the problem. 'Perhaps a simultaneous thrust to the heart. Unlikely but possible.'

'They didn't die simultaneously — one died later from his wounds,' Derek said. 'Funny to think you can be already dead yourself and can still kill someone.'

'It's still possible,' Barbara went on. 'Two swords, or any weapons used at mathematically the same instant. They could have done it. The odds are tremendous, of course. Be interesting to work it out.'

'Bet it was like a Douglas Fairbanks sword-fight,' said Jamie. 'You know, up and down stairs, jumping on things—'

'Bit before your time,' Barbara laughed, 'and mine! Where did *you* hear about Douglas Fairbanks then?'

Derek waited, frightened, on the boy's answer.

'Children's television — in 'Filmclip', and there was this man, y'see, who—'

'Later, Jamie, later. Let's get on with Arreton,' said Derek, relieved.

They moved down the stairs, Derek's hand still trailing on the pitted wood like a trolley on wire. He thought of flashing trolley buses outside Shepherds Bush underground station. Then, clanky trams before them, always in rain, always above glistening clobbles.

On the ground floor, back past Charles's candle, there was a sudden secret door, now unsecret, leading to a gun room and the kitchens. A welcome message and an arrow awaited them there, pointing them through and outside.

Refreshments were served from an old scullery at the back of the house, and on a lawn once part of the kitchen garden. It was a well of honey-perfumed warmth. A very English clink of cups and discreet conversation filled any gaps left by the shadows.

The grass was cosseted by textured silver-ochre stone and heavily established trees. They chose a bower as ancient as the pitted balustrade. Derek opened the guidebook. Barbara sat with James, ready to discourage the speed he would take on to get through his coca-cola so as to create a belch, and to emit drain-like noises with the straw. This was always to annoy people sitting near. Usually old ladies.

Despite Barbara's efforts, James, as usual, finished his drink much too early, while they each had half a cup left. She nipped the belch in the bud with a sharp jab in the ribs. Jamie set about rescuing it. Barbara had other ideas.

'Jamie, what about exploring? There are some shrubberies round the other side. Find some secret paths, give us a quarter of an hour or so. Got your watch on?'

Barbara spoke enthusiastically, hoping for some respite. He vanished obediently. Tea clinked on, the lawn gradually filled, the sun moved imperceptibly, and quarter of an hour went rapidly.

James appeared round the corner of the long house, followed slowly by a dog which resembled, uncannily, a stone one brought back to life. James attracted dogs as babies do old ladies. Boy and hound picked their way through the metal tables and gentle tea drinkers.

Jamie reached Derek and Barbara. His face was puzzled. The dog settled in the shade, its mouth open foolishly, eyes closed against the glare.

'Crazy! Do y'know Mum,' for Derek was still deep in the guidebook after glancing up briefly, 'it was like the Secret Garden – lots of different paths, secret ones leading to a door in a wall. I went in, then suddenly there was this girl—' he broke off looking puzzled again, 'she was very quiet and she didn't come very close. I felt so hot, all sweaty. She just smiled, her face all pale, then she said hello, but it wasn't to me. Some other name,

68

to someone behind me. Then she smiled again and I turned round to see who she was talking to. But guess what, there was no-one. When I looked back she'd disappeared. Completely vanished.'

'She was no ghost,' Barbara laughed. 'More likely school sprint champion! Think so, Derek?'

He looked up from the book. 'No doubt of it,' he said lightly. Yet he worried.

'But there was nobody behind me either,' Jamie persisted.

'She was playing a game of her own,' Barbara reassured him. 'You'll get used to the female mind one day!'

'In a hundred years!' commented Derek, his mind on the guide.

James *was* worried about the incident in the garden. They'd have to play it all down. Then, into the tea-garden walked a family, their heads moving like searching birds. The mother was carrying a small white cardigan. She started to talk to complete strangers as worried mothers will.

'Has anyone seen Fiona?' she said, darting to the various hot rickety metal tables, questioning everyone.

'She's eight, wearing a long skirt, a pinkish colour, and a white blouse, new only last week. She's got dark hair. Has anyone seen her?' Her eyes were full of worried tears. 'She's very pretty.' She had almost reached their table.

'It could have been her in the shrubbery,' said James, shyly. 'Don't know where she's gone now.'

'You must have seen where she went, you must have done,' the woman rounded on James. 'She just couldn't disappear.'

'No... I think it was the same girl,' said James, a little frightened by the woman's questioning manner. 'I just didn't see where she went. Sorry.'

'Don't worry,' said Barbara, soothingly, 'she'll be about somewhere. No traffic to worry about. She's probably in the house. Have you looked there?'

'Not recently,' said the woman grasping at a straw. 'Perhaps you're right, we'll go back.'

They did. Derek said nothing, thinking back to the guidebook. He thought of the young girl, pushed out of a top floor window by her brother and killed. He thought of the ghost, seen frequently by many, but notably by children. Arreton was a place of passions.

The child James had seen obviously belonged to the woman. He reassured himself quite unsuccessfully. But to whom did she speak?

'That little girl,' Derek turned to James, 'what *did* she say?'

'Hello, I think,' Jamie's forehead screwed up with effort, 'then something else, but not to me, to ... some name. She had a funny voice — sort of echoey. Like psalms.'

'Yes, yes, but which name?' Derek said impatiently, trying not to sound it. He had to know for certain. But Barbara broke in cheerily.

'Come on, forget it, there's so much else to do! All this talk of little girls! What about the gardens, Jamie, you show us. And I want to look at that Hall tapestry again.'

Derek pictured the Hall. Viols and Este's Peccavi. How well it would sound here, enclosed by Jacobean panelling, watched by Charles the Martyr's candle. And the little girl...

'You do dream,' said Barbara. 'Come back to earth, to us mortals.'

They got up. She automatically tidied the teacups together, and removed the coke bottle, with its shattered straw, from the edge of the table where Jamie had drained its life blood.

They were in the shrubbery. James had just re-enacted the encounter with the young girl. Derek looked up. Glinting in the glare was a high window which should be ideal for a fine photograph of the grounds.

'Won't be a minute,' he called to them as he strode towards the house. When he finally reached the window from which the little girl had been pushed, there below him was the gravel, and the lawn, but he couldn't see the petrified dogs. They were tucked away, masked by the eaves. There was a glimmering vista of valley, of foliage jumping with heat. An illusion of movement, or real?

There to the left, like Hampton Court Maze made small, lay the shrubbery. Barbara was bent over a rare plant and there was Jamie looking up at him. No little girls. But down below him on the gravel a loud coach party had just arrived. Their guide told them what to see with stentorian voice.

'An hour 'ere. Back on the dot if you don't mind ladies and gentlemen.'

They crunched towards the house, scattering small stones onto the smooth grass, ready to ruin the motor-mower. Derek sighed. While they thundered through, Arreton would be one more museum. They would sense no viols, see no little girl. Perhaps just as well.

When they had disappeared he took a photograph. He was just able to see the edge of the shrubbery and the walls round the kitchen garden. Two minutes later he himself was part of that view seen by other eyes from that window. But they were not looking through a camera lens.

They walked up the narrow white lane away from the house towards the car, Barbara a few paces behind the others.

'That girl,' whispered James, 'her clothes weren't the same.' Then reddening he said: 'But ghosts don't do what she did. Do they?'

'What?' Derek was intrigued. But James wouldn't say what she did. 'Wow, it's hot,' he turned and said suddenly, 'can I have another coke, Mum?'

'All right,' said Barbara reluctantly, 'but we're not made of money.' She looked meaningfully at Derek, who could see a railway signal at danger in each of her eyes.

Jamie soon returned bearing his treasure like a lone Magus, the incident in the shrubbery apparently forgotten.

The car was a tank of heat. The metal of the yellow signal had magnified it. Their eyes felt lead-heavy and prickly even looking in. It was hypnotic, yet to climb in was impossible. The tortured air seemed reluctant to escape even with every window and every door open.

Derek hurriedly rubbed out the name written in finger-tip on the dusty window before Jamie could see it, a name he would remember from the shrubbery. The name which gave Derek the answer he feared. Once again he had pushed it from him, but this time because of Jamie.

When the heat in the car was bearable, they started off back to Totland, ready for the cool salt sea. Derek swung the wheel, causing the white chalk to scream out under parched tyres as they crackled abruptly out of the car park. The dust cloud spread wide and high in that stilled summer, turning proud parked cars into lepers and dark foliage into Constable's snow. What had Jamie meant about the girl? *What* did she do? And for whose benefit? (Should they get away, *now*, today?)

Out of the corner of her eye Barbara saw, but did not note, the child watching them from the bower of dry lilies.

ECHO

Our house smells of secrets, and so does St. Luke's. Saw some super modern German houses in Illustrated London News at the dentist's. I'd like to live in one, but you couldn't have any secrets. Those huge windows. You can be seen too much. If we could have special glass that'd be all right. But I'd still like it quiet. Too much noise gives me a headache. Like when Mother has the wireless on too loud, because she's a bit deaf. I hate Henry Hall's programme anyway, especially his voice.

My school's noisy. It's on three floors, made of all this brick, and there are weird little towers on the corners with a kind of dunce's cap on top. And it echoes with noise. The bell is awful 'specially if it's shaken near you on purpose by the monitor.

We've got a playground on the roof as well. And its got railings, huge ones, all round, much higher than anyone. They curve over towards you. You play with a ball up there and it hardly ever goes over. I like that playground, 'cause instead of playing I like looking over at London. You can see the White City Exhibition grounds and stadium.

There's Queen's Park Rangers ground too, and Paddington Station's not far. The steam looks like big white feathers waving out of London. It's like being a giant, I've only got to move and I can squash all those little people. My puppets. Knock over their buildings. Could if I wanted to. Our attic window's not so high as the school, but I can just see the Green, near the White City entrance.

It's like a funny railway tunnel, very white with towers, and big enough for a train. Can't see Father's shop, but you can see into lots of windows. I know all about those people, and the things they do. I write it all down in my book, I'll show you when you come.

I like reading newspapers, and I've got loads of children's books. My *favourite is* The Young Readers Edition of David Copperfield, *by Charles Dickens. I like his funny names. Peggoty. And Mister Dick. That's a good one. Fancy being called that!*

Father doesn't know all the books I've read from his secret shelf. There are lots of things they don't know — like my telescope. They think I'm keen on astronomy!

They won't have a dog — it's too much trouble, too messy. And they say the germs will make my catarrh worse. Who ever heard of that? Anyway I've got the inhaler. The dog could live in a kennel, and I'd take him for walks. They still said no.

We've got a cat. He's called Benedict, and I call him funny names. He's a big ginger cat, flat wide head and a bushy fluffy tail 'specially when he's angry. He comes in looking very angry and ginger, all kind of ruffled and plump. Everything of Benedict is ginger. He'd be ginger inside if you cut him up. All striped.

My best name for him is Animal Man, 'cause he's a small person, lives in our house and is one of the family, and he's my friend. We talk to each other. They don't think he understands anything but he does. He talks to me in bed. He's like a little brother all wrapped in fur. He can't be very bright with that flat head, there isn't much space for his brain. But I like him and he likes me.

He rubs himself all the way round, standing up to cling on, his little hands imploring me to talk to him. It's not just for food. I know it's not. I love to watch him catch a bird. I keep very very still so as not to disturb it on the grass, and so Animal Man can get close enough to pounce on it. What a squawk it makes. He kills it gradually, and I like to watch it struggle.

He lets it go, then just as it thinks it's free he smashes down on it again. Then he's in charge and won't let go until it's dead. He always pulls its head off. When he's eaten some, he leaves the rest for me. Not to eat — I cut it up warm to look for its soul. Never found one. Perhaps Benedict has eaten it. He must be full of souls. He stands up and tries to turn door handles, with his hand. Anyway, he's very clever.

I make up bird names. Shit Warbler. Flem Tit. I've got lots of them. Turd Hopper.

This summer we're all going away, to the Isle of Wight, all except Benedict. Father announced it this morning. The Isle of Wight. Sounds smashing. It's hot where we're going. Near Freshwater, exploring, swimming. Playing with other boys.

Father said he'd been saving up for us to go to a proper hotel, one with everything. And I'm not to worry, they're taking a ground sheet. When I meet those boys, we'll have real fun. There'll be places with bushes. I'll take masks for all of us. There are castles, Father told us about them. Especially Carisbrooke.

He said he'd plan it all out, really good. We're there for a week. There's this book he brought back from the library, all about the island, with loads of pictures. There's one of our hotel and beach. He says the sea might cure my catarrh. Something needs to.

There's a proper railway over there. It goes almost everywhere. It must be like a toy railway on a toy island. I'll take some snaps with my Brownie camera. When no-one is looking. Secret photos.

Build a raft! I could sail it from the beach, the one by the Hotel. I shall build myself a raft. I can fish on it. Maybe someone will come with me, another boy to come and fish with me. The water will be so clear, I'll be able to see right down. Like Coral Island on Swiss Family Robinson. Not like canals with dead fish floating on top. Even if nobody will come with me, Benedict would like to be on the raft – all that fish. He'd hate the sea though.

It'll be end of July we're going, into August. Before then I'll read that new Isle of Wight book.

Just remembered the name of the place. Totland Bay. The railway goes as far as Freshwater, but not Totland. That means it's more quiet.

There'll be people strolling about. When I undress in the bushes and put my mask on, I can choose one girl and show her.

WEDNESDAY

It was disappointing. Motor boat trips round Colwell Bay and over to Hurst Castle had long been discontinued. Whilst hiring a rowing boat with outboard engine, Barbara had chanced the remark that they could make their own way across to Hampshire, for Hurst Castle was a sliver which speared into the Solent approach from the far shore.

The boatman's reactions were dampening. He refused to let them have the boat at all if they intended to venture beyond the confines of the bay. So much for their deep sea crossing.

'Bet they didn't stop the King racing in Britannia,' said Derek unexpectedly, a remark which puzzled everybody else.

Even close inshore it was still enjoyable to meander up and down, describing salt spirographs in the clear sea, and braving the ordeal of swapping places for all to have a turn steering. Having nearly caused serious injury to a serious swimmer with no sense of humour, they ran out of time and back into shore, surrendering the boat reluctantly to the dour boatman. He surrendered their deposit equally reluctantly.

Once again, to Jamie's disappointment and Barbara's surprise, Derek elected to sit and guard the clothes while they swam.

'I'll read my paper,' he said, and his eyes were on Barbara and the body he'd once needed so much. She reached the sea.

He closed his eyes, hoping that the now inevitable small figure away over there on Warden Point would vanish while he counted a hundred, adding as many fractions after ninety-nine as he could remember existed. His throat felt dry and croaky, though not through heat. Sleeping with mouth open again. It was regular now, a definite regression. But it was the taste, foul and metallic. It took several swallows of water to clear now each morning, and it returned after an hour or two.

Slowly, he ticked off his life in blind seconds. Sounds surrounded him, the beach engulfed him, he became more aware of the smell of the sea, everything was closer. He realised for the first time how eyes keep things at bay. You can be uninvolved if you wish, because you see all in advance. Close the lids, shut off your vision and you are invaded. No choice; with no eyes the world is terrifying. God, to be blind.

Transistor radio away on the left, plumping of a beach ball and feet thuds, cries from gulls and kids, the swosh of the sea. Warmth, comforting with eyes open, was claustrophobic with them shut. Drone of a light plane, a whisper of wind. Rustling of newspaper sheets. Tang of soft salt, seaweed, sand, damp at a distance, hot and dry near him. Crowding in. Closer. Closer.

It almost hurt as the numbers ticked away. *Could* he open his eyes at the hundred? Would the boy be gone? Or would he be nearer? ... Ninety-nine and nine-tenths. Open not too fast, the blur of slow grey curtains, brightness beyond, a shape in front. *That* smell mingled with seaweed. Eyes flicked fully open. And there was nobody.

He was, as before, isolated on his island of beach kit. The newspaper was scattered about. But two small footprints lay like New Zealand to his Australia.

On his foot's first impulse he destroyed them, angrily, with a nuclear heel, regretting it immediately. The mirror image all over again. Why must he destroy?

It seemed instinctive, the panic of a drowning man smashing at the engulfing water instead of even trying to swim, thus contributing to his own death. And he was the fool who'd smashed the mirror, scattering the fragments wide, which had only to be gathered up again. Yet the pieces could never be reassembled while he thrust them away, or tried to escape. Perhaps *he* alone should stay on Wight, but how to explain?

He gathered up the newspaper sheets and reassembled those instead. England badly beaten in the Test against West Indies. The Watergate trial rambling on in the United States. Economic gloom in Britain.

When he looked again, the figure had gone.

Barbara felt intensely nervous in the gift shop in Osborne House, fearing another signal incident. She needn't have been. Derek seemed unmoved by what was on show; in fact like James he didn't bother with the guidebook at all.

Something had decided her to drive this morning. Jamie and he had seemed apart from her, once out of the car, running off to chase each other down the drive towards the house. Like a stateroom outdoors, the grounds offered rich hiding places. Derek and Jamie exploited them, until a solemnly peaked man, gold crown on cap, pursued them in uniform.

Had this happened before the railway incident, it wouldn't have worried her beyond slight embarrassment. She would have just looked enviously at the conventional tread of other family men walking contentedly, keeping to the smooth gravel drive.

Derek would have laughed at her as he sped past pursued hotly by Jamie, or vice versa. And she wouldn't really have cared; being married to him was interesting.

But the railway had changed all that. Standing on the pier that first day, she had been right. After this holiday nothing would ever be the same.

She had lost sight of them only three minutes from the car park. They were still being tracked by the navy blue Sherlock Holmes. Only when he had disappeared up ahead had Barbara panicked into a run. What would Derek be doing this time, climbing up the balconies to the Royal Apartments? Swinging like Tarzan on priceless chandeliers? Her mind kept repeating don't let him be, as her feet crunched fast on the crackling gravel.

Then her knees felt weak with relief. No sign of the crowned keeper. Outside the open doors, peering into the dark interior, by the turnstile were her two boys waiting to be paid for.

For it was like having unidentical twins, Gemini made visible. Derek seemed like her longed-for second child. Again she recalled, shuddering, his behaviour on the train. That he was under some sort of mental strain was only too obvious, how seriously was not.

Desperately worried, to her surprise she found a detachment possible. Perhaps it helped to regard him as a child, or better, an adolescent: child and adult. Two people.

Discreetly, she had taken over all control of the family.

Thank God no real organization was necessary while they were away. That marvellous timetable. Almost as if Derek had known. Almost as if he'd sensed his mind was going. So he'd planned everything in advance so as not to worry her. A cry for help in advance.

So much was up to her now. Derek's guardian angel until the psychiatrist, she'd not fuss or add to his problem. And they'd go on with the holiday; that day at Osborne, it still seemed a good idea.

The sumptuous Durbar Room was like an Indian Tutankhamun. She followed her boys into it, but they soon disappeared. Maharajahs' treasures filled it to the heavy ceiling. An abstract Kama Sutra, it was amusing to associate it with Queen Victoria.

The Indian influence waned through the corridor beyond the Durbar Room. After Arreton, Barbara found Osborne's richness crude, though equally absorbing. A heavy ambience. Every fibre, every over-decorated molecule, was impregnated with the Queen's grief and it affected her increasingly, like a pain coming on. There was little charm in most of the fittings, and an overblown vulgarity in so much. Yet it was strangely poignant.

A pair of hugely hideous glass pedestal vases in the Queen's drawing room seemed to preserve death, like see-through reliquary urns. It was impossible to imagine children living in this mausoleum. Perhaps it was once different.

Did grief harden this house, did it finally petrify for all time that moment of death one sepia January day in 1901? Is rigor mortis confined to the organic? Her mind felt unusually perceptive.

Barbara was glad that other pilgrims had spread out. Like Derek, she hated a queued tour. In this case it would have resembled an auction viewing after a funeral.

Resisting the temptation to see if the curtains would crack, she moved quietly round the crowded burial antechamber. Such a monumental grief.

Inexorably, her mind came to a future bereavement: Her own. She was realistic enough to expect Derek to go before her, the usual pattern. How would she be? She would not bury herself in the past, but in Jamie's family, a large one she hoped. Yet she couldn't even imagine life without Derek.

What a powerful place, its influence was immediate. She felt cold. Despite the thick warmth of the summer and of over-full Osborne, she almost expected to see her breath like winter. The Snow Queen's palace.

'Morbid woman,' she spoke out loud, catching sight of a still face in an encrusted mirror. A child passed behind her, and she coloured up. Talking to herself now. She'd be the next for the happy home.

But there was enough preposterous humour in so much here that it began to lift her. She admired, by forbidden touch, a huge penile stand with a glans of imitation flowers on top. She often asked herself whether she used to notice such things before knowing Derek. She usually answered no, but wasn't sure if she should believe it.

The Private Suite lay, appropriately upstairs, past an official pointing hand, plumply Victorian. An impulse turned her on the main stair. Though he'd gone ahead with Derek, she half expected to see Jamie below. It felt even colder here.

A heavy chair stood importantly on the half-landing. She sat down into it dizzily, uncaring that she snapped the official cord.

Derek was Derek in front of Queen Victoria's bath and shower unit. Perhaps it was the act of laughing at the coy wardrobe-like edifice, and the idea of the Queen not being amused in it.

Jamie had happily gone along with his father's antics. When on proper holidays you behave utterly differently.

Derek turned and saw his son. Only his breathless body remembered the last half-hour. He himself wondered where thirty minutes had gone. Still in amused admiration, they were joined by a white Barbara.

'Whatever's the matter, my queen?' Derek greeted her. It must be the heat. 'Thou look'st tired. Dost thou wish to sit down?'

She ignored this, looking at him sharply with searching gaze which he interpreted wrongly. His mood changed.

'Sorry, I didn't know you weren't well. We sort of forged ahead. I feel a bit tired myself.' He put his arm round her. 'We'll find somewhere to sit.'

'I'm all right, don't fuss. Perfectly all right. You don't look too good yourself for that matter.' Derek moved close, put his lips to her ear. 'You look shagged out!'

'So would you be ... so would you be,' she whispered. She controlled herself, angry at nearly failing this first test. She must be utterly unflappable with Derek as he was.

'If what?'

'If you were a woman ...'

Derek grinned.

'Sorry, nudge, nudge,' he bowed theatrically and hissed back, 'monthus periodicus. Say no more.'

'Facetious idiot,' she mouthed into his ear. 'That's right, tell the world.'

She'd won.

Derek said, absently, 'Wonder where the King and Queen stay when they visit?'

Barbara said nothing. His third or fourth reference to King and Queen. Another oddity.

The Private Suite was noticeably more relaxed, the scale not so vast, the design of everything not so monumentally muddled. Here was a gentler sadness, the desolation of a widow not a queen. Barbara looked closely at her own consort. This would be a good test of his mental state. His normal self would pick up this atmosphere at once and it would show. She remembered his acute sensitivity to buildings.

West Wycombe. They had seen the house, explored Dashwood's Hell-Fire caves. The church remained. It stands over the caves, on the crown of the hill, next to the Mausoleum. No sooner had they entered than she'd heard Derek stop abruptly behind her, his feet scuffing the gritty flagstones.

She could still remember with loathing the square grey nave and dark tubular chancel, with Thou Shalt Not in usual eighteenth century fashion on the panelling. But here it mocked and winked through layers of decaying varnish, as if remembering past perversions with pleasure.

She had found Derek outside, a ghastly colour, whispering, 'evil, just evil. Can't go in,' over and over.

Barbara had left him on the grass and tried again. The chill was more than momentary. Derek was right. This time she'd felt the full force of a virulent putrescence. This was no house of

God. It was unbearable. And it threatened her.

It was their shortest visit anywhere.

'I like these rooms, there's a personal feel to them,' Derek said. 'She must have felt shattered without him. It hits you even now.

He sounded normal. But what of his real state of mind?

'What did you think of downstairs then?' Barbara probed. 'Impressed?' Derek stood very still. Albert's walking sticks stood stiffly, ready for the next walk which he never took.

'Downstairs...? I really can't remember much of it.' He spoke slowly as if puzzled.

'That's a change, you're slipping!' She affected surprise.

'Must be! I'll go back later, Jamie and I'll go...'

'No,' she interrupted hastily, 'I'll take him with me. We'll wait for you there.'

She pointed through the window into the grounds. But should they all go back together? No, the crowds were surging at them. They'd have to swim against the tide. It was not allowed, anyway, but one man could do it unobtrusively. But first, there was more to see here.

They surveyed a hideous square piano decorated in black and white candy.

'My God,' Derek said in his music-hall voice, 'takes All-Sorts to make a world, don't y'know!

'Playing that'd be like performing in a pier pavilion!'

'Very witty,' said Derek. 'I'd toss myself off rather than perform on that! Into the sea that is!'

Barbara glared but ignored him. Jamie must surely understand. But James was morbidly interested in the great marriage bed, its photograph of very dead Albert lying waxen just above the pillow.

'Did she actually sleep there?' he said, aghast. 'It'd be like sleeping in that tomb thing – the one by the transept door in the Cathedral.'

They explained about Victoria's extended and intense widowhood, but he continued to look uneasy.

'I couldn't sleep there. I'd always feel he'd come back to get me.'

Derek's stomach jerked. The familiar phrase hit home.

'What I mean is,' Jamie continued, unaware, 'you'd be there alone in the dark and he'd kind of return to get you in the black. There's no bedside light. You'd have to creep to the light switch by the door. Spooky. Was that light switch there then, Dad? *Was* there electricity?'

'Oh yes,' said Derek faintly, 'very likely.' He didn't care one way or the other about historical accuracy. He dreaded what was coming, and couldn't look at Barbara.

'Unless somebody came and put the light on before Albert could get you, you'd get lost. You'd have to be smart to find the switch.'

Smart? Word-play, used purposely, worried Derek, because he *knew*? Or just coincidence?

'Jamie, what a lot of nonsense you talk,' said Barbara quickly, noticing Derek's expression. She recalled something he'd said at the railway, about Alec Turton and a dark church. He now stared at his own son as if terrified, his tongue playing weakly over lips which looked suddenly dried.

'See you in half an hour,' she said firmly, precipitating James towards the exit. 'I expect you're sick of questions,' and she was gone and Jamie with her.

Derek was thankful to see them disappear. It was all true, and Jamie was being made a mouthpiece, to torment him. Or *was* it merely coincidence? Derek stood by Prince Albert's writing desk. He'd never have left it as neat as that. Nothing was ever just chance.

He wandered aimlessly, a living lump in the tourist bloodstream. He had no desire to go back downstairs. Remembering nothing of it, as on the railway, was bad enough. Hearing Jamie speak those words was worse.

A red-faced keeper, in peaked cap and crown badge, stood observing him closely like a sheep-dog. Derek had noticed him before somewhere. Most odd the way he stared. Rather like that old hotel porter ...

Resisting the urge to say 'you'll know me again when you see me,' he wandered again round the small cluttered suite until he had seen too much of everything. Except one very framed, very early photograph in the bedroom, in a dark corner.

The royal children stood stiffly righteous, four boys standing in proud uniform, the girls sat, demurely, hands in white laps as if to protect the neat royal genitals.

All the children's names, with dates, were at the back of the Osborne booklet Barbara had left in his hand. Identification was easy: the names were painted under them on the central plateau of the frame moulding.

Little Beatrice was placed, doll-like, on Princess Victoria's adult thighs. *Princess Beatrice lives at Carisbrooke Castle. She was visited last Sunday by the King and Queen.* The voice came from within him. King and Queen ... ! But however old was Beatrice? And still at Carisbrooke? Yes. Surely.

How bright the eyes trapped inside unbending 1860. How cold the list in the booklet, which stated bare facts of birth, career and death. He refused to look at Beatrice's dates, afraid of what he knew would be there.

But Geoffrey would not be thwarted. The photograph distorted into a Monty Pythonesque photo-montage, the eyes, oddly large with prominent whites, following him, the lips moving puppet-fashion as they initiated balloon captions, dirigibles fifty years too soon.

Beatrice's baby mouth had the biggest balloon of all. It squawked at him: 'I'm one hundred and fourteen, I'm one hundred and fourteen,' endlessly in a ventriloquist's rasp, taunting, mocking, in a tone which found raw nerves in every part of him. It grew louder. The whole room oscillated on the 'teen' like a distant dentist's drill.

He covered his ears. The guidebook fell to the floor. After an interval he uncovered them cautiously. A heavy silence in which he was aware of Prince Arthur in sailor's uniform, aged ten. His blurred head gave almost a dual face, very like trick photographs on ribbed card.

The second face would not be still, flickering back and forth as if living. It was not Prince Arthur's, but another head smirking on top of the small uniform.

The name on the frame. Geoffrey, it was Geoffrey, it was Geoffrey. That bloody Geoffrey, with Jamie's head, and Prince Arthur's body in 1860. That name *had* been Arthur not Geoffrey, Prince Arthur, born 1850. Now it read 'Geoffrey 1923–1933'. No doubt about those dates. Geoffrey aged ten looking like Jamie aged ten, but who died aged ten.

Haunted by a name, a boy, an itinerary, a place, he was a marked man, a man apart. Chosen almost. Geoffrey wanted him, Geoffrey was after him, in the light, not the dark. Come back from the dead to get him. The phrase rang louder than anything gone before.

Geoffrey was a dead boy of ten. But who? Looked like Jamie. Jamie has begun to talk like him ... like ... Derek's mirror self? If only he understood. When would he? ... Not only when, but *where* is the place of understanding? The Isle of Wight? The words of a verse anthem by William Boyce came up: 'Man knoweth not the price thereof, neither is it found in the land of the living... the sea saith it is not in me ... seeing it is hid from the eyes of all living...'

Understanding can't be found in the land of the living? Therefore only in death? Did Victoria find understanding here at Osborne? She had turned her holiday island into a land of death, with Osborne a mausoleum.

Derek still stood unmoving before the photograph. Geoffrey and he face to face inside the mausoleum. Only glass divided them. Mirror. Smashed image. The hotel bedroom. Putting together the pieces. The urge to shatter was still on him but he dropped his glasses case back into his pocket. Control. No more pushing away, or erasing. No smashing. Anyway he couldn't smash Geoffrey — he'd always be back until he got what he wanted.

He stood trembling as before his first sex experience. 'There's no one in and I'm just going to take a bath,' she'd said on the stairs. 'Please wait — I'd like you to.' He had, and they had, eventually at least. And in a way there was a similarity: nerves at the prospect of knowledge. Almost the biblical sense. He sat down suddenly on a chair, still facing the photograph.

'You all right sir?' a voice under a peaked cap. 'You don't look too special.'

'Oh yes, fine ... thanks.' Derek turned tried to smile and not be irritated. To be interrupted now, just when. ...

'Sure you don't want no fresh air?' the attendant persisted, ' 'ot 'ere, all these people.'

'No, I'm all right now, thanks.'

The attendant looked unconvinced. Derek turned away back to Geoffrey. But it was Arthur and so was the name. Arthur born 1850.

Derek fumed. He had been on the edge, and something irrelevant said had spoiled the moment, just as with Maureen all those years ago.

With her, there'd been a second chance.

But here there was not — the figures remained obstinately royal children, the names, royal names. Arthur remained Arthur. Derek suddenly hated the man who had dashed the mirror pieces out of his hand. Gone, quite gone. That fool.

Barbara stood waiting outside by a Teutonic flower bed. 'Jamie's exploring. He'll meet us in the cafeteria. He's looking for camps with another boy. ... Whatever's wrong?'

Derek couldn't reply.

'Surely you can't object to that — he doesn't often play with other boys. ...' Barbara stopped short, frowning. 'That's nonsense — what made me say that?'

'When did this boy arrive?' Derek tried to sound casual.

'About ten minutes before you. I didn't see him properly, Jamie met him over there.'

'There' was two hundred yards across the dry grass, under the shadow of the Queen's bedroom.

'Jamie shouted could he go,' Barbara continued, unaware. 'I said yes. Y'know, that boy's voice gets louder!'

'Oh God, I need strong coffee,' Derek said strangely.

His tone alarmed Barbara again. Just being with him now was like living on Stromboli.

Derek felt like the Ancient Mariner, the albatross a dead weight over his shoulders, one claw into his stomach, low down. But the Ancient Mariner was no coward, like Derek, who couldn't bring himself to search for Jamie, even in his despair.

Converted from a large conservatory away from the house, the cafeteria was becoming full but no less resonant.

They sat, guardedly, with two insipid English coffees, and pretended to discuss Osborne House objectively. Like early courting, it was essential to avoid certain subjects. Say the wrong thing and all is lost. The game diplomatique.

The tension was considerable, and Derek's leg, jammed against the table, shivered the coffees and chattered the spoons. It was the weight of Barbara's arm which steadied them somewhat.

'Dad.'

At last it was Jamie's voice from the door. Derek managed to turn. There was a boy with him, fair-haired, of similar appearance but slightly shorter. The boys moved like marriage down the aisle. 'Mum, Dad. This is Stuart. From London. Stuart ... Rose.'

Stuart stood smiling cheekily, a nice enough lad. They made a suitable response. Suddenly, Derek was happy. So Jamie had been with Stuart! The albatross dropped from his shoulders.

'Come on, you two, have a fizzy drink, and cakes! Come and choose.' He was all happy generosity. His dreads were unfounded. There had been no need to search.

The table piled too high for the Henderson budget, the boys pushed their way through the unexpected feast. Barbara sensed that Stuart was the key to Derek's obvious relief. It wasn't clear why, but then nothing was.

'It's like a birthday tea, this is,' said Stuart, 'and my birthday was yesterday. Do I look ten?'

Congratulations crowded in on him. It appeared that he was on holiday with his family, and had been released to explore after an enforced tour of the house. He was to meet them in two hours.

'Away that long?' asked Barbara, surprised.

'His dad laughed,' Jamie put in, 'and said "so Stuart Rose's fed up with museums." He told you go and play in the grounds, didn't he Stuart?'

Stuart nodded happily, and both boys worked through to the audible drain belt at the bottom of their pop bottles.

Eventually, leaving a table of crumbs, all four set off for the Swiss Cottage. It lay half a mile down a tree-lined avenue. They had walked instead of using the minibus service, and arrived wishing there was a bar. No luck, the chalet was innocent of any refreshment.

Situated in gardens and surrounded by great conifers it looked incongruous. Though genuine Swiss, it somehow didn't look so, nor Canadian as it might have done: a great log cabin, with balconies, on the edge of the backwoods. It was a giant toy, a queen-size doll's house. The royal children had played there. It really was their own house, furnished and undisturbed since 1854.

It proved larger inside than expected. The boys were much taken by the model grocer's shop, a perfect miniature. Alice would have wanted for nothing. If a tiny flask marked 'Drink Me' had been there, Derek would willingly have obeyed. He found himself longing to walk through the little door. The Incredible Shrinking Man. Another existence. As long as there was an antidote, a way back.

Was it a real shop through the reversed telescope, seen from the cathedral spire? Or from an attic in Shepherds Bush?

He had always been obsessed with entering into the lives of others. Now Geoffrey was doing the same to him. But not benevolently. The relief over Stuart had not solved anything. Geoffrey was still there. Everywhere on this island, his kingdom.

He looked back at the model shop. A half-memory—he was a giant surveying his puppet-like subjects − from a height − London − not Swallowfield − he remembered it − all so long ago − seeing into bedrooms − many a private scene made unprivate − White City − not the stadium but the old exhibition entrance − blank − end of film − four − five − six − cross − seven − flash − glare. The film was gone as abruptly as it came.

The boys were intrigued by the kitchens, the small-scale equipment inviting experiment. They fingered the guard rope enviously.

Here the past lay docile. Derek now wished that all things past would stay locked away. He sensed that his preoccupation with time already lived had turned on him, for the advent of Geoffrey could almost be seen as a calling up of a spirit. Like Saul and the Witch of Endor. Like Mr Smart and the pedal trombone. *What could that mean?* It actually sounded like the title of a short story. Or like Felicity and Dolls. He recalled the Stanley Spencer book at home. Resurrections everywhere.

The Hendersons emerged from frozen Victorian childhood. The museum, situated almost next door, was given perfunctory attention. Out again into the hot light, the grass proved ir-resistible. They sank into wiry comfort, surrounded by fruit trees.

'You boys must see this,' Barbara said from within the booklet. 'There's a little fortress behind the chalet, built, it says here, by Prince Arthur when he was only ten ... Do you know Queen Victoria had a daughter Beatrice? Was she the mother of the one at Carisbrooke, Derek?'

Derek had been waiting for the next fragment to go with Mr Smart and the pedal trombone. *The* Princess Beatrice still lived at Carisbrooke. He knew it, and ignored the question.

'I won't come to the fort,' he muttered, feigning to yawn. 'I'll stretch out here.'

It was Barbara's turn to persuade. 'Where's this "doing things" holiday then? You could sleep on the beach! You need rousting about, that's what!' And her hands curled under his arms onto his maniac zone. Once tickled there he was helpless.

He wished she'd use more deodorant. How she smelled when hot, and it was getting worse. Jamie leapt on, and it was an upside-down tortured world, for a few moments. Stuart stood not liking to join in.

Derek begged for his life and made an unconditional surrender, tucking in his shirt. The grass inside would be with him until the evening. So preoccupied was he with grass, that Barbara's extrovert behaviour had not struck him.

Stuart returned after reconnoitring with news that a boy had told him where the fortress lay. They came upon it through an arch in a wall. The fort was full boy-size, and set square, with low brick ramparts and redoubts. There was a flag-pole. Wooden cannon of boy-scale were placed strategically, and a boy could have walked down steps under one redoubt to disappear under the meticulously shaved turf. Surrounding the fort was a shallow indentation resembling a moat. The drawbridge looked as if it would really work.

It was a boy's dream, and Jamie and Stuart moved into it by instinct, complete with sound effects.

'Come out of there. *Stop* them Derek.'

But Derek was with them.

Barbara drove them to Ryde that afternoon. Derek and Jamie sat together in the back. The Osborne visit had ended abruptly, and Stuart had disappeared diplomatically after the disastrous episode at Prince Arthur's fort.

Barbara still could not think of it objectively, despite her intention. The considerable audience, which had gathered to watch the noisy game in the fort, had embarrassed her. In vain she had tried to restrain Derek. He never heard or saw her. In fact the sheer noise put out by the boys appeared to worry him. One hand or the other was constantly over his ear as he ran about, stick in hand. Yet he didn't seem able to break himself away.

As the crowd had increased she had merged successfully with it, and had watched the eventual arrival of uniformed authority to deal with this idiot man and his gang. She'd almost managed to convince herself that she was just an onlooker.

The ejecting of Derek, James, Stuart and six other boys, or was it five, she found more upsetting. For Derek, as natural leader, had been like a spoilt footballer gesticulating against officialdom and the little black book.

Peaked officialdom had replaced the overturned cannons and tried to smooth over the weals and scuffs in the turf. It was more difficult to replace the sticks ripped from near-by trees. Particularly those jammed in the redoubts. All this was in the book too. One keeper had eyed the new wild game raging on heavier grass nearby, the other had telephoned discreetly.

A few minutes later the police car had arrived and the game had broken up. Barbara had overcome herself and managed to plead on Derek's behalf. The interview had come to an end:

'Well, Madam, seeing as how you've established some excuse for ...', he looked at his notebook ... 'er, Mr Henderson, and, er, we have all his details, we'll say no more ... for the moment. He'll probably have to pay for any damage. Might go to court if the Department of the Environment decides to take it that far. Make him see a doctor, that's my advice ... and soon.'

The other boys had been cautioned and dismissed. The sight of police had not brought Derek to himself as Barbara had expected, and he stood head down with Jamie. She saw a changed personality. As he had behaved, so he looked: different. Somebody else.

Barbara knew very little about mental illness, but she'd heard of schizophrenia. She understood it as two personalities in one body. She thought of the railway incident. Derek's aberration here was more marked and longer lasting than at Haven Street.

The remaining keeper had requested them formally to leave his area and hopefully to leave Osborne, but Jamie had run over to Queen Victoria's bathing machine. Worried, Barbara had followed, making certain that Derek came too.

'What's it for?' said Jamie, stroking a tall wheel, 'its's like a caravan.'

'Sea bathing,' replied Barbara, 'she changed in it.'

'Caravans change people. Horrible things,' said Derek after a pause, and then Barbara knew he was himself again. He certainly disliked caravans, and once had almost told her why.

An eye was kept on them all the way to the car park. Two eyes to be exact.

Barbara found a parking place eventually, way down the Esplanade at Ryde. Thank God they'd gone to Totland: this place was chaotic with big time holidaymaking. Luckily the tide was out. What could it be like with the hordes pressed back to the concrete front by the blue Solent?

There was too much to spend money on. The town fathers in their financial wisdom had seen to this. Unfortunately the Wight-style Acapulco appealed to James. He was promised a turn on the boating lake and limited time in an amusement arcade. While they sat, two frigates passed in mid-channel, and the ferry approached the pier end. Some children could be seen on a coloured raft.

Barbara was relieved when Derek, now seemingly normal, wanted to go on his own to explore the town. She knew he'd hate Ryde Esplanade in the holiday season, and that it was only in the itinerary for Jamie's sake. So despite the dangers, she was glad when Derek strolled away.

She'd been waiting for a quiet opportunity to talk to Jamie about Derek. Jamie's bewilderment was obvious. She had been successful so far in suppressing his questions, but it couldn't last. The Osborne episode forced her hand: Jamie had to know something of Derek's mental trouble.

But it was Jamie who spoke first:

'What'the hell's the matter with Dad?'

Derek walked into the town. He could forget holidaymaking. And Osborne. He could not tell Barbara that this time had been different. He remembered everything at the fort. This was a development. He was now aware that this Geoffrey was in him permanently.

The phrase which had so sickened him at Blackgang was now reality: 'Geoffrey took over.' Who the bloody hell *was* he? He felt frightened. What would happen? Being conscious but helpless while in the fort was something new. Boy Geoffrey had been only too real, but always at a distance. It had been like sleep-walking before. Did I really do that, or say that?

Not true now. Derek was a puppet, worked from within himself. He tried to think when the change had occurred.

A frenetic music hit him point-blank from a pavilion theatre. One of today's odd jerky routines was being rehearsed by a pop dance group. Derek's hatred of noise, recently even more acute, was oddly suspended. He felt himself drawn in by it, sucked in by the pressure.

Unisex Peter and Petra Pans burst identically on to the broad low stage, all limbs and tossing heads. How contemptuous they all were, how scornful. But they are just puppets, Derek thought. The overtly sexy music, with its heavy throbbing bass and vicious syncopation controlled each one. That twitching and thrashing. That flailing hair. The wide eyes flickered to order.

Despite himself, Derek was secretly taken by this suggestive, masturbatory choreography and rhythm. Not that he could ever admit to it.

Round they jerked, now reacting, pointing to the spotlight suns, then thrusting away imaginary suitors, now protecting their bodies with jealous hands which became abruptly provocative in an opposite instant.

They danced round their own crotches, the movements either sticklike, sinuously suggestive, or both.

But it was the puppet element: the unrelenting perky beat was king. It wouldn't end. It can never end. It has pervaded us all, he thought. All. He remembered Sandie Shaw's old song *Puppet on a String*. Had she spawned today's marionettes by parthenogenesis? Can we change now? Possibly. But some never can: they are punch-drunk.

The Peter and Petra Pans never change either: they are slyly replaced when they show age. Age, the new obscenity. Time, the enemy. Old, tired, they are put away to breed, and new bright-eyed ones spring, at a cord's jerk, into their places. They need no tuition. 'Dolly birds' for the 'guys'. We must all be called guys now. We must all seem American, mourned Derek.

He watched the youthful bodies now seemingly at the point of collective orgasm. Is it all merely a living parable of human existence? A harnessing of rhythmic instincts? Or does it really tell of an insidious takeover? The music industry rules, O.K.? Americanism rules, O.K.? For what is a guy, but a doll, a dead effigy?

But suppose by accident, a new puppet were snatched away after he had barely begun? There waiting in his box, a hate would build. Tomorrow shall be my dancing day. For him somehow to escape back to the stage would be death to the dance. That huge resentment would be too powerful, would blow the show.

The orgasm never quite finished, there was no relief, and the routine did not end. It faded, the last disappearing puppet rolling its eyes and little bum as it left the stage. The implication was that it all continued beyond.

Its disappearance freed Derek, and he backed out of the sequinned door like a courtier from a court of marionettes. It was only then that his head exploded with five minutes' accumulated noise.

George Street. Esplanade more distant, the town became more normal, and so did Derek's hearing. He spent a long time in a second-hand shop in a back street, watched morosely from a desk in the far gloom. Harmsworth's Encyclopaedias, chests of drawers and ancient deceased clothes made the air smell like old women, dead books, No 22, Poplar Grove, Shepherds Bush and father's shop.

He came upon a set of Great War histories bound in brown. One lay open at the degradation of the Somme. Corpses rotted in liquid, filth-filled craters punctured by torsos of trees. He slammed the book shut. It wasn't just abhorrent, it was unbearable, and he hurried from it surprised at his own reaction.

Eventually he came out happy with an early Victorian copy of Handel's Acis and Galatea, price 25 pence in a box of musical flotsam.

There were some attractive buildings in Ryde. A high spire in superb proportion and Victorian Gothic took his eye. He would have tracked it down had he not seen the large music showrooms in John Street.

There was an impressive Steinway in the window, and some quality electronic organs stood at ingratiating angles; a maze of somehow American gadgetry. 'Pipeless' organs always held a dreadful fascination for him, but they always seemed to await plush transatlantic lounges and Mormon hymnbooks, or *Home on the Range* by numbers.

When in music shops he enjoyed pretending he was a potential customer. It was specially rewarding as he had once worked in one. Since then, he had toured showrooms on playing sprees, only to say after half an hour: 'Sorry but you don't seem to have quite ...' The actor within usually forced him into his pet Yorkshire accent. A new identity.

As usual, no sooner was he inside the hallowed door, than a salesman, Steinway-smooth, moved forward in shiny black silent shoes. Instinctively, Derek remembered Mr Smart.

They began the charade, for it always seemed to him that the assistant was acting too. A ritual one-upmanship game. Three pianos, a harpsichord, and five electronics later he was attempting Bach on two staggered manuals quite the wrong length.

'Flute! I ask you! When will they realise it can't be done? And when have you heard a passable artificial diapason? This one sounds like electric spaghetti with a condom on each note,' he remarked chattily to the discomfited salesman.

'You must have learned the organ as a boy, sir, easy to—' But Derek had collapsed open-eyed onto the manuals like a dropped doll. His elbow hit the trombone tab.

Mr Wilkins could not drag him off early enough to prevent a gargantuan discord screaming fortissimo through the music sanctuary. That shiny shoe stood heavily on a pedal note, jamming it for a moment.

Fortunately for his sanity, Derek never heard it, but Mr Wilkins dreamed of it for many nights. And of Derek's face.

94

'... so your Dad's ill in a way. He's been under a strain recently. Doing too much. And he's been worried ... about his voice.' Barbara had almost finished. James's reactions had been low-key throughout. Was it a mistake to have talked their way round the amusements? 'You know how uptight he gets over his voice.'

'Hasn't seemed worried to me,' said James. 'He's been great fun but sort of silly. Daft.'

'Well ... just don't be surprised at anything he says or does. He'll see a special doctor when we get home.'

They were back at the beach. By a miracle their place was still vacant. Barbara felt a twinge of concern for Derek's whereabouts now she'd talked to Jamie, but it was soon gone.

Jamie deftly changed for swimming. She lay down, her eyes closed. It was so hot. The sounds shimmered from the beach around her, a dog sprang up, spurting sand onto her face.

A giant foot planted itself briefly near her half-closed lids. It jumped away. A toddler cried. A snatch of Radio One, small as if tinned. Then began the warm beach coma she'd looked forward to. Her ears stopped listening.

'Hey, Mum, look. It's Stuart.'

Osborne. The fort. Barbara felt initial embarrassment, but kept her eyes closed. Perhaps it didn't matter. Derek wasn't here. There could be no recurrence; even if he returned too soon the boys could be out of sight.

'He's on his own. He's coming over.'

There was a comparative silence. How that seaweed attracted flies. She could hear their lazy buzz as they attacked it.

'Hey, Mum, it isn't Stuart, it just looks like him.'

'Never mind, doesn't matter, play on your own.'

She settled down again. So it wasn't Stuart. Big deal. Another comparative silence, then she heard Jamie's voice in distant conversation. Curiosity got the better of lethargy. She sat up.

He was standing with a boy very much like Stuart, and indeed similar to Jamie himself. Very similar. Were all boys on the island the same? Blue eyes, fair straight hair, big feet. Long legs, upright stance.

But the newcomer was fully dressed. His heavy jacket must be wearisome. He looked extremely hot, his hair flat and wet-looking. Both boys turned and approached her.

'Mum, this is Geoffrey. Here on holiday.'

'Hello,' said Barbara, looking more closely. So old-fashioned. Those baggy shorts, right down to the knee. Surely he wears braces. And long socks, with garters. His lower half resembles cigarette-card footballers in Derek's prized collection. Those boots, big and roundly toe-capped like old men's, but scaled to a boy of ten. She didn't like those spots on his face and knees.

'Where are you staying?' Barbara felt her stares needed justification, 'In Ryde? Enjoying yourself?'

'Yes, thank you Madam,' returned Geoffrey, politely, smiling slowly. 'I'm here with my family. Come over from Freshwater by train. To play with James.' He nodded towards Esplanade Station. He had strange eyes. Cold in spite of their smile.

Barbara smiled back, 'Jamie *was* feeling a little lonely. Where's your home then, Geoffrey?'

'Shepherds Bush.' His smile faded.

'Jamie's father comes from there, originally that is. What a coincidence!'

Barbara's tone was bright: her coffee morning intonation. Geoffrey made no answer. His hair did look wet, and his skin was so pale next to the almost blackened tans of the beach.

She was interested in dressmaking, and always disappointed not having a daughter. Her accurate eye continued to run him over. There was a strangeness in his manner too. Almost a slyness of eye.

His shirt. A separate collar. The striped square-ended narrow tie was too short. So were the front buttons. She'd not seen that sort of shirt for years. It didn't open up fully. The heavy jacket had a peppery colour and darts let into each pocket. One lapel proclaimed him an Ovaltiney, and there was a Hornby Club badge in the other. He looked wet all over with perspiration. Even his clothes.

Geoffrey's parents must be poor, keeping him in jumble-sale clothes. Some poor part of Shepherds Bush. How then could they afford the Isle of Wight? Relatives?

'May we play then, Mrs Henderson? I don't have long.'

Geoffrey's voice reminded her of her manners.

'Sorry, I was thinking how much you resemble James,' she said, hoping her analysis hadn't been obvious.

'Do I? Isn't that interesting?' She could swear he was

mocking her. That faint smile wasn't pleasant.

'Going swimming?' she said uneasily.

He smiled properly now, shaking his head slowly, then looked directly at her. 'Do you want to see me with nothing on? I've no costume.'

'That'd cause a stir!' she said. Then: 'James, don't go too far.'

Geoffrey's smirk was still there, but it was Jamie who laughed: 'What a fusspot, Mum. O.K. We'll not go beyond the station, and I'll put my tee-shirt on.'

They went off in the direction of the pier, in appearance like brothers forty years apart.

It was even hotter, and the smell almost objectionable. When she'd settled again, eyes closed, she realised. Unlike the average boy and his love of detailed explanation, Geoffrey hadn't said where he was staying. And his smile had almost been suggestive.

'Ridiculous,' she corrected herself. 'Suggestive at his age?' Geoffrey was just unhappy. She sensed it. An old-fashioned unhappy boy from Shepherds Bush.

Mr Malcolm, manager of Truelove's Music Showrooms Ltd., in John Street, lifted the telephone to contact the hospital. It really was too bad, this man collapsing onto the Hammond. It would be churlish to mention the bad scratch on the wood veneer.

He'd not moved, despite the application of Miss Simmonds' smelling bottle. Surely he had merely fainted? Doubtfully, Mr Malcolm addressed a prayer to the God of Retail, but the man looked laid out. Stretched on the sofa in Mr Malcolm's large office, luxurious as the salon, he gave the premises the appearance of a musical funeral home.

Most unfortunate, just when he was due out to tea with that charming young lady from this morning. Very annoying. There would be a fuss, ambulance, people in the street watching the stretcher men, a newspaper report, maybe even the police. He shuddered. Perhaps the man was a criminal. Not that he looked the type. But the carefully nurtured exclusive atmosphere would be shattered by ambulance men and curious onlookers.

He grieved, remembering the affluent gentleman he'd noticed

examining the Steinway. Nowhere to be seen now, of course. And that managership just coming up in Southampton, too. Staff of twenty. Hadn't sold an expensive instrument for three weeks now. If one couldn't sell just one top-class pianoforte how could one expect promotion?

He was glad that boy had not loitered about. The less onlookers the better, one boy would soon attract others, and he always objected to children with dirty hands. He could never forget that awful group with the ice-lollies.

Mr Malcolm sighed. Perhaps the man would recover before the ambulance arrived. He'd position young Mr Wilkins ready to head it off. It hadn't occurred to him to search the man. Perhaps his wallet would help. His hopes rose. A relative. Someone to come and take responsibility, to remove the patient.

There was no wallet, but a diary told him the grim truth: he was a visitor. There was no way of contacting anyone nearby. Not that there was mention of relatives or dependants. What a ridiculously old diary.

He hesitated, and passed a spotless handkerchief across his moist bald head. He wouldn't telephone yet. This Henderson man was surely only overcome by the heat. He looked healthy enough. He'd surely regain consciousness soon, and an ambulance would not only be embarrassing but unneccessary.

All that was needed was time. He opened the window wide and left the smelling bottle propped under the patient's nose. It was now 4.15. He would return in ten minutes by his Accurist watch, and would telphone the ambulance then if needed.

'Keep an eye on the gentleman, Miss Simmonds, if you would be so kind.'

Mr Malcolm hastened with dignity to the returned figure by the Steinway. He could see a Daimler through the window, newly parked. His tubby form had a crispness about it as he headed towards promotion. Tea could wait.

Barbara woke suddenly. A fly had singled her out for attention. How she hated flies. It was 4.25, she was thirsty and needed some tea. Not that she could leave the Henderson belongings and their beach claim for other prospectors to discover. About time both Jamie and Derek were back.

The afternoon had moved round a little, the heat if anything was more intense. She watched, with satisfaction, a large man angrily silence a transistor radio belonging to the inevitable beach cowboy.

The tide was just beginning to encroach. Smell of fresh sea. Hot sand, long dried seaweed infested with busy insects. It looked dirty, dead, a tangled husk of corpse in a pitiless desert.

There was some near her. Lolly sticks and hints of filth sheltered beneath the tangled decay. There was a smell of death and excrement. The salt water would scour and cleanse. Would it revitalise even this death?

Despite the heat, she remembered with a cold shudder the final frames of a Dracula film, in colour, which had stayed with her for days. The sudden shafts of dawn sun had flooded in, to disintegrate the vampire caught out of his tomb. There followed a horrifying drying and shrinking sequence followed by the cracking to disgusting powder of apparent flesh and blood. The face caved in, the clothes went down like a punctured balloon. A breeze had removed all but the ring of the Prince of Darkness.

She looked again at the seaweed. The rich sea would reverse the process: this death would spring to unspeakable life, the green monster would once again swim deep to rise and feed on the feet of children.

The weed lay on parched sand, tormented by salacious flies, waiting for a corrupt Easter. Barbara hated it, dried and dead, but the idea of it wet and dead was positively abhorrent.

THAT WHICH HAD ONCE DROWNED WOULD BE FREE TO LIVE AND PREY ON CHILDREN. The phrase jumped into her mind suddenly, like one of Derek's quotations. What a nightmare. More of a daymare. Had she unsuspected depth, a suppressed imaginative side to her? It had happened at Osborne. This holiday was having a strange effect on her too. She who possessed an almost eighteenth-century sense of pure reason. What had spawned her unaccustomed fantasies? She looked again. It was, after all, just dried seaweed. But the phrase remained.

'Mum, Geoffrey's gone. Did he come this way?' Jamie appeared through the assorted live flesh of holiday humanity. 'Guess what. He's building a raft back where he's staying. And he makes masks. Told me all about it. Said we could play his special game in them next time, not now, it's too crowded. Then we played his sort of hide and seek, but I had to hide all the time while he hunted. Then we went under the pier. There were some lovers in the dark part at the back. We hid, and threw tiny pebbles at the man's bottom. But he didn't even notice! Then Geoffrey went off, and I can't find him. Been looking for at least ten minutes.'

Barbara suppressed, with considerable misgivings, one interpretation of the scene under the pier.

'Perhaps he's had to go back to his parents. Or catch a train? Did you quarrel?'

'No ... but he's a bit odd. Keeps saying he's mad on Smarties. Then laughs.'

'Well, perhaps you are better off without him. Where did you last see him?'

'By the pier of course, wading into the sea. He'll be in trouble – he didn't seem to *care* if he did get wet. What've you been doing, Mum?'

'I've been asleep. Oh, and thinking of seaweed.'

Derek was woken by a sharp pain in the sinuses. His eyes watering and red, he sat up. His mouth tasted filthy. What the hell was he doing here? Where was this anyway? Then he remembered. The Hammond. He understood. The door opened. An oily managerial person entered.

'My dear sir, you have recovered. Capital. And how do we feel?'

Mr Malcolm rubbed his plump hands together. No ambulance, no fuss. And he'd just received a fat cheque into his soft palm in outright payment for the Steinway. And now tea as arranged. God was human after all. He reminded Derek what had happened:

'... and so we thought it best to let you rest here. So much better than to fuss, don't you agree? And we've recovered your spectacles from between the organ pedals. Staying near here, Mr Henderson?'

'However do you know my name?' Derek stared.

'I ... that is to say we, took the liberty of searching you for identification. Your old diary gave us your name and address.

You don't look your age, if I may say so! No offence of course. All's well that ends well then, Mr Henderson. Please excuse me, I have an appointment. Just leave when you feel able. Give my regards to Shepherds Bush on your return. I once had an aunt there. The Holland Park side, of course.'

The beach was much smaller, more crowded, and even noisier. People were overflowing back onto the Esplanade. Jamie and Barbara were sitting on the wall waiting for him. Derek wished she'd cover herself more – she hadn't the figure for a swim suit.

'Do you feel all right now?' said Barbara, concernedly, after hearing about the showroom episode. This sudden blackout business was worrying.

'Perfect. Never did that before; the heat I expect.'

Barbara hoped so. She said:

'We've had a visitor. Thought at first it was Stuart. But his name was Geoffrey. Jamie and he went off enjoying themselves while I slept like the Sleeping Beauty. Don't say it!'

Derek wasn't about to.

'*Slept?* While Jamie went off?'

'You can't talk, asleep in a strange man's office! And Jamie *was* with another boy. What possible harm ...'

Derek couldn't reply.

'Anyway,' Barbara continued,' what's interesting is he came from Shepherds Bush – such odd clothes, looked positively pre-war! Those trousers! And he wore *boots*! In this weather! Still, he spoke well and seemed harmless enough. That's something these days.'

Derek listened, his stomach now in spasm, and a throb behind the frontal bone of his forehead.

'Where is he now?' he muttered.

'Gone now,' Jamie said. 'Last time I saw him, he was peering under the pier! Get it? Probably had to catch his train back to Freshwater to get on with his raft.'

'I suppose he was about your size,' Derek said after a pause, 'looked like you a bit?'

'How did you know?' James was surprised.

'I think I've noticed him once or twice,' Derek said finally.

Barbara stood silent. She was watching the seaweed. The water had reached it.

THURSDAY

'How could a king be prisoner in his own country?' Jamie turned to Derek, who was into the Civil War in a cannon flash.

They were surveying Carisbrooke from the ramparts. The heat bore down into the crater of the castle courtyard, shimmering the stone into a transformation scene. Unlike the William Crotch anthem it never resolved. Look well, look well if there be any way of wickedness in me ... And in fact there was a well, known for its donkey wheel. They had crowded round to hear the pebble hit the far-off water.

They had explored the keep museum, had wandered the undulating rampart path. Here at the site of King Charles the First's prison rooms, a sliced chimney flue in a wall and a glassless window remained.

Yet another sad place, Barbara thought. She was almost collecting tragedies. How many more? But it was fascinating. She felt more sensitive to place and time than ever before. The atmosphere round them seemed charged with continuous electricity.

Did Derek feel this? Normally yes, but what was normal about this holiday, particularly that pathetic group of mentally subnormal people on a trip to Carisbrooke? She'd had to divert Jamie's stare as they'd lolled by, children in adult bodies.

Derek and Jamie were still deep in the Civil War. She herself seemed to have really caught Derek's feeling for buildings, something she'd never really known before this holiday.

'So you see, Jamie, the Royal Family in 1641 was a bit like the Russian one in 1917. Destroyed or abolished. Then there followed a totalitarian regime as bad or worse than the old system. And think of the destruction, think of poor Swallowfield.'

But Jamie had begun to lose interest in Derek's hobby-horse. 'What can we do next, Dad?'

'I'll tell you what I must do next,' Barbara interrupted, 'visit the Ladies — and none of your usual comic remarks about porcelain thrones! I felt a real fool talking to that keeper. No royals have lived here since 1944!'

She disappeared down pyramid-steep steps in search of relief. Jamie settled into a niche and watched the broad sweep of downland beyond the town change colour with the passing clouds, like a live version of his eiderdown. This was the place for his telescope. But that was in Swallowfield, trained across the moat from his high bedroom window onto the maids' bedrooms of the Angel Croft Hotel. Mum and Dad thought he liked astronomy.

Eider-down, eider-down. Ida Down? Could be. Those small hills were called Ida Down. Because they looked like Ida. He thought of Ida Craddock, daughter of the school janitor. He remembered the boiler room. Ida Crack, that's what the older choristers called her. Good name. He giggled.

The heat felt like the boiler room and made him conscious of his hot body inside his clothes. Glancing quietly at his father, he wondered if he'd ever felt like this.

Derek had begun to walk idly along the uneven stones. The path was about four feet wide, and curved round inside the curtain wall like a medieval rail viaduct. Chunks of inner castle, sometimes buildings, sometimes green banks, touched the outer walls at intervals.

Two figures began the ascent to the ramparts up the far steps. There was something very familiar about the woman. She stared, turned, and went down, two steps at a time. The man called to her but she vanished round a corner. He continued to the top.

Derek and he approached each other along the narrow walk. Derek felt his stomach move. It was Hazel's husband, Alan. There were about twelve seconds. Jamie was behind him, and here in front was shy, inhibited Alan Roe. No hope. Nowhere to hide, nowhere to merge into. Just this confrontation. High Noon. His mind raced. Had she told him? He'd soon know.

Alan was a few paces away. Be positive. Be innocent. An actor. Somehow.

'Hello, Alan, on holiday?'

The heavy blow on the side of the jaw rocked Derek, dislodging his glasses, but did not fell him. The surprise was staggering, not the punch, for he'd failed to see the hate spring into Alan's eyes. Turning, flabbergasted, he managed to move his mouth.

'What did——?' he stammered at the retreating figure.

'That's what I think of *you*, you bastard,' shouted Alan Roe, walking backwards, nearly over the unrailed edge.

'But what did——?' Derek's astonishment was both real and sham. But Alan was farther back still. Afraid of him! All along. Instinct had struck out at this bugger who'd had it off regularly with his wife. But now he thought the smaller man would hit him!

Derek's charade faded. He became aware of faces gazing from the grass below. Alan had disappeared fast down the steps at the other end. Hope to God he didn't meet Barbara coming back from the Ladies. They *had* met, just once. They might click.

Then Derek remembered Jamie. He was not there. He was running fast across the courtyard towards his mother.

Derek ran along the path and hurtled down the steps. They were waiting for him, Jamie crying. What had he said? What would he say, the one witness of importance? But his crying would not be silenced, nor would he explain.

'Whatever's happened?' Barbara spoke urgently. 'Why's Jamie so upset? And whatever's wrong with your face?'

Derek hadn't considered that the punch was visible, nor how to explain. Thank God. Obviously she'd not met Alan. He had to get them all out of here quickly.

'Had a bit of trouble. It's upset Jamie. All's well now.' He was hoping to avoid further explanation. It didn't satisfy Barbara.

'Oh come on, Derek, what's happened?'

'I've just got hit by a lunatic,' he huffed desperately.

'You're joking.'

'No, I'm serious. Complete stranger, real nutter, came straight up and smashed me one. No harm done. Poor devil's off his rocker and it didn't hurt.'

'We must report him. Where's he gone?'

'Don't know. Forget it. More to be pitied than hunted for.'

'But he can't go round hitting people. Supposing ...'

'Oh come on, he's probably with that party of nuts we saw from the local mental home. Why spoil their outing?'

Jamie stopped crying, Derek waited. Then Jamie said, 'You called him Alan.'

It was out. Could he stop his voice shaking? He felt weak, as if with flu. She'd never believe him a second time.

'No, no, he called *me* Alan! Poor devil doesn't know what year it is.'

A pause. Derek waited again.

'You didn't hit him back.' This was what upset Jamie. 'And he didn't *look* mental.'

'You don't hit people if they're mentally ill,' Derek spoke quietly, 'and many look normal.' Silence. Jamie didn't look convinced.

Barbara remembered her fears. Mental illness seems to be common here. A cell of lunatics, an infectious colony? That is if Derek was to be believed. She looked at him. Was he? The bruise could not be doubted. Her mind turned it over. But Derek's mind was on being out of the castle before encountering the Roes again. 'We must get a good place for the carnival,' he said.

They walked out down through the splendid gatehouse and towards the car. Barbara did not feel in a carnival mood. So far the week was a saga of disasters. For the first time she considered abandoning the holiday altogether.

Derek had a fresh headache. Not only must he keep Geoffrey from his family, he must now prevent a second encounter with Alan and Hazel.

Judging by the intensity of the attack, Alan had not known about the affair for long. He was obviously angry, but would he make real trouble? A letter to the Dean of Swallowfield? Anonymous obscenities about him to the Bishop? A telephone call to Barbara? He wished he'd seen that priest. But it was a bit late for God now.

'Let's stop for a drink.' Barbara pointed out of the window. 'Oh *yes!*'

Jamie reacted visibly to glaring posters enveloping a cafe in the heat outside Newport. There was a convenient drive-in, and Derek failed to think of a reason to ignore it. He shuddered. Suppose the Roes stopped here?

Cool drinks and ices flaunted themselves on garish signs attached to the old wood building. Watching the carnival would be thirsty work, and it had been sweltering in the castle. Their sudden departure had precluded the ritual refreshments, though Jamie had cried out vainly as they strode past the cafe in the long dry moat.

Now a new interruption. Derek pulled in to the lay-by. Perhaps Coca Cola was the antidote to Jamie's clear dismay over his apparent cowardice? More important, now Alan knew, what would he do? Look for him? No, probably not. He had committed common assault in front of witnesses. Surely he wouldn't risk more trouble and a possible court case?

The Morris halted reluctantly, and James was out of it immediately, walking towards the crowded building. But engulfing, bursting the doors, was a school plague. Too late. Jamie was among heavily built teenagers pushing and chewing open-mouthed. They ignored the mild older teacher obviously regretting the whole trip. They smoked all over her trendy young colleague, desperately be-jeaned and hopefully identical with his pupils to the last American badge.

Jamie had vanished into all this. There was no recovering him. Did he have any money? Derek couldn't remember.

'Look, no point in both of us suffering,' he said to Barbara, and moved in after Jamie, who had left no track behind him in the warm bodies. Far off, his head was just visible, amongst breasts.

The atmosphere was heavy. It wasn't possible to walk. It was more of a pressing into softness, persuading a gap to open. Loud pop music throbbed through several speakers, scratched through a few ostentatious transistors. Derek thought immediately of the puppet dancers in the Esplanade Theatre. Pressed against these pubescent girls he could sense that same perky but heavy beat absorbed by each young body.

These were the real puppets, but they didn't perform. Though not so obviously controlled from outside like the Petra Pans, these lovely girls certainly didn't own themselves. They were as possessed as — *I am.*

107

All pressed together. I bet I could creep round and touch ... But I won't. I'll just choose one, as usual. One in a nice short skirt. You can see so much. Like with Dawn.

But these girls aren't looking at me. I'd make them look if I had my mask. Have to have my mask. Look at me, I'd shout, who's this? Mr D., that's who!

Anyway, there's boys here too. I like just girls for my mask. Well one girl really. And not in a cafe. Somewhere lonely.

There's one like Dawn, dark hair, and plump legs, and ever such a short skirt. I want to put my hand up under all the secret clothes. She's got a nice mouth with wet white teeth.

I put my hand flat on me, and press on her. It's all soft under. Lovely. She still doesn't know it's me. Thinks it's the crowd, pushing. Move my hand round. Slow. Slow. Nearly.

But she knows — jerks round — her elbow—

the pain cut through him. It was Derek, turning and thrusting back through bodies to burst through the door, just as sudden pain had just jerked Geoffrey out too.

'Can't take it — too hot — feel faint,' Derek gasped to Barbara. 'You try.' And he sat on the grass nursing his stomach, secretly thankful even for agony.

But as she entered, the teachers were persuading their mob out to the sticky coach and its greasy driver. Derek turned away, feeling several pairs of eyes on his back as guys slouched and dolls giggled past, dropping polystyrene cups and cartons.

'Filthy bleeder, felt 'is 'ands trying' to pull up me skirt.'

Panic fought nausea. Derek rose and entered the cafe somehow. Barbara had reached James, lonely by the counter as a mooring post with the tide out. The sweaty, composite floor was latticed with cigarette butts, squashed straws and rolling coke cans.

Barbara ordered some iced drinks. Derek sat at a plastic table to wait. Through smeared glass he studied those last tight denim plums climbing into the bus. A last girl said something to her friend. Both looked back towards him, and he turned his head hastily. He still ached from her elbow.

Barbara. *Could* she have seen?

Geoffrey again. And this time Derek hadn't just been aware

of him. He'd enjoyed it. Geoffrey was building up to use him. But for what? It was his purpose which escaped Derek.

They had fought for a front place in Newport. The carnival bunting fluttered only slightly in the heat, but there was continuous movement in the excited crowd. At last the procession arrived, and passed them like a slow train in bright colour.

'Look – a green gilbert,' said Derek unexpectedly, as the Carnival Queen's float went by. But he meant the gathered phlegm which he spat into the road towards the Queen's float.

'Hob goblin!' He laughed, his voice strange. Barbara felt sick with disgust. Jamie put his hand into hers and held on tightly. They left the carnival shortly afterwards. Silence in the car until they reached Totland. Even Jamie said nothing.

'Jamie, what about running to the beach for a swim.' Barbara did not ask: this was instruction. 'Get your trunks on upstairs. Back in an hour. Go now.'

He vanished, glad to escape the atmosphere, avoiding his father's eye.

'If ever you do that again, God help you,' Barbara said quietly, 'problems or not. And another thing—' Barbara strode ahead of him to a seat. He had no option but to join her.

It was hot near the cliff edge, overlooking the beach. The pier stretched out into silver ocean from just below them, a skeletal finger into both future and past. The seat slats burned into Derek; Barbara seemed impervious to them.

Derek waited, but Barbara said nothing. Behind them, the hotel spread itself high and wide, its turrets saluting the sun, a holiday cathedral with sculpture come down and walking round it.

Barbara still said nothing. The air hung over the hill. The cries from the beach were faint, the sea swell heavy. Distant music, recalling the Ryde pop dancers, rippled from the pier end, and drifted out to the horizon.

Far out, the Queen Elizabeth II edged towards the Solent. The sea waited like Derek. What was coming? Had Barbara met the

Roes? If so, when? At the carnival? Not possible — he'd been next to her all along.

All right. He'd spat filthily in public. Or rather, Geoffrey had. But it was a minor manifestation. Barbara was naturally disgusted. If she only knew! But there was something else. She was now in charge, powerful, confident.

'Obey' had been left intact at their wedding service. Derek had insisted. Yet it was he who now obeyed her, that is when not obeying Geoffrey. When had it happened? He couldn't think. His imagination? No.

A scientist's knowledge is based solely on repeatable proof or evidence. But Derek, no scientist, had instinctive knowledge. And evidence was certainly repeating, even though he couldn't control it.

She fired the first salvo. Barbara the battle cruiser, he the unarmoured torpedo boat.

'I saw you through the cafe window.'

'What?'

'Touching up that kid,' she said sarcastically. 'Didn't you realize you could be seen?'

She had noticed. No wonder she'd been distinctly off him at the carnival, even before Geoffrey had made him spit. Derek put up a smoke screen for time to think.

'What *are* you on about?'

'People noticed. Couldn't avoid doing, could they? You'll get yourself arrested.' Now she pretended indifference, turning her nose up, and her head half away. He bluffed:

'I told you — I was faint. Put my hand out to steady myself.'

'Funny you had to support yourself on that girl's thigh.'

'Honestly, it was the heat. I felt really odd,' he persisted weakly. She looked utterly unconvinced. In the heavy silence he wondered whether this was the moment to tell her everything. Everything that is except Hazel Roe. That'd really finish it. He'd probably end up as a battered husband.

He tried another torpedo run.

'Look, I didn't actually do anything,' he finally broke out. 'It was all nothing.'

She looked coldly at him.

'Just try "nothing" again, that's all. You're perverted. I never knew. Little girls.'

Barbara had finished. She rose as if the interview was over. As an afterthought she added 'and you can cure your own hang ups now. Talking in your sleep, for instance. I've had that to put up with.'

Derek stared. This was new.

'Talking?'

'It's not been flattering.'

She refused to say more. Embarrassed, he looked away. What the hell had he burbled at nights? Curse this Geoffrey. How could he fight him? How can you fight a spirit?

Barbara tried to put aside the recent past, her voice quite changed from a minute ago. Now she tried to keep her family intact. 'Look, we could go home, you know. I could settle our bill today. I'd have no trouble with ferries. They're easier mid-week. Let's forget all about the last few days.'

There was a kinder tone. One of reconciliation, or was it a last effort at reason, thought Derek. But it would be impossible to leave the island. He, probably they, were trapped. That ferry would never sail. And if it did he'd never be on it. She could never know, never understand.

Inside him was an unholy guest. Derek was only partly Derek. And who was speaking in the night? And what about? It couldn't be about Hazel – Barbara would have left him for that.

'Jamie's enjoying the week. Let's try again,' he said, but he couldn't look at her. His rejection of her solution was clear.

'Suit yourself,' she said curtly, 'but I'll be watching. No more cheap thrills.' She walked off.

He couldn't confide now, anyway. In any case, she'd never have believe in Geoffrey the unholy spirit. She'd have listened while reaching for the pen and committal form in his own interest. Nod while ordering the yellow van for his own good. The eyes from the hotel window watched down, two eyes which never lost interest.

She never understood him. Never came to hear him sing. Father had done, once or twice, but only from the back of the church. Mother was always cooking dinners. She lost his brother. And she wouldn't adopt.

Their hotel dinner was a large mixed grill. Barbara failed utterly to restrain Jamie eating as though for two. Derek noticed that she herself ate too heavily for her figure, but had little appetite of his own. He felt uncomfortable with the aged porter's eye on him from behind, through the open dining-room door. All week he'd stared. All week Derek had wanted to ask why.

He recalled an Edgar Allan Poe story, about an eye. Or was it Sheridan Le Fanu? He glanced round again. Yes, those eyes, intense through the wire glasses. Strangely bright for an old man. His mind became wholly occupied. Geoffrey. And that old man ...?

'I'd like to make a raft, and wear a mask on it.'

Jamie spoke into the silence. Nobody responded. Both were preoccupied.

'You've put Tennyson Down and Cliff Walk for this evening,' Barbara said, studying Derek's written itinerary. 'I'm ready if you are.' Barbara's voice was firm, almost deep, as she rose from the table.

'Geoffrey loves Smarties,' Jamie said slowly.

'So you said before,' said Barbara vaguely, enjoying the memory of the meal, 'but how you can think of sweets after that excellent dinner ...!'

Derek thought how the eye in the story followed the man about. He never saw it, except at the end. He felt it in his back, on his neck. It drove him to suicide. He only saw it as he drowned. Too late he knew it was his own. It stayed open all the way to the sea bed.

They left for Tennyson Down, Barbara driving, Derek staring towards the sea, Jamie busy in the back with an exercise book and pencil.

'What are you writing?' asked Barbara seeing him in the mirror.

'Nothing. It's a secret,' replied Jamie with a grin.

ECHO

This evening we've come to see a huge stone monument on the cliffs. It's in memory of a great poet. What's his name?

Up here, it's all smooth like an eiderdown, and when you get near the edge you can see the cliffs like white cake with green icing.

It was a long walk here. We felt quite tired, climbing up to the Monument. At the top, Mother had to rest. She looked as white as the cliffs, and all trembly. Father said he felt all right, but he was a bit wobbly too. They're both pathetic. They said don't go too near the edge, but of course I did. I bet I could fly down if I wanted to. We're not going to do the cliff walk. Father says too tiring. Bet it wouldn't be for you and me!

I walked right over to the great tall cross. Tennyson. That's him. When you look up, those clouds move round the top like swirly water. Makes me feel dizzy. It's so hot. I feel all sweaty.

They won't let me go out except with a jacket on even in this weather. When I grow up I won't wear one unless it's cold. Or a collar and tie. On my own I often take them off.

On holiday in Kent, I sometimes take everything off in the secret bushes. I put my mask on and play my special game, with girls who pass by in the lane. I laugh when they jump.

Here on my island, from my hill I can look out to sea. All the world's ships sail by my island for my salutes. The Times at the Hotel says the King is in his yacht Britannia today. Its Cowes Week. Over at Totland I can see the paddle steamer at the pier end. Yesterday at Ryde I'm sure I saw the Hood with two destroyers making for Portsmouth. Navy week starts soon.

Down towards the Needles the land goes to a point. Several points really. It doesn't want to end. It's the end of my world. My world ends with this island. You can see so much sky and almost all my land up here, like in Treasure Island. There's nobody. Just me ... and Tennyson. And the cloud shadows. Can't see Mother and Father. Good.

I walk down from the cross towards the cliff edge. Then I look back away from the glare. Is that you on the other side of the cross? Looking towards me into the sun?

Barbara parked the car in a chalk pit under Tennyson Down. A tight white path led up into the green towards the sky. The air felt precious despite the heat. There was no heaviness.

As they climbed, Derek looked back. At ground level the bushes now revealed hollows in which several couples could be seen hard at work. He couldn't remember ever wanting to stand and watch before. Barbara led the way, but, as she tired, Jamie bounded ahead, and disappeared round a bend in the steep white crumble of path.

Breathless at the top, they found Jamie flicking berries at a tin can. Away, up across the smooth slope, towered the tall stone to Alfred Lord Tennyson. Grey, massive, as monumental as Morte D'Arthur. Its celtic pointing dominated the Down, and the Down dominated the island.

The sun was fiercest here. It scorched the springy turf, yellow-white on fibrous green, dark for mourning. Jamie ran towards the monument, away ahead of Barbara's stride. Derek was some yards back, the sun pounding his eyes, knees weak after the climb. He had forgotten his sun-glasses.

The merciful shadow of the cross stopped him, able to see again. Clear shapes sprang out of the whirling purple in his eyes. In front the massive monument. Between Derek and the cross, Barbara, looking back, also in the shadow. Then Jamie looking into the sun. All movement stopped. Vast sky. That sculpted name on the granite, higher than the black-tailed spears of the guard of honour. Beyond that rock majestas, separating Alpha and Omega, stood the small figure Derek had come to know as well as himself. The lettering was still and timeless as Kells:

Geoffrey Ford Henderson
Aged 10 years
Drowned Totland 1933

But the boy beyond did not remain still. He moved steadily in the sun's shimmer towards both cross and Derek, who, heavy as Tennyson, could not move. Geoffrey grew nearer, one arm outstretched as if to grasp. 'Qui venit, qui venit,' who comes. It was not in the name of the Lord and certainly not to bless.

Derek felt panic rise and fought it down. So Geoffrey would have him at last, here on the hill, in front of his wife and son.

Yet it seemed that the figure was visible only to him, for Barbara's untroubled voice fulfilled the itinerary unconsciously when Jamie lay suddenly on the grass to worry a beetle.

'We'll not walk the Downs – Jamie's tired. All right, Derek?'

He nodded slowly in reply, his eyes not moving from the empty shimmer where the boy had been. The black cross stood firm, silhouetted. Dead Geoffrey Henderson, aged ten. Drowned. They even shared their name. It was all getting closer. More radioactive material to lock away, killer jewels to crackle in the dark behind the eyes.

'I'm not tired. I'll walk somewhere. Meet you at the car in half an hour.' Derek's voice felt decidedly odd, but Barbara seemed unaware of it.

Jamie rose, locked the beetle in his matchbox, and soon they were hull down over the hill, voices last to fade.

Derek turned to the monument. It commemorated only Alfred Lord Tennyson. But what of the commemoration in Totland, a death five years before his own birth? It wasn't there.

He moved slowly past the cross, and down the gentle slope to the cliff edge. It was tempting to fly down to the far off breakers. Farther out, the blue divided like camouflage, increasing as it came close in shore, the water swelling over seaweed.

Could he, should he place all this before Barbara's crossword mind? Still no. Geoffrey would then intensify work on her, and also Jamie. He'd already started.

He ought to place it before a priest, before God. But where was the priest who'd believe this? They were nearly all glorified social workers these days. And God was back in Swallowfield, locked in. Geoffrey must be headed off, without God. Derek must be the cross, to stand between Geoffrey and the Henderson family.

He sat and watched the sea. The monument stood behind to

his right. The fiery sun inched down. One less day to go, instinct said, then Geoffrey face to face. Geoffrey would get him at the last. If he could but know why, that would help. Being at least slightly armed would help.

Derek stood up, feeling old. The gigantic sweep of ocean brought his eyes once again to the memorial. Celtic veins writhed heavily near the top, which was thick and rounded with the cross inside it. Strong, proud, upright, it was a phallus, displayed proudly for miles on its downland body. Once, he'd have laughed at the giant stone cock on the hill. But not now. The lone boy in the bushes: Derek already knew him intimately. Like Jekyll, his body sheltered two people.

Yet Geoffrey was active outside him too. Every day, every night, an unholy mass brought an undivine guest. A travesty of 'Benedictus qui venit in nomine Domine'.

Geoffrey was lonely, he knew this. Like Derek, an only child? Highly prurient. Though but a child, obsessed with sex. It had a sick, disturbing feel, this obsession. Ships, railways and sex secrets. All connected. A Shepherds Bush boy, drowned in Totland, 1933. He had known so many of the same things as Derek in that short existence. And his surname was Derek's surname.

Derek was frightened but clear, for here it was easy to think objectively. He set as still as stone; the sun moved round the cross.

Geoffrey even looked like Jamie, perhaps like Derek as a boy. He could only guess. There were almost no surviving photographs of his own boyhood, so the mirror image had been almost the three of them. Was Geoffrey what Derek *might* have been – his alter ego, but with an independent existence?

Geoffrey, like Derek an only child, unhappy and unpopular in his brief life, was obsessed with finding a constant playmate. Hide and seek – the footprints at Colwell Bay. All this Derek knew intuitively.

Alec Turton – he'd have been too friendly. But would he? He would have offered love of a sort. What about the graffiti message at Blackgang? Was Geoffrey responsible? Was nothing of this holiday untouched by him?

So, when it came, what form was his claim going to take? This claim for possession. Derek was the possessed already, but it was leasehold. The freehold had yet to be signed.

It was surprising that he'd been allowed to think it out so far without interruption. Geoffrey must be allowed Derek alone. He owed it to Barbara and James, for it was his fault Jamie was an only child. His selfishness.

If only, if only he'd not persuaded Barbara to risk that car ride to his concert against doctor's orders. The inevitable crisis on the return; the final discharge into the world of their first son, dead, and no bigger than a thumb: all Derek's fault. Now he must make atonement. Peccavi.

Suddenly he thought of Mr Malcolm. His diary. Mr Malcolm had said something odd about his diary. He hunted for it feverishly. Old diary he'd said. In a strange way he was disappointed. It was still dated 1973 as always, and the address was 9, Vicars' Close, Swallowfield.

There had to be other Hendersons in Shepherds Bush. Why not a Geoffrey Henderson who lived there in the thirties? Yet why did the name of boy and place so frighten him?

A sudden cool wind blew up from nowhere, and the Down took on a chill despite the blazing sun. But the air crinkled over Main Bench, and the Needles still moved. He walked up over the spine again. In the distance, beyond, lay Totland, its pier shimmering on the blue; and the ancient paddle-steamer thrashed distantly towards it on glass. It occurred to him that he'd never actually seen it reach the landing stage.

The spires of the hotel pierced the cloudless sky, the past scratching the present. Reaching out for him, 1933 was now closer to him than ever, and getting nearer. The itinerary was the railway which led to Geoffrey. There was no return journey. But which was moving, train or landscape?

Trains and railways. On impulse he unfolded the map from the book. In 1933, the Wight rail system was quite extensive, but though one spur reached out to Yarmouth and Freshwater, the western side of the island was untouched. Geoffrey (and his father and mother?) must have travelled everywhere by train. Then, presumably, they walked or took a short bus ride.

He looked automatically for Robin Hill Park: tomorrow's visit in the morning. It wasn't there. Too small in 1933? Possibly. Blackgang Chine was hardly mentioned.

Suspicious, he examined the plan again, recalling so many

twinges of unease. Something had always been wrong. As with everything, the railway was the key. Staring at the old map would yield no more answers. Like an octopus the rail tracks searched out Eastern Wight. Wish it was all still there. Hang the bloody car, the smell of the exhaust, the modern traffic.

When did they begin to close it down? 1952 said the glossy new handbook. A short stretch from Ryde to Shanklin was left like a trunkless branch. Haven Street was isolated in mid-country, its mile and three-quarters of steam railway the only other line left. It was clearly marked as a tourist attraction and museum.

Geoffrey could have, must have ridden through it from Freshwater to Ryde. But not yesterday; it closed in 1953. One way of celebrating the Coronation. Luckily, Barbara was uninterested in railways. For her to have suspected that Geoffrey was not all he seemed could have been disastrous. Derek's attempts at containment would be at risk.

But Jamie was more worrying. It could occur to him, at any time, that the Freshwater line was long closed. He still had a long way to go before finding out that Geoffrey never reached 1934, much less 1973, but Jamie was bright and also more imaginative than Barbara.

Derek looked again at the itinerary. A question hung heavy over it. Odd about Robin Hill Park. The modern guide gave no historical details; it was as vague on this as detailed on the railway.

There was no reason why the answer came so suddenly. One second the list of visits looked quite normal, the next the entry Haven Street was so clearly alien.

How could it have been missed? Haven Street was an ordinary station in the thirties. Nobody would have visited it: there was no museum and nothing to see. It was just an unremarkable country station of considerably less interest than many others.

So, part of the itinerary was not in existence in 1933. Therefore what had Geoffrey done that Tuesday morning in 1933? Not knowing worried Derek. From knowing Geoffrey's every move in advance, he now had a blank, and there could be more. The implications were enormous.

For one thing Geoffrey was cheating, and you don't have to

when you have all the cards. Very well, he would cheat too. Beat Geoffrey by cunning.

He chose Saturday. On Saturday they would ignore the plan, and instead of Sandown they'd go to St. Catherine's Lighthouse, then on to Ventnor. It would be a surprise for Barbara and Jamie. He deliberately chose the lighthouse. It wasn't directly on the old rail network, the essential point of the choice. The power of the itinerary would be broken, Geoffrey's spell shattered.

It was the answer. Why, oh why had he not done it before? He would pretend to be heading towards Sandown, but they'd never reach it.

He would explain to Barbara that to take the long coast road would be a refreshing change. He must of course make certain to be driving himself.

He rejected Friday reluctantly. Robin Hill Country Park followed by Brading Roman Villa. The route was not so suitable for his purpose. So he must wait until Saturday. If he could avoid confrontation with Geoffrey until then, he would gain strength enough to break the sequence.

But he forgot that Geoffrey knew what he thought as he thought it himself.

Jamie had been unlucky so far. His efforts had failed to create a sand Carisbrooke Castle or to see the tide fill the moat up the long canal. Something always went wrong, or time and tide ran out.

Jamie was getting openly resentful of the itinerary. A long evening session on a quiet beach would appease him, thought Barbara, and it had suited Derek, but not Jamie, if just Barbara accompanied him. They went, Jamie looking sulky, complaining that his Dad was no fun.

Derek sat deep in a brown armchair in the lounge. He'd relaxed through the Times, absorbing a beer as he did so. Reading of today's woes had not lightened his troubles. He felt terribly alone with the responsibility. Must talk to someone, but not a priest. Someone actually *used* to the world from which Geoffrey had come.

The case of a poltergeist in East Acton gave him the answer. After scientific tests had revealed only that they couldn't explain it so it wasn't happening, and after a failed exorcism by the local vicar, a medium had persuaded the spirit to leave.

A medium, was what he needed, one who could approve his plan. Someone who wouldn't laugh and try to rationalize the unrational. But how do you contact a Contact? The Yellow Pages? A burst of laughter from the bar answered him.

A Spiritualist Church. They'd know. He got up and walked across the over-ample carpet into the foyer. The old porter looked at him, then quickly away, pretending to test the revolving door for squeaks. It moved noiselessly as usual.

Derek found the Places of Worship list quickly, framed near the reception desk. There, at the bottom, under Pentecostal and Seventh Day Adventists was 'Spiritualist Church, Hope Street, Freshwater', then the service times, and finally: 'Honorary Secretary, Miss Daphne Strand', an address and telephone number.

Derek pushed the folding wood doors of the booth tight shut with his back as a contralto voice answered the telephone.

'It is *most* unusual for us to put people in touch with a medium. You *aren't* a member of our congregation, are you?'

'No, though I *am* a churchgoer.'

'You mean C. of E.?'

'Yes, but I *do* believe in—'

'Well, come to our service on Sunday. The clairvoyant may have something for you.'

'But it's urgent – it can't wait until then.'

'Very sorry, it is our rule. You can imagine, we have to be careful. One whisper that the visiting Sensitive had been ... for all I know you could be part of a trick, a press reporter.' There was a finality in the voice.

Derek began to despair.

'Look, I'm desperate, could I talk to *you*? Now. Only a few minutes? Please. I have a car.' There was an agonizing silence.

'Very well, but it must be a short visit. I have a meeting in church. Is 7.15 possible? Meet me there.'

Miss Daphne Strand gave him street directions. Even as he wrote them down, he wondered. It was not on the itinerary. Would Geoffrey allow him to reach there?

Apparently. Hope Street was narrow, and lined with red brick Victorian terraced houses. Each one looked so thin that it was difficult to imagine there being room to keep a cat, much less swing one.

Derek parked just past the gap in which the Spiritualist Church lay, some way back from the road. There was a long thin untidy garden behind tall pillars and railings, then the strange stucco building itself.

It was not just the strangest church he had seen, it was amongst the most unusual buildings he had encountered. The sun had begun to throw it into silhouette. An extraordinary power seemed to emanate from the Egyptian facade, its tulip-capitaled columns peeling like a nightmare venereal disease. Their heavy double entasis was almost voluptuous, suggested the body, hardly the spirit.

He left the car, and opened the high iron gate, set into obelisks twice as tall as himself. Sentinels to the place of the dead. For, oddly, Derek felt here already a preoccupation with death, not eternal life.

The soil looked damp, fecund, even in hot weather, like Kensal Green cemetery. The path was of old cement and weeds. Lost plants writhed on each side like the secret garden. It was like walking a causeway from a Nile suddenly become cold, for the long shadow of the church reached almost the length of the path. A chill hit him on its edge. To enter the shade was like walking into the building prematurely.

The church had sloping walls and thin rectangular windows narrowing slightly to the top. The door was ajar as if to a 'Hammer Horror' tomb, but the interior was a very English non-conformist chapel, lined with pine boarding and divided by stiff pews, with no centre aisle. There was a low platform with a lectern, a reed organ and several imposing carved wood chairs. On one of them sat Miss Daphne Strand.

She was heavily built, and in an oatmeal suit with brogues. Her grey hair was pulled severely into a bun, making her look older than she need have done. Behind the curly frame glasses were piercing eyes of blue-grey. Behind them he discerned humour.

'How can I help you?' she said directly, her manner fitting her appearance. She motioned him into the front pew.

With no hesitation, Derek poured out everything since Swallowfield library, his plan, his great fear. She sat, occasionally asking a question, but in alert silence otherwise.

He finished lamely, but there was no immediate response. Miss Strand fingered the the edge of *The Spiritualist Hymnbook* in front of her, allowing the pages to flicker at speed. The text jumped like a movie, the numbers speeding past like an animated calendar. Certain hymns seemed to be trying to spring out with an answer for him.

'When you telephoned I was unaware how serious your situation was,' she said at last, quietly turning to him, picking the book up to cradle in her lap, 'and I feel very unqualified to offer advice. You are right, and we must relax our rule. You need a clairvoyant. But from where? Only two professionals live on the island, one of whom, Miss Ocaldo, is with us on Sunday, but away until Saturday. You cannot wait that long? Then I could telephone old Mrs Bridger, our other local sensitive, in Yarmouth. Come over to my house it's not far.'

She put the book down, and picking up a huge handbag, began to walk swiftly to the rear of the building. Her stride seemed purposeful, almost as if she wanted him out of the place, and Derek hurried to keep up.

At last somebody was on his side, someone who believed. No question of are you imagining it? You need a rest. There must be a logical explanation to all this.

Miss Daphne Strand lived in the narrow house directly opposite the obelisks, with a view up the church path through the wilderness to Egypt. To Derek's surprise she owned not one but three cats. He sat surrounded by three pairs of intense eyes from behind which buzzed three motors. Miss Strand disappeared to the telephone, and was absent for longer than he expected. Derek studied his surroundings.

It was a tiny room. The window had to be narrow to fit into the wall. The hall passage had been positively claustrophobic. Incredibly, stairs rose from it. The dining room must be even tinier than the oddly cold parlour in which he now sat.

'No luck I'm afraid,' said Miss Strand, re-entering the room. 'She's ill in bed. What can we do? We have other contacts on the mainland, but they are impossible at short notice.'

Derek's temporary hope was gone. Miss Strand clearly sensed his desolation.

'Look Mr Henderson, shall I make us both a cup of tea, and perhaps we can talk a little?'

Derek merely nodded, with thanks in his eyes. She rose quickly, and without damaging any of the myriad ornaments perched everywhere, switched on an ancient electric fire at the wall. Then she vanished through a door more suited to a wardrobe.

One cat remained faithful, with the help of the glowing bars. The others ran on delicate feet after their mistress, hearing the sound of milk bottle against jug. Derek's eyes ranged over the contents of the parlour.

There was no surface which did not support trinkets and ornaments on little square mats with beads round the edge. There were several incidental tables with perilously thin legs, all covered in bric-à-brac. One nudge from a cat would be enough to upset several, for nothing could fall alone.

The flowered wallpaper was covered mostly with photographs and curious amateur paintings. The large one of a Red Indian over the mantelpiece was the most striking. He was seen as the centre of a rainbow effect of unusual hues. It was like an icon over an altar, for everything on the mantelshelf was placed symmetrically on a miniature altar cloth. There was even an embryonic frontal and a candlestick at each end.

Miss Strand returned with a tray and two cats, then dispensed tea from beside her on the fat sofa.

'I do hope you like Earl Grey, Mr Henderson, so beautifully perfumed, don't you think?' A muffled clock ticked somewhere. 'Such a tragedy, dear old Mrs Bridger should have been so much help to you, she's so experienced. Lived in this area, so I understand, for over forty years. ... Well it is not to be ...'

They sipped their tea gently, studied by the six feline eyes. 'You know, Mr Henderson, I have to be so careful. I am not clairvoyant. For me to advise you in any way is probably most unwise. Yet I feel I must help you. But if you were to act on my word alone, I would be *responsible* and I feel so unqualified.'

Miss Strand appeared to settle herself more deeply into the sofa and took a further large silent sip of Earl Grey. 'Have you told me everything? I have to ask you this − you are not under treatment for a mental condition, at some hospital, are you? For all I know you could be ... shall we say disturbed. It would of course be easier if you were.'

She seemed slightly disappointed at his answer.

123

'Well, whilst telephoning, I also contacted our society, the Spiritualist Association of Great Britain, in Belgrave Square. They echo my opinion: unqualified advice could be dangerous to you, and in the event of something going badly wrong, to the society itself. I must not bring it into disrepute. They say wait for the medium. But you need help now, so if you wish, I'll just offer you my *reaction* to what you have told me. No more, no less. After that, you must be guided by your own feelings.'

She took another sip of Earl Grey. The Red Indian looked Derek straight between the eyes. The ginger cat stood on hind legs and tried to turn the door knob, for all the world like—

'Have you I wonder, been laying yourself open to evil influences? Meditating under wrong conditions? You don't meditate? Ah, but sometimes we can approach the state of meditation without quite realizing it. You are an imaginative person – no, I don't mean you are imagining all this – and your mind often takes journeys without your body. Night and day. We are all used to dreams. But they happen all the time, and they're not always what they seem.'

'A half-dream can be a form of meditation. Perhaps you have unwittingly produced the conditions in which the spirit Geoffrey could pass into you. And you've noticed recently, that when you wake you've been sleeping with your mouth open? That could be indicative.'

'But he's not just a spirit, Miss Strand, my wife has conversed with and my son James has played with him.'

'That's no problem, I assure you. Some spirits are perfectly capable of communicating, and creating the illusion of physical reality. I hazard a guess that neither your wife nor your son actually touched the boy Geoffrey?'

'I'm not sure of that, of course, but I get the point.'

'You see, perhaps Geoffrey has been able to pass in and out of you, sometimes without your knowledge. He appears when he wishes, and not just to you, but I would guess always at significant moments. You think back.'

'Is this possession, then?'

'Possession? That isn't quite it, but you are close. If you meditate without supervision and knowledge, you can lay yourself open to danger. Opening the *chakras*, as they're called, can happen inadvertantly. How can I put it? You see, chakras are spiritual "gates" situated in different parts of the body – I'm not terribly well up in this, let's see if I can get it right, I think the solar plexus, the spleen, neck, eyes and one more ... yes, the top of the head. I think that's correct.'

'And you think I've opened these "chak—" '

'It is a possibility, Mr Henderson, that's all I think. What is worse is not closing them. They must be closed very carefully after meditation. If they remain open, the system can be flooded by evil influences. Like a submarine putting to sea with sea-cocks open.'

Derek felt, but could not prevent himself giggling childishly. See cocks! Miss Strand looked at him sharply.

'So, if you don't realize you've opened the chakras in the first place, you'd hardly go through the correct meditative process to close them.' She stirred her tea, and sipped again, moving along closer to the old electric fire, which crackled a welcome like radiation.

'So that's how he got in,' Derek murmured. 'I suppose he picked me because of my name and background? Surely it's no coincidence?' His high voice sounded strained in the close silence.

'I did *not* say he *had* got in – I only said it was possible. But *if* he had, from what you have told me, it would appear anything but coincidence. I'd say it was calculated, with evil intent. You do realize, Mr Henderson, in that case he is almost certainly here now, with you? I may as well tell you that the minute I saw you walk into the church I knew there was something. It's your aura you see. I'm sensitive to auras. They are astral colours which appear to emanate from or hover round a person. There's one there.' She pointed to the Indian. 'It's been gradual, I wasn't born with this sense. Some people are of course. They play with children they think are there – we all know children with imaginary friends seen by nobody else, don't we? Often, these are lonely children.'

The implication struck them both together.

'But often it's not an imaginary friend at all, the child has actually *been* there. Somebody has been there, in the form of an aural projection visible only to that child. Perhaps a truly powerful aural personality can appear to others too, and have a destructive influence. Are you perhaps, unknowingly, a

Sensitive yourself, Mr Henderson? Consider it at least. It fits what we know so far. And a malignant personality has entered you, as you know only too well, *because* you are hyper-sensitive. Why he resembles your son I can't say. You had no relation who passed over as a child? We surely must discount a foetus – though I'm not sure even of that.

'Your aura is confused and most worrying because of the particular colours involved. I'd best say no more – you have enough problems.'

Miss Strand appeared suddenly troubled, stopped, hesitated, her gaze darting first left then right, anywhere.

'Anything you can tell me helps, anything. I need knowledge to fight him, please!' Derek said desperately. She mustn't stop now.

She looked at him searchingly. There was fear in her eyes, and the voice had a quaver.

'It's no good, I can't be objective, I have to speak my mind. Your aura, Mr Henderson, frightens me. Either you yourself are a dangerous psychopath, or this child is truly evil and in you. What worries me is that he can hear everything you and I say. He knows your plan to defeat him as well as you do. Either way, we are both in danger.

'Your aura is full of horrid colours. Grey-green, deceit and cunning. Odious grey with pink, jealousy. And sanguinary red through everything. That fits the boy's sensuality. And round the edge, most hideous, is the black of hate. Yet it is not of you. I sense that much.

'I have a book of auras, but *never* have I seen one so ugly and so involved. There's just one tiny glow of pale blue, supposedly the religious colour. The rest ...'

'Well, what can I *do*?' said Derek. 'Do you think my plan would work? Breaking out of Geoffrey's itinerary—'

'I can't tell you. You must decide what you feel in your heart is the right thing to do.'

'But that's no good,' cried Derek passionately 'I must have your advice!'

'Not *must*, Mr Henderson, not must.'

'I'm sorry, Miss Strand, I didn't mean that. I just feel so—'

'Look, Mr Henderson, I've explained what I think could be your position. What you plan *could* work. I just cannot take the responsibility of telling you to try it. Why not try a priest? You are a religious man. Get a second opinion. I can't recommend anyone. We favour no particular denomination amongst the main churches. We are as we are.'

'But I've told you why I can't. Geoffrey won't allow it. I'm surprised he's allowed me to talk to *you*.'

'Is that the real reason, Mr Henderson?'

Derek did not reply. Miss Strand looked at him. The cats looked at him. So did the Red Indian. Derek heard himself say:

'To tell the truth, Miss Strand, I've lost God. Or at least, he's lost me. So I can't really ask Him for help. I let it happen, no, made it happen really. I cannot go to a priest.'

Derek went on in detail. At the end, Miss Strand looked sad.

'That is the worst of all you have told me. With God ... I felt sure that your priest should have taken responsibility, not I. But now... without God you have no-one. Except me, that is. I cannot just stand by. You know, perhaps I'm meant to be your help. That must be it. As myself, not as a member of our society. As an instrument of God.'

She gazed into a distance unhampered by the clutter of the room. Derek began to feel hopeful again. The silence grew in length, and in intensity. Onto his new lightness a heaviness began to build. Odd. He tried to ignore it, tried to concentrate, for Miss Strand had begun speaking again.

'... so we have to ask ourselves, having assessed the facts, and what we know of this malevolent child, what he *wants* you to do. Then you must do exactly the opposite. You follow?'

'Yes-go-on-please.' Derek's words were what he wished, but it was difficult to say them. Miss Strand peered at him sharply. Had she noticed new tension in his tone?

'But he's listening now,' she was saying, 'I must take care. You must tell me your plan again, then I'll indicate agreement or disagreement. Somehow. I shan't say how, for obvious reasons. You will know. He is aged a perpetual ten? You did say ten? Plus what he gets from you of course. Something of you will be printed on him.'

'Geoffrey won't be fooled by *anything* you do, Miss Strand, he's smart, Geoffrey is.' Derek heard himself defending him.

'Not if I make myself subtle enough. But you'll have to concentrate. Expect anything. Something very adult. Something he won't follow.'

Miss Strand was peering at him again. Derek found himself wanting to laugh at her. Stupid women! Charlatan. What did she know about it? Geoffrey and he were being insulted. This woman was trying to trick him, trying to hoodwink him. No doubt she'd charge him a fee afterwards. It was all a con, the whole thing.

'Well, are you ready Mr Henderson? Tell me your plan again.'

What a load of crap. Derek felt scorn turn to dislike, then antagonism. He didn't have to put up with this. The electric fire was roasting. He sweated. It was that peculiar heat, the claustrophobic temperature, the beginning of that smell. Then he knew. It was Geoffrey thinking, not he.

'Well, come on Mr Henderson,' came Miss Strand's voice as if far off, 'it won't be easy. *Fight* him. I can see he's in you.'

He had to force himself. Concentrating by sheer will, Derek went through his plan doggedly, detail by detail, his voice betraying strain. Each time he paused for breath he felt Geoffrey would crash back, so he tried to sing it like fast plainsong, then Geoffrey couldn't get in.

At last he'd finished. Beads of perspiration had formed rivulets. They ran down his nose, into his eyes. His spine felt clammy. There was a sudden wailing as all three cats sped to the door, backs spiky. Miss Strand put them out, then returned to her place, looking sharply at him.

She should be put out, put out of her misery. Derek felt Geoffrey's hate. The heat was worse. He couldn't see properly. That bloody fire. The sweat poured into his eyes like glue. Must wipe them. He couldn't see Miss Strand clearly. He tried to find his handkerchief, unsuccessfully, so tried his fingers. They made things worse. Geoffrey was flooding him, breaking over him in waves.

All bleary, Miss Strand was nodding up and down, across and diagonally, like a car window dog, mocking him. Bloody cheek.

'*Watch* me, you *must* watch me, fight him. Wipe your eyes. Try your sleeve. Anything. And I'll ignore anything you say. As if you were drunk.'

Miss Strand's voice was years away. What a bag. '*Stupid old sod. Come on, come on then, come and get me!*' Words came out, not his. He drew his sleeve across his face. Too hard. A button struck his right eyeball. The pain. Oh God. Fresh tears streamed down. On his feet now, head bent forward, half-blind, despairing. Agony.

'The electric fire. Switch off. It's the fire.' His voice sounded high.

But she stumbled up from the sofa towards him, arms, hands outstretched as if to bless, or touch, one hand tipping back and forth. He heard his voice scream out, higher than ever, taunting, insulting.

'*You can't bless me you bag. Hands to yourself, bugger! Wandering hands society, that's you. Like Smartie. I'll have you. I'll stuff your bloody mouth. I could fly if I wanted to. I'll have you!* But it wasn't his voice.

Her teacup on the sofa end smashed over. Her foot caught the worn fibre flex. She fell in a welter of liquid against the orange bars of the fire. A flash, and a cry. Miss Strand had a moving electric aura for a split second, then lay still in a sea of fused electricity, expensive porcelain, tea and wreckage. A burned charred smell.

Her foot lay cocked on the cooling upturned electric fire. Derek heard words coming from his mouth, '*Poor old bag. Fancy trying to tell on me. I'm going to piss all over her.*' And he did.

Derek found himself standing by Miss Strand's body. There was a stink of burning and urine. He kicked her foot off the fire. He had murdered her in return for her kindness and concern. She had seen hate in his aura. She was right – the hate had not been for him. It had been for her. Call an ambulance? One look at her eyes told him it was a waste of time. Her spectacles were off, and her grey-blue irises were still intense, but dead. They accused him. He couldn't bear it, and moved from her dead vision.

Geoffrey had permanently removed his one hope, substituting another unbearable weight: guilt. Miss Strand was dead the moment she'd agreed to meet him.

But what could he do, Derek despaired. He couldn't report the 'accident'. The procedure might prevent the final killing of Geoffrey. Banishment to his tomb, wherever that was. But it was also true that investigations and possible arrest would in themselves snap him out of the itinerary.

But Geoffrey might have allowed for this. Geoffrey had murdered Miss Strand, wilfully, and might have *meant* Derek to telephone the police.

They would want to know why she was wet all over with urine. He would be accused of defiling a corpse. He looked at her again, and was suddenly sick.

Why couldn't evil Geoffrey be spewed out as easily? Because you can't vomit your soul.

Miss Strand was now dead too. Would she seek revenge? Would there be now two against him from beyond the grave? No, he tried to tell himself, she would not blame him.

He peered through the lace curtains into the narrow street, now dusk, with only thin bars of sun between elongated shadows. Luckily, despite several cars near the Morris, there was no human movement.

Derek eased open the narrow front door and shut it after him silently. The delicately curtained window hid the interior until the ginger cat parted the lace from within like a sunburst on the sill. Any passer-by could now see the tragedy which Derek Henderson had caused.

Legs unsteady, the twenty yards to the car were the longest he could remember. The keys wouldn't go into the lock, his hand trembled so much. The engine coughed once, then roared into the loudest engine ever heard in Hope Street. Inhabitants would rush to doors and windows. Children would run the length of the street just to watch his car, and someone would spot Miss Strand through the curtains.

But they didn't, and he drove off, a murderer, poor Miss Strand dead with eyes open over an electric fire, watched by three cats and a Red Indian.

Jamie was getting ready for bed, and Barbara was with him. The sand castle had been successful and so had the moat.

On his return Derek had managed to appear nearly normal. So he trusted. A stiff drink in the hotel bar had helped. At any rate, nothing was said when he joined them in Jamie's room, but everywhere he saw, superimposed, Miss Strand falling very slowly onto the electric fire, Miss Strand dead amid tea, urine, crockery and ornaments. He saw the efficient police.

Then Jamie got into bed and Derek walked quietly out into the grounds overlooking the sea. The sun was a red ball, like Mars, just above the horizon. Everything was red like blood, or glowing electric bars. He stood on the overgrown rockeries near the cliff which was no more than steep hill. The drive was almost empty, except for the hip-conscious walk of a few lovers as they wondered where to stop.

The beach, too, was almost deserted. Just one or two dog owners and their bounding charges looked for places to plant excreta, ready for the children to stumble into next morning.

The little town was quiet: there was no din of discos in Totland. Even the radios were discreet. In the bay the waves flopped gently on to calm sands and shingle. A few gulls wheeled away high into sky pale blue where it wasn't bloodied by the sun. A coolness had begun, stealthily, to pervade the nearly silent land, creeping close into crevices and between grass blades.

But the pier was all lights, and music blared distantly from the tiny world at its end, a world marooned except for its thin walkway of wood and metal, its tenuous link with land and reality.

There were not many figures on its length. Derek could pick out one optimistic fisherman fighting the lights and noise dancing along the gentle water towards him. His rod was just visible but not the line. Odd, that minute umbilical cord linking man with salt sea. Odd to know the link existed, yet to the unknowing observer there was no connection whatsoever between the vast dancing ocean and the human being who contemplated it.

But at the pier end all was bustle and brilliance, lights so bright that Derek expected it all to explode any minute.

A touch of breeze fingered his hair. He seemed to hear Miss Strand's voice again and again. 'Fight this, fight him.' But where *was* Geoffrey? Derek had felt oddly empty of him since Miss Strand's death. That despicable job done, he had gone, leaving Derek his guilt. He would be back. He hadn't finished. But, temporarily free, Derek could *plan*.

Something Miss Strand had said. Something which could

help. It was just before ... it ... happened. She had known that Geoffrey was flooding in. She hadn't much time to signify her opinion of Derek's idea. How desperately hard she'd tried, but failed.

Yet had she? Was it already said before she was propelled onto the fire? Had she realized that her original intention would not succeed? He visualized again her lurch towards him, saw again the outstretched hands as if to bless. Like a bishop. A confirmation ... a laying on of hands ... a touching ... 'You will know,' she'd said. 'You will know. You did say he is a perpetual ten?' She was going to touch him in some manner. She'd failed. It all came to nothing.

But he wasn't satisfied. Perhaps she'd had some reserve plan. Something too clever for Geoffrey. Some hidden thing which said this may work. Do this if evil Geoffrey beats me. Almost do this in remembrance of me. Yes, she could have foreseen her death. He pushed his memory as far as it could go.

'Expect anything. Something very adult ...' Had she said that *before* he'd repeated his plan or after? 'Watch me ... I'll ignore anything you say ... as if you were drunk ...' He saw again her right hand cupped, moving in traditional parody of drinking.

Drunk. Yes. Could be. Geoffrey, aged a perpetual ten, was not used to alcohol! He'd taken Derek's personality, but not perhaps Derek's head for drink! Miss Strand's charade had said for temporary freedom, get him tipsy. Then plan something while he's fuddled!

Brilliant, Miss Strand, brilliant. Tragic she had to die to say it. He must over-drink when Geoffrey was inside him for certain. The only safe way to plan. Taking advantage of his absence now was not enough: he could return any instant.

So although Geoffrey knew of the existing plan, Derek had one secret weapon. Not that he could use it for Saturday: he himself must be utterly sober, one hundred per cent clear for that Niton bend.

Ironically, he still didn't know Miss Strand's reaction to his St. Catherine's plan, nor ever would. One thing was certain: Geoffrey must never know of the drink trick, and to make certain Derek had to forget it himself. Essential to dismiss it, then focus Geoffrey's attention elsewhere when he returned.

He had better begin now. Willpower. The mind *could* be

controlled. Sometimes, indeed, it acted alone with amnesia. How incomprehensible, for example, that his mind could so utterly dismiss involvement in a murder a few hours before, freeing him to wonder at sun and sea on a summer evening.

Or was it really Miss Strand's way of saying it wasn't your fault, forget me, just deal with this evil? Was she here with him now? He could hear someone.

No, it was Barbara, looking thoughtful, but not at him. Her eyes gazed out over the sea to the sun, which now nearly touched the glimmer it caused, not just on the horizon but over the whole spread of the ocean. Its shimmer came down even to the pier end, whose lights perpetuated it almost to the beach.

'You really could have put yourself out for Jamie this evening,' Barbara said. 'You're mean, it wouldn't have hurt you to help him build that castle.'

'I'm sorry. Had to be by myself for a while. Needed to think.'

'Always alone. No room for us. One day he'll be grown up and it'll be too late.'

'Needed, not wanted. Anyway, you're wrong – you'll never know how much I love that boy. Just because I can't be with him the whole time ...'

'That's an understatement – you're hardly with him at all.' Her voice had begun to sound edgy.

'Barbara, please,' said Derek, firmly 'Let's not quarrel over it. I'll try after the holiday. Really. But not now – I do have problems.'

'You could say that. But Jamie's no Peter Pan. He'll grow up for certain. All boys do. You'll miss his boyhood, and you'll be sorry.'

'Not all boys,' Derek said, rashly, instantly regretting it, realizing she'd think of the miscarriage. 'You're always saying I never grew up.'

There was now red in every part of the ocean, the hill-top, the curved beach; cadmium in pier timbers, sand, rocks, all the way from Hatherwood to Warden Point, even the breakers were pink. But everything had its original colour too.

Each different hue was tinged with a rosiness lit from within itself, a moving restlessness textured like a pointillist painting. As if that crimson sun, millions of miles across the universe, had exploded, sending fragments of itself to lodge in between every molecule all the way to Totland. The hotel was lit too, its bricks, glass and turrets tinged with that same glow worn by the cathedral on certain evenings, its red sandstone alive with love in the late sun.

Derek looked at Barbara, semi-profiled against the warm sky. She was lovely too. Was that pink from the sun, or from his blurting insensitivity about boys failing to grow up? Either way, she was still lovely. He was looking at her in the old way, enjoying her beauty as once he used to do. Slowly, newly, as a lover does. Savouring.

In an instant he realized. Perhaps, for one last time, Geoffrey's absence was letting him feel for her as he had before Hazel. Before Geoffrey had bent him.

Her face. He easily recalled the effect she first had on him, smiling behind that Trinity desk.

Odd about desks. His first sight of Hazel had been behind a desk. And pews like desks had been in front of somebody else ... that other name ... the name which still caused goose-pimples ... as if he were still adolescent, vulnerable. Elizabeth-Marie.

There was the slighest lifting of air as newer, cooler currents disturbed the tired warmth of the dying day. Barbara's hair moved minutely, one thick strand straying across her face. She seemed not to notice; indeed she now seemed almost not with Derek at all, just standing coincidently at the same spot on the hill.

The gentle light touched her superb mouth, proud on the strong but very feminine jaw. He always admired her lips, the lower just a fraction more forward than you would expect, pushed sensuously by the white clean teeth it covered. The red of the upper lip was nearly as full, but flatter and almost tight round the maxilla when she smiled.

The nose was short and very twentieth century, but it was not the common characterless snub of the girl-next-door. Instead, with its mere hint of upward curve, it suggested slight disdain which Derek had always found enchanting. The effect on the fluted upper lip was delicious, for it raised it minutely, giving a delicacy both disapproving and suggestive. He liked that slight pout in profile.

They were good cheek bones, high and prominent, with just the right amount of hollowness below. The eyes were large and blue with heavy upper lids, and the evening light imbued them with even more mystery. They were the eyes of a dreamer, not a mathematician. Derek could never come to terms with the anomaly. And now the sun made her like Elizabeth-Marie from long ago, in a blurring superficially like the Osborne photograph. But living and so beautiful.

The hair was thick and swirled round, swinging when she walked. But Derek always found it most voluptuous when styled short or tight, to follow the curve of the head behind and above the ears. He needed to see that part, remembering with what erotic pleasure he had first run his hand over the sculpted tightness caused by the elastic band stretching the straight brown hair back into a graceful ponytail. He had always loved ponytails. 'Tighter the better!' he would say, not daring to add 'like pulling the skin back'.

'It's so real there's horse manure on your collar!' he used to laugh, and she would turn, her mouth and nose expressing slight disgust while her eyes laughed back. It had excited him to imagine she knew what he really thought.

All this time Barbara had never spoken, never taken her eyes from the glory of the sun. Now she turned, her large irises softer, bigger than ever before. There was no blurring now.

'Derek, if there's anything you want me to know, now's the time.'

There was so much he wanted her to know. So very much. But it was too sudden. He was caught utterly unprepared, still in his erotic dreamland. Could he tell her everything? Could he? There was a silence broken only by a few gulls and the somehow faded boom, bah-boom; boom, bah-boom of the pop rhythm from the pier. It was, despite this, a genuine silence, or perhaps more a vacuum into which something could now be placed. But how the hell do you explain a dead Geoffrey, live? His murdering of Miss Strand? His evil? But he'd try. He'd try now.

'Is there anything really wrong? I'll understand anything humanly possible! Try me,' said Barbara slowly, her eyes serious despite the tone of voice. But he couldn't. He did not have the courage. 'Humanly possible.' She had scuppered him before he began with that killing phrase. This had been his last chance. His opportunity was over before it began.

'Barbara, whatever happens, I do love you. Remember that. Please.'

'What do you mean – whatever—'

'Just remember. It may not be easy. At this moment I need you so much.' His voice shook, he knew it and she sensed it more than heard it. He kissed her, experiencing the softness of her lips for nearly the last time. But she persisted.

'Then tell me whatever it is that's wrong. If you love me, tell me,' she insisted. 'There's something.'

'Not yet ... but please remember. However else it may look. ...'

He was surprised that she said nothing else. Despite the café episode, they made love in the dusk, like a courting couple, in thick bushes near Turf Walk. The ground was warm and hard and the perfume was of flowers. It was almost spoilt just before the climax. Derek had to fight away the sudden image of Miss Strand falling on to the fire, faster and faster, and faster.

They walked slowly back into the hotel. The sun had gone, its light remaining only in the pier end behind them. It had been a kind of farewell, but only Derek knew it.

Goodbye my love. I love your lips.

FRIDAY

'Do you think I'm really a counter tenor?' said Derek. 'My voice is different. Perhaps I was never a tenor.'

He made as if to launch into a demonstration, clearing his throat and taking a hasty swig of ale.

'Not here! You do embarrass me,' Barbara whispered.

'Oh, come on, you're so inhibited,' Derek replied. And even in her new firmness, she was.

Robin Hill Country Park stretched round the trellised beer garden, luxuriant green spread richly over undulating ground. They had explored the 'zoo', tried the radio-controlled boats, fallen foul of the stacked gift shop and left Jamie at the assault course. Jamie's horn-handled knife and Barbara's polished wood ibex lay in her pagoda basket.

'We'll have these place mats too,' Barbara said firmly. 'I love the Bewick wood engravings. That tiger!'

She had bought them with all the detachment of Derek and the railway signal. They nestled in between the ibex and her handbag.

Robin Hill appeared to be very recent. Derek had looked secretly for clues. Could it have been open in 1933? Surely not. Another leak in the itinerary, another doubt. But there was no doubt that Geoffrey was back. He had known, at the moment of waking, on feeling coldness at the sight of Barbara next to him in bed. He was a different man from last evening and it saddened him. He longed to have told her, to have shared his terrible secret. He knew his love for her was gone irretrievably, and with it his last chance of telling anybody. It was finished. She was now the woman with whom he shared Jamie. There was perhaps some affection, nothing more. Geoffrey was here. Geoffrey didn't like grown-up women, didn't like pubic hairs.

He had lain awake in their tall hotel bedroom all night, churning it over. Especially his plan for Saturday. He now feared his mouth opening in the night, too. A door for Geoffrey. So he felt tired for lack of sleep. At least he couldn't have babbled anything crazy in the night, so he told himself.

The strain of the last few days was evident. A rich cornice stretched unbroken round the room. Under it was a Greek key decoration. Derek lay wondering which would unlock the moulding.

Should he try his key, his plan, on Friday, at the first opportunity? Was he right to have chosen Saturday?

The Robin Hill commando assault course had captivated James; half commando, half monkey, he was now part of a ten-boy game, reality forgotten entirely.

At length, tired of waiting, Derek and Barbara had retired to the nearby bar, outside which they now sat. The sun and wasps kept them company, as if excited by the prospect of drinking a genuinely brewed local ale.

Derek's first pint had lubricated his larynx and it was his relaxed beery hum which now encouraged vocal demonstration. Temporarily, drink had washed away his fears for tomorrow and the horror of yesterday. He felt his usual self: the singer concerned with the vagaries of voice.

'I've almost an extra octave upwards,' Derek persisted. 'Notice any change?'

He looked anxious, took a pull of 'real ale', and despite her, suddenly produced a top B quietly and effortlessly. It had a bell-like quality that she usually associated with John Saville, the best of the Swallowfield counter tenors. The cathedral altos always insisted on their ancient title. All except old Eric, who didn't care. Titles like 'Bitter', 'Mild', 'Pint', 'Jar'; these were names which meant something to Eric.

People glanced round in British surprise at the resonant head-tone cutting through conversation.

'My God, that's a good note,' Barbara exclaimed despite herself. 'It's so clear. You're right, it is different.'

'How?'

'It's ... less thick, and sounds sort of easier up there than usual.'

'*Told* you. Not so scrotal. Trouble is, the low range has gone,' he went on, utterly engrossed in vocal problems.

'Oh, come on,' Barbara said firmly. 'The holiday is responsible. You've not sung for a week. Every day for a term, then a week's break. Shows how good your top notes'd be if you sang less often.'

Derek, sensing the approach of another well aired subject, his inconvenient cathedral commitments, steered himself away. 'You may be right ... This beer's good. Wish we had it in the Midlands. I'll go and get Jamie.'

His empty glass was textured with beer head from top to bottom. Barbara's shandy half remained. He rose, disturbing the wasps, passed the eager queue at the bar, and went out through the open trellis gate.

He walked between clumps of cave-like bushes towards the assault course. The ground became soft sand with twigs struggling for survival, a miniature Australian outback. Children raced about in games energetic, which involved much shooting, dying and resurrecting, and games explorative, which were taking place inside the bushes in the quieter areas.

Derek paused on the hot deep sand. There was a voluptuous smell of cow parsley, and it transported him instantly to boyhood and Kent. Deep green, secret places where you could see all but not be seen from outside. And always the one delicate flower ready to open. ...

When the deep urge came to him to join the junior doctors and nurses in a cavernous bush, he knew it was Geoffrey, not he, Geoffrey drawing him into another encounter. Yet he wanted to be drawn, wanted to touch. As at the cafe.

He managed at last to run, his urgent feet scattering sand powder into the air, and soon reached the assault course. It lay in a sand-filled valley. He sat breathless on a wiry tussock overlooking it. Small figures were placed on the apparatus like crotchets on staves.

Jamie was about to spring onto a ginger-headed boy from a rope. Hardly daring to, Derek slowly turned his head the way he'd come. Far off but clear, just inside the bush, stood Dawn Rollins, frock right up, no pants. Her laugh drowned all other sounds.

He snatched his gaze away abruptly, savagely suppressing

Geoffrey, and ran down to grab James from a pile of struggling boys. As he steered him back past the ice cream stall, he reflected it was only a matter of time before he did what Geoffrey wanted, and fully.

Oh Christ, what was he to do? Geoffrey Henderson was to blame, but Derek Henderson would get the blame. Any time now. He would try to explain: 'It's not fair, wasn't me, t'was him' in Geoffrey's phrasing. Would the police believe him? Of course not. 'What did *you* 'ave in yer 'and, then sir? Bastard. I've a daughter 'er age.'

Slam. The police car would bear him away to court, coat-over-head, Sunday papers, gaol. Humiliation. Child molester. Murderer of old ladies. Useless to say 'it's unjust. Am I my brother's keeper?'

He who once said that was concerned to conceal a death. He who said it now would manifest himself in his own.

We are all brothers. We atone for each other. Peccavi.

Barbara sat in the beer garden, reading the Robin Hill booklet, her drink still unfinished.

If you left the wasps alone they left you alone. Derek seemed better today. His voice was, as usual, his immediate concern. But, last evening apart, he had changed towards her. She kept catching his eyes on her body, assessing, criticizing. Yet last evening had been beautiful. He was a strange man.

People were strange. She herself must look so to others, but surely not so ridiculous as that fat woman suffering inside the tightest trousers ever.

The quarrelling group of young executives and wives, in carefully casual gear, was becoming louder. An extravagant gesture destroyed a coy Babycham.

'Charles, how *could* you say such a thing. How *could* you? Now you've upset Valerie. And spoilt her drink.'

'Oh God, all I said was, there's nothing to bloody well *do* on the Isle of Wight, except screw.'

'Charming. Keep your voice *down*. We'd have *gone* to Ibiza if you hadn't. ...'

Barbara turned away. The small enclosure was quite full, mostly with families: children who had finished their lemonade, parents whose glasses were only half empty. Her wasps had broken allegiance and were spreading to the crowded nectar on other tables.

There was something familiar about someone just arrived in the far corner. The man, thin on top, was almost completely turned away, but the woman faced her. A little girl with a fat face and fair hair sat between. There was a constant movement of impatient kids between Barbara and the far table, so a clear view was impossible.

Where *had* she seen that woman before? Swallowfield? Watford last year? Wellingham? Wellingham. In a busy street. But somewhere else too. An office. A typewriter, with photographs behind her blonde hair. She'd had a younger smile than this tired one. A 'can I help you' smile, 'I'm efficient.' Was it Trinity College? But somewhere else too, somewhere ancient, stone and grass. The cathedral?

Her memory bank chased information relentlessly. The image of the street involved introductions. She recalled embarrassment quite clearly. Derek's. He had seemed ... ill at ease. Then it was clear at last. Up came the radio-photo. There they were, all four, in New Street, Wellingham. The traffic had swept by, making conversation difficult. But why were they there, and who *was* the blonde woman? Barbara looked again.

The intervening party rose suddenly, like slowly startled pigeons, and swept out noisily, leaving Barbara's view clear. Their table was taken by an attractive man in his forties, whose eye caught hers every time she stared past him. He clearly thought she was interested, and his gaze ranged over her still trim figure then back to her face.

Awkward, she so wanted to continue looking, but couldn't. Instead she fell to analysis ... photographs behind the curled blonde hair. Concert artists with gleaming teeth, bow ties, crisp shirts; signatures; successful, confident. ...

An agency. Derek's ex-agent's office? Yes. She risked it and darted another glance. Hazel Roe, the attractive secretary. Definitely. She looked older, but who didn't? Was that her husband?

She remembered Hilary's gossip linking Hazel with Derek. Nonsense of course, but... Hilary was a cow. Barbara could still hear her excited voice husky with feigned concern:

'I'm only telling you for your own good, love, but they do say he was seeing her several times a week. That harmony class, the Wednesday teatime one? Didn't exist.'

She had laughed, but had satisfied herself that the classes existed. All lies then. The prospectus could not be wrong. Derek had laughed too, when denying everything.

Everybody knew spinster Hilary's interest in Derek, even Derek. He and Barbara had giggled over it many times at home. And over the Chapter Clerk's obvious relish for Barbara herself: 'His qualification's longer than your arm!' Derek would insinuate with coarse arm action. This was a double joke, for pompous Mr Dixon couldn't raise a degree to his name.

So she had put it all down to jealousy. Hilary had maintained that the whole thing had been going on for years, since about the time Jamie was expected. She even hinted that, subsequently, Hazel had borne Derek's child. At this, Barbara had lost her temper utterly, and Hilary had not appeared in Vicars' Close for six months.

Derek had known nothing of Hilary's more serious allegation, and Barbara kept it that way. She was thankful to hear the Roes had moved to London. Hazel was gone, out of the way, out of her thoughts. She never existed. Derek would never have been unfaithful. She just knew it.

As for fathering another child, when she herself was pregnant. ... She'd hated Hilary passionately for several months. Now she wondered. Almost face to face with Hazel, it was all forced back to her. A coincidence, the Roes being here too. She sipped her drink without tasting it.

The husband rose with empty glasses, and strode past purposefully towards the inner bar. Barbara looked down at the booklet. 'Opened to the public in 1969, Robin Hill Country Park is. ...' she read, but her eyes would not stay on the page. Hazel Roe and her daughter were now preoccupied with wasps. The wasps seemed to be preoccupied with jam sandwiches.

'Mummy, Mummy, get them away, Mummy!' the girl squealed in panic. The fortyish man left, looking meaningfully at Barbara, and his place was filled simultaneously by a vociferous group, part, if she was not mistaken, of the be-jeaned party seen at the Newport café yesterday. It reminded her of

Derek's behaviour there. *Was* he so faithful? Had she maligned Hilary? Then she remembered last evening. Never had she felt such love from him.

When Stuart appeared she thought at first that he was somehow with the school party, now all sitting feet-up on the table. He *was* like Jamie, he really was. Startlingly so. ... But to her surprise, he went to Hazel's table and sat next to his sister, whom he resembled not at all. Either Barbara had to walk over before Stuart recognized and greeted her, or she had to get out unnoticed. She got out unnoticed.

As she bent for her basket, two wasps took possession of her unfinished drink. One pushed the other under the liquid, almost as if trying to drown it.

A third arrived on the rim of the glass too late for anything.

Brading Station was still in use by British Rail, one of five on the pathetic remains of the network.

It wasn't the Hendersons' intention to be there at all. Barbara driving, they had reached the main Ryde-Sandown road at a T-junction. Brading spread both ways.

'Right here,' Derek had said, 'then fourth lane on the right.'

But despite her firm intention, Barbara had turned left. It alarmed her. Was her mind so much on Hazel Roe that she couldn't control the steering?

'*Right* not left. Prune,' exclaimed Derek irritably.

'Oh, shut up, the wheel turned the wrong way.'

'Women drivers!'

She really was quite plain, and getting fat, thought Derek, whistling O *Where Shall Wisdom Be Found?*, a favourite anthem. Barbara, understanding its implication, pulled in suddenly to the kerb, causing a blare of horns about them.

'All right, *you* drive.' She really was angry. 'I'm sick to death of you, your hangups, your problems, your snide remarks.'

How *dare* he criticise her when she had been making so many allowances for his bloody behaviour? And after last evening too. He didn't love her at all. Derek, normally ready to do battle, could do no more than mutter penitence:

'Look, I'm sorry, I was only joking. You drive.'

He took her hand, but she snatched it away. Jamie sat silently in the back, pretending to read the Robin Hill booklet and wishing he were not an only child.

'Very well. But cut out the remarks.'

She restarted the engine, and drove off more confidently than she really felt. Hazel and Derek? Derek and Hazel? And how *could* the steering wheel turn left when she'd moved it right?

Derek knew how, when the first right turn for reversing was Station Road. Of course. Geoffrey had come by train. The station still existed, so they had to come here to reach the Roman Villa.

Yet not all the itinerary was the 1933 original. Presumably the original was more powerful: you couldn't step from it. But where Geoffrey had superimposed modern places perhaps there was more leeway? It was easy to test this theory, but he didn't dare: he'd need his full strength for the next day.

'That old station, Jamie,' said Derek. 'It's almost unchanged in forty years. Look at the old oil lamps. And there's a train coming.'

There was. It stopped precisely where they did, and out came a few passengers, leaving the crowded coaches hardly lighter at all. Doors slammed. A pause, a whistle, and the sterile electric coaches glided out, sounding like several milk floats on rails. They clicked off in a line towards Sandown to make more deliveries.

Derek noticed a sign to Yarbridge Roman Villa, pointing with an arrow down an old cinder track by the railway. Geoffrey went that way in 1933, Derek remembered. He'd turned right at the Anglers Inn. How hot it had been.

To attempt now to drive to the Roman site would be stupid: why fight Geoffrey now, when he needed all his strength for tomorrow? 'Let's walk it,' said Derek, 'and leave the car here. Parking will be difficult.'

'Unlikely – surely? It's in open country.'

'I just feel like walking.'

'Suit yourself, but we'll ride,' she said coolly. 'Meet you there.' (Those Wednesday classes, *were* they real?)

Derek got out, smiling weakly at Jamie, who avoided his gaze.

Inside the station entrance stood a vintage Nestlés chocolate machine, solid and red. Amazingly, it was working. He bought three bars, as he'd done before. The car had gone, so he pocketed two and began the third.

As he munched he wondered how the Hydroplane motor boat trials were going for Miss Britain III on Southampton Water. Would we win in Detroit in September? He thought of the 'Speed' set in his cigarette cards. He kicked a stone along the kerb. Bugger his shoes.

Barbara glanced automatically into the mirror as they turned left into the main road. Derek had gone. Silly fool, walking in this heat. But could that be Geoffrey with a tall man and a dumpy woman, emerging from the station on to the cinder track? Eating a bar of chocolate? There was something oddly familiar about those parents.

Derek found some satisfaction on arrival at the Villa: there was a parking problem caused by several coaches. It was evidently going to be a congested visit.

He found the others at the entrance. Thank God, there was no sign of the Roes. Barbara greeted him briefly.

The Roman remains were protected by a plain prefabricated structure resembling a small aircraft hangar. Inside, the tripper atmosphere evaporated quickly, as if everybody sensed the power of the past. The superb mosiac floor was rich, and demanded more than superficial glances. There were almost too many Roman domestic items, and eyes glazed over like the pottery itself.

There was a raised stone walkway with railings, making it possible to see closely almost any part of the floor. Slowly, jerkily, the crowd shuffled along this.

Jamie was drawn to the intricacies of the Roman locks and keys, and the coin collection claimed his long attention. Derek stood before the pottery and tiles.

Barbara found herself swept gently along, onto the stone walkway over the mosaic floor. Owing to the damage, the original design had been patched expertly here and there with flat cement. This had the effect of an unfinished jigsaw; in repeat patterns you could quite easily see what once was there, but never know the missing detail of certain diamond-shaped tablets, which were lost for ever.

Most, though, were beautifully complete. Always fascinated by mythology, and knowing the major stories by heart, Barbara began to identify the deities systematically. It took her mind off Hazel Roe, temporarily at least, and off Derek's regression today. The designs were especially bold and looked as if they were by the same artist.

That Medusa was very fine. Hercules stood astride in the next table and beyond it Icarus fell, never to crash. A Bacchanalian scene occupied a large rectangle, then the diamonds began again. The last one lay in comparative shadow in the corner, and was slightly damaged, making identification more difficult. She tried to move nearer through the narrow crowd, but made little headway.

Barbara looked down and along. She was struck by the accidental effect, brought about by patching on the edge, of a miniature Isle of Wight. Remarkable. Almost as if done on purpose. She found a passable Sandown Bay, and there was West Wight with the River Yar exactly right. Totland even had a pier. Cowes and the Medina estuary looked a bit odd though, and St. Catherine's Point was too pointed. Ryde was uncannily correct.

So far, the actual design had not been visible. Suddenly the crowd shifted and Barbara found herself right above, able to see properly at last.

It was an animal with a dragon's tail and three heads: lion, snake and goat. What the devil was it called? Chimaera. It was snarling hideously, the mosaic creating an unusually evil expression on each of its faces. An odd thing with which to decorate your house.

At first, she was annoyed that Bellerophon wasn't there at all, much less depicted slaying it. The irritation changed to nagging worry. A myth is only safe because the end is known. Chimaera had to be killed, but Bellerophon was not there.

The beast was enormous and spread to every part of the Isle of Wight. It was the three heads which triggered a development in Barbara's mind. One moment she was seeing an ancient mosaic with a mythical design, the next her mind was working rapidly, flickering through like a computer making up lost time.

It built up quickly and alarmingly into a picture she did not wish to see, and it was still developing fast. She hated it, but had to look at it, for the body of the creature lay over Carisbrooke.

146

Hazel Roe. It *was* true, all the time. She knew suddenly where else she'd seen Hazel: Carisbrooke, hurrying away across the yard, head down, pale. She was here on holiday with her family. The children were elsewhere at that moment. The husband? With them?

Just afterwards there had been that business of Derek's attack by the mental patient. Punched hard for no reason. But Derek had been strangely anxious to play it down, and to leave the castle without delay.

Jamie had seen the attack. It had worried him – his father a seeming coward, not hitting back. What was that name business? Alec ... 'You called him Alec,' Jamie had said, and Derek denied it. No, *Alan*, not Alec.

So Derek had known the man Alan, who had hit him hard without warning, so Jamie said. She paused. It had to be faced. Was the attacker Hazel's husband? It fitted.

Perhaps he had learned only recently, by chance, of Derek's affair with Hazel. Then, who should they meet on holiday? And what about the coincidence of Jamie meeting Stuart?

Hazel had seemingly avoided meeting Derek, but Alan had exploded with a punch into his face, the instinctive action of a betrayed husband. And the worry about it all was affecting Derek very obviously. He'd had plenty to tell her, all right, but no courage with which to do it.

She looked at the Chimaera again. It was an eternal triangle: the heads were Derek, Barbara and Hazel, bound together in one body. What was the biblical phrase? Something about a man leaving his parents, taking a wife and they become one flesh. Wrong. They and the man's mistress become one flesh. Her skin crawled.

What if she were wrong? *Was* Hazel's husband called Alan? Her memory would not help this time, but she must know for certain.

If it were all true, could she control the bitter accusation in her body? Would she, like Alan, strike out too?

It would not be a mere blow if she did. She was by nature a thorough, methodical woman.

Derek studied the people almost more than the Roman

147

remains. There had to be a time when that one tall figure would appear out of nowhere, just like Carisbrooke. But no menacing Alan, no frightened Hazel seemed about to occur from this crowd at least.

There were now two pressures on him simultaneously. How long could he endure it? Both natural and supernatural fought for him. It was only now that he admitted the question which had battered to be heard all week: why had he thrust God away in this most spiritual of problems? Where was He? In Swallowfield Cathedral, locked in by him, and the tragedy was that the great Derek Henderson could not do it all without God. His arrogance was pathetic.

He should have tried to talk to a priest. He hadn't. Not even dropped to his proud knees, alone somewhere, to say 'I can't turn to anyone but You.' Could he ask now? No. For in one way his lack of faith had caused Miss Strand's death. He had that on his conscience now. Too late... he must handle it without God.

He wondered how Alan had found out, but hoped he'd never be close enough to be told. Had Hazel confessed as she'd threatened? It was all a nightmare.

Derek had suffered nightmares since Carisbrooke, not always while asleep. The ones which occurred last night, in the dark heat, were more frightening; but those of the day were insidious, further weakening his grip on reality, his grasp on himself.

Always the castle, always the rampart path. Sometimes he himself would be tiny, the path like a deserted motorway and Alan running hard at him like a sprinting Goliath. Other times the path was so narrow that he couldn't keep his feet at all, and fell as Alan reached him. In this version Alan would laugh as he trampled little Derek. The enormous echo would smash the castle and bury them all.

One particular dream was the clearest of all. Hazel had with her a boy with no face. As she and Alan reached Derek, the boy was flung forward at him like a doll. They were laughing.

Derek recoiled in horror, stepping aside, letting the boy who had become Geoffrey hurtle off the edge onto the stones below. Miss Strand stood applauding and nodding. He looked down. It was now he himself. And the stones were Somme mud.

Then Alan and Hazel were changed into his own father and

mother. Distorted with echo was Saville's penetrating voice on the phrase 'O my son, my son, my son ...' from Derek's father's mouth. His parents' huge tears filled the castle courtyard the shape of the hotel mirror. But the brown filth corrupted the clear tears.

As the boy's head sank beneath the ooze, the face disintegrated like his footprints in the sand, that first morning early.

For light relief they had visited the Brading Wax Museum in its unnaturally pink Tudor home. Jamie and Derek had wandered off while Barbara was in the Ladies. It always had been a family joke, her frequent trips to conveniences all over the country. Derek had even suggested she compiled a loo guide or her memoirs.

When she emerged she was confronted by two grins, and a large irregular bag in Jamie's hand.

'It's a secret until later,' Jamie said.

She knew they'd been in the wax museum's silly shop; it would be something funny. God, she needed to laugh, but the way she felt, it would be an uphill task.

The waxworks had not taken Barbara's thoughts from Hazel Roe. All the time she was conscious of herself watching for Jamie to be alone. She must ask carefully about Carisbrooke: must dig deeply without seeming to.

There was no chance yet. Derek seemed determined to get back to Totland without delay, promising Jamie a swim before dinner. It was a tempting idea to Barbara too: they'd not swum for ages, it was hot and sticky, and the clean West Wight salt might clear her thoughts.

She would have a talk with Hilary on her return to Swallowfield, not, of course, admitting anything. Poor Hilary, right all along? If so, Barbara did not like her more for it.

If it were true should she leave Derek? Not necessarily. Hopefully he'd got it out of his system. It was after all in the past. But by God, she'd teach him a lesson somehow. Thinking it over in the cool sea would perhaps soothe the hurt. Or would the salt aggravate the wound?

Jamie had bought a cheap plastic kite at the pier shop, and they had promised a trial flight.

It was the Friday evening. A firm breeze had sprung up about tea-time, as if to say I'm ready for that kite now. Headen Hill seemed to be the nearest suitable place after an abortive and nearly disastrous maiden flight on Turf Walk. It had taken half an hour to extricate the fragile framework, with its plastic membrane, from the tree. They were watched suspiciously by an aged resident, with stick, muttering 'vandals', to Barbara's embarrassment.

During the process, Derek had crashed down the few feet from the Walk onto the sloping bank and its dense bushes, scratching his eye painfully. Half blinded for some moments, the eye watered freely. Everything was stretched round his flooded eyeball, like the glass globe lamp on the carriage ceiling. It felt as big as Hell's Head at Blackgang.

He thought of Miss Strand, the agony in that little house. He saw her fall and burn. Suddenly he had seemed to stumble, in his pain, onto the ethyl drums and raft wood he knew he'd hidden there. But surely he'd finished the raft?

When the eye was dry, the pain gone, so had the raft pieces. So had physical proof. It was all happening, but there never seemed any way of proving it. Nothing he could take to Barbara and say 'this shows I'm not mad!' Real evidence! Now, please help.

But all he would ever have, in Barbara's eyes, would be hypotheses, if you didn't include an elderly lady, dead on an electric fire.

Headon Hill was clean, perfect and overlooked Alum Bay. The sky was egg-shell blue, and the Needles stood like sculpture against it. Here was one of those evenings in summer when time stands still, and nothing can ever change. The sun was low but still hot, though the long shadows from the rare trees rippled in a slight breeze that was growing firmer every minute.

The hill itself was deserted, apart from the Hendersons. The grass was mostly short and springy with wiry clumps at intervals like buried overgrown heads. The combination of hot air rising and a wind off the ocean seemed ideal for kite flying.

After adjustments, the kite was ready for the air. It was highly coloured, and a snake design coiled all over it, a snake whose head was enormous and whose eyes lit as the light streamed through from behind. There was an impression of almost hypnotic power.

The tail of the kite formed that of the snake. There were two vestigial wings suggesting mutation. The wind plucked at it in Jamie's hands, or was the reptile anxious to fly? It worried her.

'Close your eyes and only open them when I say,' shouted Jamie, laughing as he picked up the large bag from the Wax Museum. Barbara obeyed. The sound of giggling, of rustling paper. A twang of elastic followed by 'Ouch'.

'Not yet, not yet!' yelled Jamie.

The breeze rippled the grass. Swishing footsteps retreating. Flap of kite. Silence.

'Come *on*,' she said irritably, always hating to be kept waiting.

The wind fingered her hair, whistling slightly like some ghostly errand boy.

'Now!' shouted Jamie from afar.

Her eyes clicked open like the instant sight of a doll. What she saw remained in her mind long after most of that week had faded mercifully away. Only that last scene at the pier end was more powerful.

It was Chimaera, just as at Brading. It was small yet, but alive, and enveloping man and boy. For the bag had contained masks, masks of a particularly puerile design, recalling Disney.

Separately they were laughable, ridiculous, but together with the snake kite, and given life by the human bodies beneath, they formed the resurrected Chimaera. There was no Bellerophon, and the snake with its whooping tail thrashed in the air while the earth-bound lion and goat cavorted with frozen features below.

Barbara stared at the open mouths. There was an instant when all three heads were turned to her, leering, mocking and obscene. In that instant, and before she screamed out, there was just that lone figure of a boy on the road far below, next to their car, seen through the pattern of kite and figures.

Even from where she was, she could see the fair hair glinting in the sun, and the knee-length trousers. Geoffrey? Or Stuart? Which?

'No, no,' she rose up and began to run, unevenly, down to Derek and Jamie. 'Stop, for God's sake stop – it's West Wycombe, it's like West Wycombe.'

Her scream echoed round the hill, the words soared into space. The kite plummetted to the ground, the masks were jerked away in alarm. Barbara bore down on them, feet tripping over hummocks of grass, hair like wild woman, mouth like the Potemkin nurse.

Wide-eyed, breathing crazily, she reached them at last, gasping 'the *masks*, you mustn't—' Her gaze was past Derek and Jamie, though, onto the empty road below.

James never knew, and she never told him, why the fun they were having, two boys in masks, with a kite, had to stop on that perfect Friday evening under the blue sky. She just said:

'Bloody idiot – those infantile masks – you could have broken your necks.'

There was something in her manner which told Derek that wasn't it. Later, he put his mask carefully in the car behind the back seat so that she couldn't see it.

Wide open to catch any air which moved, the large hotel windows could not keep the rooms cool. What it was like in the more recent building, Derek could only guess.

The heat had become more intense with the coming of night. Moths fell in love, went insane round lights, reached paroxysms at the still bright pier end. The night air felt like black baize over the water and the town. There were few who could sleep until the chill of dawn crept in.

James lay on top of his sheet, too hot even to feel himself. Sandown would be good, but the week was racing by. He sang softly to himself one of Tippett's Negro Spiritual arrangements from '*A Child of Our Time*' which they'd performed last term. He'd had it on his mind this week.

Next door, Barbara was as far away from Derek on the bed as possible. She told herself it was the heat. One movement and she'd be on the floor. Her mind raced over the last few days, and ended, always, at Hazel Roe via Derek and Stuart.

Despite the heavy heat, she lay cool inside, and this surprised her. For it was not her nature to remain cold, analytical, after receiving final clear indications of her husband's infidelity. Strange, as was everything about this week.

Her reactions to the kite and masks worried her. All so utterly out of character, like her feelings in Osborne and the Roman Villa. Lying in this incubator room, she could almost believe some force was affecting her, changing her.

Derek too? She suppressed again that image of the Chimaera on Headon Hill. Too preposterous. Could Derek's behaviour be ascribed solely to the presence on the island of the Roe family? Not solely, for his oddities had begun well before Carisbrooke. Her mind span round and round.

Together on the dark bed, Derek thought of the morrow. Curse this heat. All right for Edward Prince of Wales, asleep in the cool on the Royal Yacht at Cowes. They'd both need all their strength for the next day. But Derek certainly couldn't sleep. 'Miss Strand, it was my fault, my fault. I'm sorry. Forgive me.' Geoffrey, who didn't need to close his dead eyes, didn't stop Derek's nightmare.

So the Hendersons lay in their two hot rooms. Saturday crept closer in the blackness. The railway signal stood in the corner, propped at 'danger'.

When at last even Derek slept, a trapped moth might have noticed the open-mouthed smile on their face in their sleep. The expression of an imbecilic corpse, soaking with salt sweat.

Funny to die with hand inside pyjama trousers.

SATURDAY

There was no way that Barbara could have got into the driving seat ahead of Derek. She was not good at reversing from the garage yard, so he did it and was therefore already in situ. She could hardly order him out, though she wondered if she should try.

He drove faster today and seemed determined, almost anxious. There was no other trace of abnormality in his present behaviour, but she was aware of a subtle change of appearance over recent days. Not just his increasing untidiness, though he was usually so particular.

'Not another hair wash,' she would say, normally, as he passed with her hair dryer, as if her mission in life was to prick his pride.

'I'm on *show* all the time – a performer. Must be right,' he would reply impatiently.

Now his hair was uncombed. Unshaven for three days, he actually looked dirty, and it wasn't mere holiday use. He had one or two sores near his mouth. She wished she were driving as she watched him at the wheel, hardly slowing for corners.

The car sped on towards Niton: the same smooth route they'd taken to Blackgang, the ocean glinting continuously at them. Derek was conscious of Jamie's whistling. It grew more insistent, and he found himself trying automatically to place the words with the melody of the Spiritual – surely the Tippett version?

Finally, he gave up exasperated, and blurted out, 'Give it a rest, Jamie,' whereupon it faded away.

Derek had half expected Geoffrey to begin before they reached

Niton. This wasn't happening. In fact it was feeling easy, but he knew from the Mottistone episode that this wouldn't last. He steeled himself as they made the sharp right turn at Niton towards St. Catherine's Point, and it was here the tension first began.

Each building they passed was like teeth on a ratchet, the spring tightening ever more strongly. About three-quarters of a mile later was his planned take-off point, and here he was prepared for the biggest battle of his life.

A leaden weight in his stomach, heavier than any dread of an audience in earlier days, now spread to his chest and threatened his arms. He'd heard of people under forty having heart attacks.

He put his foot down firmly on the throttle. Just this short run in, and they'd spring out of Geoffrey's hands, break the puppet elastic. And they'd smash him. Now, *now*, must be, foot hard on floor. Lucky no traffic, no wavering pedestrians.

The car flies forward. Barbara twists sharply, shouting 'What the hell are you doing?' I ignore. Few hundred yards then take-off point, no return, he's beaten.

Done my homework – Ventnor road's sharp left. He's no chance – can't drag us round at this speed. We'll break out at the bend. Then straight to St. Catherine's Point. Seconds now, just seconds. She's screaming. Close my ears.

Oh God, get off the wheel silly cow – you don't understand – stupid bloody silly cow. *They all are.* Somehow keep control. Shoot across junction. Thank God – no traffic.

Road to Buddle Inn. Car shakes crazily. Sixty's too fast, narrow lane, wheels jumping mad. Near the end. Buildings. Tiny track to the Point. But there's a bloody bollard. Not on map. Christ. Can't stop. Footbrake. Too late. Alternative left loop, turn the wheel, turn the wheel. We're dead if I don't. *Already am.* He's won if I do. *Yes, cunt.* Oh God, it's all gone wrong. Swerve left, left. Screaming tyres. They'll burst. Skidding round broadside. A wall, and boy on bike. I'll pulp him. Christ! It's going to hit, going to hit. Wheels grip again. Missed him. Miracle. Barbara's still screaming, 'Stop, you bloody fool, stop.' Grass bank now, low wall on top, red flowers. Slow film, it's all flickered down. Feel head jerking towards car door frame like thrown puppet – is this dying?

James had been whistling: 'My Lord, He calls me, He calls me, He calls me. ...'

Hurt my head on the way to Sandown, standing up in the train. The window was down, we'd stopped at the signal. There was a cottage by a lane and red flowers on a bank. A boy on a bike was flicking flowers with a stick.

The train jerked suddenly. My bag fell over. The mask! I looked down, it was showing. Had to stop Father seeing. Bent down to hide it. As I got up the engine jerked us really hard. Crikey. I was by the door, and hit my head against the window frame, just as the boy lopped off a flower.

When I woke up, the train was in Sandown Station. I was lying on the seat. I got up feeling all dizzy and sick, but it went off when they bought me a cup of tea at the buffet. But my head was swollen all round my ear. Mother was angry because I stood in the train. Father said it was my fault I got hurt. No control, like at nights.

The ache mostly went when we reached the beach. Just as well, because I wanted to feel all right for using the mask.

And for meeting Leslie later.

Barbara had endured enough. She sat angrily by Derek who lay half-dazed on the grass by the road. The car was bent, but a little brute force should make it driveable. Her nerves were shaken, James tearful and on edge. She was embarrassed, self-conscious and was waiting to accuse Derek of attempted murder. She could never trust them to his driving again, ever.

The crowd was melting away, as at Osborne. An off-duty nurse had pronounced Derek probably all right, but urged a hospital check. Barbara had refused her suggestion of an ambulance, once Derek was thought merely to be shaken. He was already half sitting up, head bowed, ashamed, as well he might be.

The police had come and gone. It seemed likely that legal action would follow. The sturdy Morris Traveller looked sadly crumpled on the offside front wing, and the driving seat door wouldn't open at all. They'd have to pile in from the nearside.

Scars in the grass bank, and some mutilated flowers like blood-drops marked the only damage, except to Derek and the car. The boy and the bike had been untouched.

Barbara, impatient for an explanation, fumed inwardly. Three cups of sweet tea had come from the landlord of the Buddle Inn. Something even stronger would have been better. She controlled herself. No point in questioning Derek about the crash yet – she must do it without James.

As if by fate, a woman with two children stepped forward kindly. Would Jamie like to look round St. Catherine's lighthouse with them? 'While your husband recovers, dear.'

Gratefully, Barbara accepted. She could do without Jamie's keen ears, and the woman seemed trustworthy.

They went, James already looking happier. A diversion, not a rest, was what he needed after such an experience, and he looked excited at the prospect of an unexpected bonus.

Barbara was not just angry. She was puzzled and frightened. For, semi-conscious, Derek had mumbled oddly of railways and something nastier even than the Haven Street episode. Luckily, Jamie had been examining the car and talking to the indignant boy with his bike and his audience.

Mr Smart again, and now this Leslie. A nasty sounding pair. All this time, was she denying the most obvious interpretation? Derek was or had been homosexual. Yet there was absolutely nothing to suggest this before, nothing she'd seen. Thinking of the café, he had a problem just the opposite way.

Now he was sounding more bent than the car, and, if so, had been for far longer. Or was it a guilt thing? A guilt caused by Hazel Roe? Or about a homosexual episode in the past? A perversion hidden all these years? A perversion which also included young girls?

No, it was Hazel plus something. But she couldn't accept Derek as 'A.C./D.C.', even remembering his rambling sleep talk. Hang the proof, she'd accuse him of the affair at Sandown. And should have done long before this. Jamie would be out of earshot on the beach, or anywhere, and Derek would not be half-dazed as he was now. Yes, at Sandown.

His reaction would decide her. She'd not torture herself anymore. The strain had obviously produced that Chimaera business.

And as if the clearing away of indecision was responsible, her mind made the most obvious progression of all. A progression which explained everything, including Derek's state of mind.

He had spied the Roes early on in the holiday, probably that first day. Perhaps on the way down to meet Jamie and herself at the pier? Or at Alum Bay? Thereafter, Derek was frantic that he'd encounter them again, this time with Barbara.

It happened, inevitably, and Derek was hit by the husband at Carisbrooke. Since then he was desperate that she, Barbara, would discover the truth. Not just that his affair had lasted for years, but about the unforgiveable. Stuart. Odd that he'd not worried Derek at Osborne, but how scared he'd been on Ryde beach thinking little Geoffrey was Stuart.

Stuart was born in August 1964. She remembered his mentioning his birthday that day at Osborne. James was born in December 1963. You didn't need to be a mathematician. No wonder Derek wouldn't confide in her. 'Stuart Rose's fed up with museums,' were Jamie's words. Or were they 'Stuart *Roe is* fed up'?

The smell of warm grass. An almost indigo sky, but, unnoticed except on the Solent, a quickening of wind. Barbara sat feeling very lonely, her world in pieces. She was sure now. The puzzle was solved.

The truth must be that Stuart was Derek's son.

Men do cry, and not just eye-watering during Bach. Not just the lump in the throat, at the mention of the sunset bugle at the Menin Gate; or *Peccavi* on the viols. No, crying like women when disappointed, hurt or frustrated.

Derek was still inert on the grass. Hot disappointment welled in tears born also of claustrophobic despair: there could be no sharing, no unloading onto Barbara. Understandably, she was distant, cold, and becoming more so. He'd left it too late, as with so much. No escape now. Geoffrey had won.

Derek couldn't think now how he'd even touched, much less made love to Barbara on Thursday evening. Yet the cooling off had actually begun with the book. The first few nights he'd told himself it was emotional strain; after all he was a psychiatrist's paradise, always had been. This Thursday was the only time in weeks that they'd made love.

Geoffrey was killing, soiling everything he touched. A dead Miles corrupting a live Quint. Nastiness in a dead child is horror indeed. Here was rabid infection from a wet grave, the humidity exploding spores spread by the hands of a little corpse, and a mind which refused to decompose.

'Christ is risen, Alleluia,' was now bad news, for evil was now resurrected too. God had not stopped it, agonized Derek. St. Paul said 'If Christ is not risen, then we are the most miserable of men.' Yet it had been better had He died on the cross, for Derek was the most miserable of men because Christ *had* risen. Surgens Jesus, the first fruits of them that slept. Now Surgens Geoffrey, the corrupt second fruit, out from a sepulchre in the sea.

We'll have a few pleasures Derek, you and me. Until tomorrow. Haec Dies. I am your Lord.

Derek felt Geoffrey giggle, a half suppressed, high-pitched staccato giggle as when a chorister farts at Evensong. It was all he could do to avert his face from Barbara. Laugh now and she'd kill him.

Perhaps that would be the solution? Geoffrey and Derek together were too much for one poor mind, one weak body. He felt like a doll with 'flu, a ventriloquist's dummy. And, like Gandhi, a prisoner. Derek remembered *The Times* at the hotel.

Then thought, before Geoffrey took over completely, of the most terrible thing of all: the total loss of God.

ECHO

We've come to Sandown. To a special play area. The noise is awful. Nobody else seems to care, though. This amusement place is in a big dip. The beach is over that bank with rockeries.

My head hurts like in the train. The screaming and shouting makes it ache. Mother and Father have gone for a walk to see some boring plants!

'I'll stay here,' I said, but I'm not going to. There are some hedges and bushes over there to explore. They aren't boring. You know. Mother and Father are miles off by now.

I've brought my mask. That's the kind of fun I like, quiet fun. Leslie the porter wants me to meet him this evening. We're really quiet. Nobody knows we're there. It's ever so nice, and his voice is gentle and soft, like his hands....

Deborah Ransome felt great, and ready to meet Paul. The sun shone on her red hair, smooth and fresh from the fingers of a queer but expert hairdresser. The new style suited her. She knew it instinctively, and was aware of the open admiration in the eyes of men walking towards her on the path through Sandham Gardens.

She had taken trouble with her perfume too, and knew she smelled beautiful everywhere. Her smooth hair was left loose and shortish, and without lacquer, so it was easy to toss her head a little to feel the quality cut settle back, exactly as placed by Charles' exquisite hands. Pleasurable to feel it curve under to touch her long neck.

Each movement brought forth the subtleties of a Chanel fragrance, and she was perfectly aware, too, of the gazes which she inspired behind her. She knew of the effect her legs had on men, and she chose clothes which accentuated this.

Today her perfect buttocks moved smoothly inside tight shorts starting just where the male eye most wanted them not to be. The initials D.R. were conspicuous in badge form on the pure white material, placed in just the right way on the curve of the left thigh.

The result was like a Design Centre award. In that position the badge drew the eye to the area with most merit of all. She knew it well, but would never have admitted it.

The path took her through some tall bushes, winding a little as it did so. For a moment she paused, looking back. Did Paul say the miniature golf course, or was it the canoe lake?

She decided the golf course, and resumed her walk. Used to being watched at all times, she had become acutely sensitive at any hint of an appreciative audience.

There was someone in the bushes up ahead. She knew it rather than saw the movement, and it was of no special interest. Probably a kid. The Chanel Number Five was proving useless against the stink here. As bad as those French pissoirs.

Under her superb self-assurance, Deborah was really quite a nervous being, and what happened next affected her nerves for months afterwards.

The bursting out of the bushes to her left was so sudden that her heart paused in mid-beat. A scream caught itself in her tight throat. The ridiculous lion mask that jumped at her leered sickly, frighteningly; but most horrible of all, it was worn by a naked man with swollen hammerhead gripped in moving hand. His pelvis jerked lewdly at her as he leaned way back on his heels.

She turned to run, but he was there; then the other way, but he was there too. Branches pricked her legs as she backed across the narrow path. The scream would not clear itself. Her stomach contracted. It was a dream; one of those when you can't run and your legs are leaden.

But the rape did not happen. Instead, the man seemed content to stand almost still, once she herself stopped trying to escape. Her shoulders shook, her panic exploded, tears of fear spilling down her cool cheeks. Her sophistication was in ruins. The mask grinned inanely at her, while the stocky figure below it shuddered desperately at last, the papier mâché contorting crazily to one side, the eyes almost glazed. The sun caught their artificial whiteness but failed to melt their frozen orgasmic roll.

For a second or two Deborah and the obscene figure faced each other, her body shuddering, matching his in a lewd dance. But she had to watch him: what was happening was to be watched by a girl.

When it had happened, he stood shivering loosely. Then he was gone, smashing bushes, his urgency lending him ten-league boots, great plunging jumps which must have hurt his naked body.

Crashing foliage became abrupt stillness. *Was* he gone, or waiting, ready for the kill? Panic made Deborah's legs work at last. The leaden weight went, leaving her wobbly as if violated. Her mascara in rivulets down her face, lipstick on her teeth, legs bleeding, she lurched back down the track, from side to side, not able even to step over what was left of him, pale on the path.

Once out of the bushes the scream materialized somehow. Its impact was small at first. Excited children's voices almost covered it, toned it down. It was Deborah's despairing stumble which finally caught attention. She must tell them, must tell them. Then, her foot caught in something and she crashed down, striking her forehead hard on the iron grounds.

So she couldn't tell anyone yet.

The bushes smell, there are flies and someone has spoilt the best place by shitting in it. I'd spoil their camp for them if I had time. Anyway there's another place.

I feel excited, you know, tingly in the stomach. And special below as I undress. More than usual.

Always trousers and underpants first, then my tie off, then shirt up over my head. Vest last. Keep shoes and socks on, might need them quickly. Mother might come along. But today the trousers won't go over them, so off come the shoes.

The air feels good round me, like dry warm sea. Especially round you know where. I walk round my little camp and it feels nice. Now, mask on to wait. There's a hole in the leaves and I can see along the path.

A young woman. She looks pretty. My mother's not pretty, she's ugly. And old. This one's quite close now, short reddish hair, curled under, with a fringe. I like her legs. You can see so far up with those shorts on. And she's smiling with red lips.

She's stopped and turned round. Oh no, don't let her go back. It has to be this one, because of her head.

You know, smooth and rounded, then a ridge, then the neck. She's a beautiful shape. Because it's parted in the middle there's a dent.

Now she's walking towards me again. I jump out like a monster, shivering, but it's not cold. There's more strength than usual, more of everything. Better than before. More like Alec. More like Leslie.

I AM BECOME AS IT WERE A MONSTER UNTO MANY.

Barbara was walking back, though not too quickly, rehearsing her accusation. She'd rejected several cliché-ridden over-dramatic openings. Now she knew what she'd say. She'd say 'Derek, if what I'm going to talk about turns out to be true, I shall leave you ...' She rehearsed it through once again. Her cold anger turned everything grey round her.

It was like walking through a monochrome zoo, children swinging like monkeys, screeching like rare birds; parents, lying prostrate like seals or bears, dozing on the grass. And the fencing everywhere. But all in monochrome.

She still wasn't clear what action to take when Derek admitted his guilt. Divorce was so messy, and what about Jamie? Did Derek's mental problem change anything? She could forgive *almost* everything except that Hazel Roe had borne her child. The boy she'd conceived but lost, James's brother and friend. The greys became flecked with pink.

Derek had caused it all. And now justice. Perhaps a separation to think things over? Would Mummy have her and Jamie? What of his schooling? Perhaps Daddy would help with the money. Or he could leave the choir school. Were there still grammar schools in Hertfordshire?

She turned the corner, expecting to see Derek reclined on their blanket. But all she saw was her *Telegraph* proclaiming more sensation in the Watergate trial, and an Alsatian rooting in the hold-all, Henderson belongings tipped out like truffles by the dog's nose. No Derek. No carrier bag. Then two policemen sprinted by, and the Alsatian bounded after them. She replaced things automatically in the bag.

It really was too much. She was steeled for this moment and now it was gone, and Derek too. Tonight before bed would have to do. But, inside, she sensed it wouldn't happen, for something else was dreadfully wrong.

She began to read 'Foul Play not Ruled out in Wight Tragedy', small on the *Telegraph*'s front page.

My bloody shoes and socks. Can't get them on. Quick. Oh Christ, oh Christ help me – I'll be caught. Gashed my ankle. Blood. She'll tell, she'll bloody tell. Shoes, with no socks. Nobody's looking. Out of the bushes, my shoes rubbing, blood in them, wet and soggy.

It's all so normal. All except me. Oh Christ, say it's not too late. Help me. I'm that panicking man. I'm the filthy boy.

People lying about in the sun, kids playing. Jesus, why don't you help me? Main road. Green Vectis bus coming, says STATION in large letters.

People at bus stop. Looking at me. Stop looking. Bigger bus than before. Pulls up, throbbing, diesel fumes, heat. People staring from windows. 'Look well, look well and see... any way of wickedness in me....' There is, there is and they *all* know. They'll shout as I get on. But they don't, and I step off at Sandown Station slightly less unsteady.

Booking office. Crowd with lolling tongues: the Carisbrooke

mental cases. They're harmless, and allowed out. I shouldn't be. Pervert at large. Comedy film. Some bloody comedy. Stand with them. Blend in with them.

Now the ticket man's looking. He *knows*? Hang on to the group. A patient smiles vacantly, reaches for my hand. No. Can't touch anyone again, even this idiot man, even to protect myself. Some jump up and down like kids when the train appears. Others cling to the supervisors.

It roars in. I loathe its noise. My head *hurts*. Coaches are right-through ones, like the Push-and-Pull, only green. They flicker against my eyes, slowing gradually.

An end seat, slightly away from my fellow lunatics. One or two passengers move away. We start with a jerk. Must think. What did I do before? Where did I go? Back to Totland?

Yes, changed trains at St. John's Road Station. But the Newport-Freshwater line's not there any more. What'll I do? Can't think while that bloody mask is in my carrier bag. Must purge myself of it.

The window's open. The mask flies out, high like the boy's cap, but not through smoke. Nobody noticed. But, fool, they'll find it. I should have buried it. But after Sunday who'll care?

Train jerking, slowing. St. John's Road Station, oddly misty. Storm threat crinkling everything.

We've stopped. Empty platform. Through empty barrier. Out into St. John's Road, I walk automatically west towards tomorrow. High Street. Must do as he did up to Haven Street Station.

These buses go there direct. He'll not know until — don't think it, fool, he'll know. Everything must be on impulse. Mustn't fail again.

The bus pulls in. A queue shuffles slowly into it. But no, it's too soon. Once knew a Miss Strand. ... I feel like a drink. Several drinks. Whiskies. Always could take my liquor. Not like some. Oh God, it's not yet opening time. And shops are closed. All of them. I can't wait for the pubs — he'll know. Even they are on his side.

I catch my bus.

It was the end for Barbara. First the commotion and police.

Then her first feel of fear. 'Rape attempt by Masked Man' someone whispered. The gardens buzzed with shocked rumours. Then somebody said: 'Joker dressed in comic lion mask'. It was enough. Grabbing their belongings and the amazed Jamie from the canoe lake, she ignored loud-speakered police requests for anyone with information to come forward.

She'd not give Derek away, while he was still her husband. But that was it. He was finished this time. Bastard. They bundled into the battered car. We'll get off this cursed island. Grey was now red.

Half-way back towards Totland, she realized. No ferry until tomorrow. And tomorrow was their last day.

'Where's Dad? Have you had *another* row?'

'Don't ask damn stupid questions.'

'Where's he gone then? How's he going to get back?'

'By train. I don't know. At this moment I couldn't care less.'

'But the railway doesn't go to Freshwater any more. Didn't you know *that*?'

Haven Street. Level crossing. It's hot. Sodding flies. My arms flail like lunatics. Fool, mustn't be noticed.

The station's closed. Past the platform, a distant figure picks its way across the lines. One locomotive clanks slowly away onto a siding. Holiday cars pass, but no eyes for me – all for the engine.

That fragment of track went once to Ashey Station, then Ryde. I'll jump the long gate, then that thin fence beyond hot dusty trucks. It's the end of the line. And what's beyond that? Geoffrey.

To break Geoffrey I must reverse 1933, walk *back* from Haven Street along the old track lane through Ashey to St. John's Road, Ryde. No car to crash, no family. But no rails, no help, no whiskies. Just dead Geoffrey and me. Off the end of the old line, I'll be fighting both him and the past.

And he's here, he knows – he's blurring everything. Concentrate. I am *Derek*. I am *Derek*.

Father will beat you if you spoil your shoes. His voice. Outside or in? Both. So it must be now. Up onto the gate. Then jump down into a slow explosion of ballast. I reach the ground in forty years.

I *can* kill him. I can. Just keep going. Barbed wire. Thousands of finger-nails claw, scratch. But can't stop me. No more rail. This is it. Heat on my neck. The sun. Or him? Lumped ballast hidden like graves. Sharp grass tangles. Burrs. Thistles. Swarms of insects rise as I wrench us through low sly brambles.

Feet wet. Blood? Crowding bushes, heavy, smelling voluptuous. Come in. There's Dawn Rollings, frock right up, no knickers. But I plough forward. Always forward, but slower, slower like the recurrent dream. Pick-up ploughing a record in reverse. And time slips, slides. Slow-motion nightmare.

Electric scurryings. Big Brother's eye burning head and neck. I'm stretched round hot glass.

'I hate you, I loathe you, corpse,' I shout, wild, over and over to myself and trees.

Now it's all huge flat leaves. Like water-lilies from some primeval lake. Red *pain*. Ankle on a buried bolt. Another fence. I catch my calf. Trouser rips as I fall, heavily. Miracle, glasses stay on. Lurch up, it's agony but I run somehow. Momentum. Like that Niton bend, but no bloody car.

'Not this time, you sod,' I shout, feeble. Can't breathe, can't breathe. Everything's tight. Can't breathe. There's a storm near. Or is it him?

It rains, huge, warm like solid blood, running behind my lenses. Light's going. Hate helps eyes to see, lungs to find breath. To scream, 'I loathe you, corpse. Every step I kick your balls.' Stitch. Terrible.

His teeth bite, suck. Draw blood. Surely. Good – my pain's his pain. Can't run. Can't run. God. Agony.

But a clearing. Old Ashey Station. Half way. Respite. A place to draw breath, let pain fade, rest against the soft platform. Trains stopped here. So can I. The soaking rain smashes down. But cold numbs, new cold, it fades pain. Even mine. I see again.

Old sleepers, piled rusty lines, cancered creepers. Inevitable old coach, now a peeling shed. A coal bunker on the platform near the house. A shelter. Fields beyond. Still bushes, tall, like old steam turned to foliage. The rain should melt it back but doesn't.

I *can* see again. For he's not *in* me. He can't operate now because my wait is like his in 1933: the down train paused longer than usual. They weren't searching for him. But, crouched under a seat, he wet himself worrying.

The up line's safe enough. The soft mossed platform reassures. No movement though, in the toy station house, like Jamie's 'Brick player' set: red with tiles. That station shed. There's me in the window. But is it him? He's waiting somewhere.

The rain stops. Changed light. Dull metallic, yellow. But the station's changed too. It's not Ashey, it's Bridge Down, the Canterbury-Folkestone line. One of us came up that curved station road, tar-bricked path hot, slippery. Iron railings at the top, but blunted by undergrowth, steam-proof now.

Alien plants wait to burst asphalt platforms. Yellow brick chimneys, corrugated roof. Wooden posts for the canopy. Yes, it's Bridge Down. Between platforms, a lake of lank grass deep enough to drown in. Stillness.

Suddenly, livid Geoffrey reverses the video. Years race and twitter backwards, shrinking undergrowth, freshening paint. Voices, posters, chocolate machines, excited children, buckets, spades. Hats. Picnic bags. Adults with raincoats in case. Porter. Ticket Inspector and barrier. Rails gleam above crisp ballast and fresh cinders. Kent 1933? Or Ashey 1933? Contrived for me? But who's me? I'm Derek. I'm Derek. And Derek must walk on. Out of the end. Have I strength to fight again?

'Why fight?' whispers a voice, 'you're on holiday with Mother and Father. They're waiting on the other platform.'

They are – in a window. The dark mirror? Instinctively, I know they too are a contrived distraction, like Dawn Rollings. All to stop me walking to St. John's Road. I know, but can't resist. 'Tell me, I'm grown up now,' my voice shouts. But they don't see me, they never did. I cross towards them. And a train is coming in hot and fast to my right.

Panic, but I reach narrow land between Up and Down. Hot sucking tempest thunders past my back, shuddering to a heavy halt, hissing, dripping, metal. No escape now – I'm on the wrong side. But still I shout: 'Mother. Father. It's Derek. Please. This Geoffrey – is he me? Me in the glass?'

They don't look. They've gone. But Geoffrey's smirk looks instead, Geoffrey the cheat, staring back, wet dead eyes, green, evil. Corrupt.

He's not me. And he's not in the glass. He's above me, close on the platform. His smile broadens like a diseased Cheshire Cat, mouth gathering oddly. Slowly the lips distend, slowly the putrescence behind threatens to split and burst. Enormous hobgoblin. The dead face a swelling mask. Corruption just contained.

Only now I hear the other screaming train, yards away. I'm dead. Unless I reach Geoffrey's platform. Only a few feet. But vault up to Geoffrey and I'm dead. Or could I reach the platform end? Before the engine? Go on, choose, mocks Geoffrey's steady smile. 'I won't. I won't. He'll not win,' I cry out instinctively from a Golgotha between seconds. Not 'Eloi, Eloi Lama Sabachtani,' but 'I *can* win without you, God.'

And there is an answer. Stand firm. In the engine's path. Hot. Huge. Stand firm. The suck of fear. My throat hurts, screaming, 'Get to your grave, corpse. I've won. *I will not turn, I will not—*' Impact. Yet no impact except boiling wind. Geoffrey's face contorts, cracks to fury.

He gobs large, his tongue uncurling like a chameleon. The phlegm bursts into my face. In one instant, mind numbed by screaming engine, I know the vomit-fear of rail suicide, the absolute evil of Geoffrey, that travesty of Jamie, of me.

Then utter silence. Utter stillness. The serenity of the absolved.

Derek in the lake of leaves and wild flowers. Derek at Ashey Station. It's raining hard, but brightening. Filthy phlegm still runs down his cheek, towards his mouth. Geoffrey trying to re-enter? Wiping it off hurriedly just stops the sick from rising.

He'd beaten Geoffrey? Trembling, shocked, he now knew how poor Tim Wyatt felt on Swallowfield Station last year. Suicide is the ultimate bravery. Yet they call it cowardly.

Geoffrey exorcized. He himself disgraced, wanted for indecent exposure and the Miss Strand tragedy, but surely Geoffrey was beaten and he no longer his pitiful zombie? New strength flooded through him.

At any rate, there seemed no need, now, to slog up that track lane to St. John's Road: Ashey had been enough.

What had Geoffrey wanted of him? Perhaps he'd never know. He thought suddenly of Barbara, and he felt all his love for her. He wanted to go to Barbara and say, 'It's all right now. I've beaten him, you'll understand now.' He wanted to hug Jamie. But what had happened to them at Sandown?

Now to find them. Now to throw himself on Barbara's considerable mercy. But had she any left?

SUNDAY

It was somehow a shock that St. John the Evangelist Church, Totland Bay, should be mere Victorian Gothic, grey and over-neat in the still early light. Disappointing that despite its generous size, the general proportions were so poor.

It was instinct, coming to a church. But he knew it was long overdue. He should have seen a priest at the very beginning, but exactly when was that? His ever more shallow observance of the faith, the seduction of its outward trappings. The arrogance of the cathedral singer. Despite these, God had helped him beat Geoffrey, forgiven the obstinate pride which had brought death, ultimately, to poor Miss Strand.

Derek had slept heavily at the far end of the beach at Totland, past the Warren. It had been dry under the bushes, but he'd woken cold and stiff from a new breeze round the headland. He ached everywhere.

A luckily open public convenience had almost restored him, though he was very hungry. The mirror showed him a battered Derek Henderson, eyes faded, face stubbled. There were scratches over his hands, head and neck. The sores round his mouth looked better though. At least he was himself. He controlled his own body and mind.

There had been nothing but a milk machine outside a grocer's, and he had only enough change for one small beaker-full. Now he was less hungry, but chillier than ever.

Euphoria over his new freedom had cooled in the newly crisp night air on his way back to West Wight. The guilt had come back. That poor girl. The police could hardly have his description from her, except in a novel way, but you never know. He could have been seen rushing from the bushes. Even now there could be an island-wide search going on. And poor Miss Strand. He had brought tragic pointless death to her.

Barbara and Jamie must be faced. Could he bluff it out? The ferry. What time? Midday? 1.15? Bugger. He didn't have either copy of the itinerary. Barbara had both. He'd go to the hotel in about an hour. Presumably they were there. Yes. Prostrate himself on her mercy. Surely, the circumstances. ... Tragic she'd never know how he'd saved them all. What he'd been through.

Meanwhile he needed warmth and comfort. The notice-board provided his second shock. St. John's was 'low' church. It mattered. Bible-thumping had always repelled him. As had wax polish and a vase of flowers, if you were lucky, on a bare Communion table. Now, just when he most needed Anglo-Catholic incense and a high altar it wasn't there.

The church was open for a Remembrance of the Lord's Supper, at eight. It was now seven forty-five. It might be warm, but could he stand the starkly clinical service? He entered the pitch pine vestibule, ignoring the personal evangelism leaflets on the dark wood table.

Derek had not registered the Totland of the Past Exhibition posters outside, so it was a shock to find half the nave filled with it. It was a formal exhibition gallery, not a place to find God. But it felt warm.

There was just a morose verger moving sadly in and out of the vestry. Derek was surrounded by a hundred years of Totland. It was an absorbing collection, demonstrating how Totland had happened because of the hotel, and it because of the superb coastline.

It was *Highways and Bridlepaths* all over again, but compressed into a small area. The same blurred figures, the oddly stark photographs. Modern ones never achieved that etched greyness, that simplicity. That innocence. There was that blurred man in the still street again. Surely taken in Totland?

There were several articles about the lifeboat station, and the proud crew posed stiffly before the First World War. There were views of the High Street and the beach, the hotel looming over all as if painted on a backcloth. The steamer stood at the pier landing stage, its smoke vertical in a windless sky. There was so much frozen activity. Carriages waited at the shore end. Porters with bandy legs heaved heavy luggage for cool clients with sovereigns to spare. Ladies with no 'Lib' to trouble them looked lovely.

Derek moved along to photographs dealing with the reconstruction of the little esplanade, then on to the construction of the church. Time went by. People started to arrive for service, but nobody joined him. It didn't hurt any more, this past. His feeling for the place where wisdom would be found now felt entirely objective, free of Geoffrey's evil pursuit. But now the service was due to begin. That last stand, with its back to him, must wait.

Derek sat in one of the unctuous back pews, shiny with zeal which would never polish candlesticks or crucifix. Towards the front, the small congregation sat forbidding anything wonderful to happen.

At eight precisely, a mournful minister with preaching bands emerged alone from a door in the transept and walked speedily into the chancel in cassock too short and surplice too long. Once in his place at the north end of the Lord's Table, the service was quickly into all the Ten Commandments.

Derek tried, but there was nothing here which spoke to him of mysticism and liturgy. He managed to find private words which said thanks across the stubbornly prayer book service, but his eyes ever strayed back to the exhibition. It was difficult to avoid. He tried the walls. On them were a number of perfect white memorial tablets, on black marble slabs. They had never a Latin phrase between them, but much pious hope.

Then, people were moving sadly into the chancel where the minister stood simply with flagon in hand. Derek got up. Utterly unworthy of the Sacrament, it was because he doubted this *was* the Sacrament that he stepped into the aisle. Even a wafer and a moistening of wine would be welcome. He started forward, past the exhibition stands.

He was last to the communion rail, and received slightly more wine than his due. As he returned back down the green carpet, the shafts of bright sun spotlighted certain areas of congregation. The brass eagle lit up, black Bible on back, ready to speed to the mission fields in Africa.

The last exhibition board now faced him. The sun had

reached this far, and lit the end of the metal and board framework. Heat was reflected back at Derek. There was a marked increase in temperature but only at this point. He was imprisoned before the stand. He forgot the service.

The church was utterly silent. Even the traffic noise did not penetrate. Nobody but Derek was alive. There was pressure building now, like the pier on that first day. The heat was even more powerful, and radiating with it was a faint familiar odour. It sickened him, frightened him, and he knew why.

The display concerned the hotel itself. In the centre were pictures and a page from the *West Wight Gazette*, Saturday 12th August, 1933. A savage pain hit his stomach and pushed pressure up his body into his head, behind his eyes. The hard floor and grey walls swayed round him. The roof seemed lower. Pressure even higher. Surely that was a boy giggling.

The report covered two columns including pictures. It had a prominent headline.

BOY DROWNED IN PIER TRAGEDY

Whilst playing on a home-made raft, by the pier end, last Sunday, Geoffrey Henderson (10) of 22, Poplar Grove, Shepherds Bush London, W., strayed into the path of the ferry steamer at Totland.

The boy's father, Mr Derek Henderson (30) and a pier official, Mr Fred Hunt (25) went to his rescue, but were unsuccessful owing to the fierce current and the danger from the paddle wheel by which the victim had been struck already. The steamer withdrew from the landing stage in order to facilitate the search.

The police were informed, and dragging operations were carried out, but the body has not been recovered to date (Saturday). Witnesses said that the boy was naked, wearing a mask at the time of the accident, and seemed to be playing a game. His clothes were piled next to him, on the raft. The water at this point is about 20 feet deep at high tide, and the boy, who could not swim, apparently lost control of the raft and was struck a series of blows by the paddle wheel before he disappeared.

When interviewed yesterday, Mr & Mrs
Henderson were stunned. They didn't know how
they would cope with Geoffrey's death. Certainly
they could never bear to have another child, even if it
were possible.

Next to the account was placed another, dated one week later.
Under a headline 'Shocking Aftermath to Pier Tragedy', it said
that the complete body was still unrecovered, but how, together
with fragments of the boy's clothing, the head and hands came
ashore under the pier one week after the drowning. Recovery of
the head made identification possible.

The account continued:

The remains extant were interred in St. John's
churchyard. In his funeral address, the Revd.
Ambrose Townsend spoke of a happy holiday which
ended in the tragic death of an innocent child.
'Though deeply shocked, we should try not to be too
sad. Little Geoffrey was now with God, and what
better place could there be than this?'

A formal inquest report was the third item.

Derek could not think or move. He was into the mirror. No
metal brush to hurl, but useless anyway: the glass was closed
behind him now. Little Geoffrey with God? Anywhere but with
God.

When he could move, Derek sat down suddenly in a polished
pew, feeling physically sick. Here was the information he had
craved, in hard cold phrasing, charged with power. He knew, at
last. Knew what Geoffrey had wanted. His brother to play with.
And *he* was his brother. *Brother* to a filthy, undead boy.

His own parents stared at him from 1933. No wonder they
were embittered. But it didn't excuse their treatment of him,
born unwanted. Why, oh why had they never told him? Why
had nobody told him?

Geoffrey smirked from his grey rectangle, wearing his choir
cassock and surplice. Beyond death, he had still waited for his
brother. Waited, until now. But why now? Had he to claim him
from the Isle of Wight?

Anyway, Derek had beaten him, his scheming and his evil.

By reversing part of the itinerary he'd smashed him. So there was nothing to fear. He was off the railway. Safe. Not that he'd have been much use to Geoffrey. Far too old. Catch him being lured onto a raft!

Then the silence exploded. *Jamie. Jamie* was ten. *Jamie* had been playing with Geoffrey already. *Jamie* had said something about a raft.

Oh, what a fool! He cursed himself out loud. It was Jamie whom Geoffrey wanted, all along, arranging that Derek would end up separated from his son. Murdering Miss Strand just as she was about to give him away. He fixed everything, exactly as it happened.

And, even worse, Derek, by fighting and defeating Geoffrey, had signed Jamie's death warrant. However indirectly, Derek was going to kill his son. 1933 would happen again unless he could get to the pier in time.

He lurched to his feet, and ran full-speed down the nave, slammed through the doors, scattering people on the warm pavement. Traffic. Slower. Everything slower except those snatches of radio. Thirties dance music. Old black cars.

People in hats. Lights too bright like over-exposed photoplate. Breathing's more difficult. Turn off High Street. Don't recall those shops. Nearly trip on camera tripod. The panicking man in the street. *Me.* The hotel smarter. More people, all in hats. Worlds of Great Western and Southern, mixed. No colour. But brown, cream, beige. Different smell of air. People strolling. Into tidy grounds to the hotel front. There's the pier, below. Paddle steamer approaching. No time left. Down the grey bank, destroying beige flowers. Thud, onto the cliff path. Then down between brown rocks, miraculously, feet never slipping, down near Turf Walk Bridge. Jolting, not running now. Eyes closing with fatigue. A zombie again, made to lurch for ever. Zombie with crippling stitch and chest pain. The heart will surely burst out. '*Me not him!*' But it's my tiny voice, 'This time me not him.' Pier turnstiles. Once again scattering, knocking people away, plunge through, then over the turnstile, jarring the spine. Ambrose or Roy Fox from somewhere. Now lines of wood stretching away. Like in the Push-and-Pull train. Mr Smart, rubbing his hands, in his cassock and split organist's surplice blowing in slowed sea wind, A.R.C.O. hood proud against the

175

sky. Miss Strand in tweeds, not angry but mouthing me on like a goldfish. No anglers. No peeling paint, rails new, smooth to the bright terminus at the pier's end. I careen uncontrolled. By the rail the boy's mother, but beautiful, like before that filthy war. 'Beatrice, help – the boy – raft—' God let me be in time. Plunge on, jacket streaming. Money tumbles, rings through slats. Now she's running too, but what use now? The pier end. The steamer. My son. O my son. Smoke vertical like Tennyson's monument. A slow sea tornado. Something small sliding, shooting out on salt glass under the pier. A boy paddling, on a raft, naked in a funny mask, a pile of clothing near him. I try to scream out words.

'Look— steamer, the steamer.' But have I a voice? He ignores me, trying to race the ship, surely trying to race it. Flash. Somme corpses, faces wet masks, slime brown.

Plunge down. Lower landing stage. In time to see the raft pushed deep through the mirror and wedge for a moment between the two worlds. Then it disappears under the chopping paddles, smashing the glass into fragments, into liquid, and my boy to pieces. 'Padre, they're not shot – they're bloody drowning in mud. Help me, padre.'

Dive in. Warm green sea. Round the pier timbers. No razor slivers, no chunks of mirror. Powerful swirling and pulling in several directions. But always downwards. Towering steamer. Darkness. I'll be crushed. Salt froth, seaweed, floating things, bits of raft. Then giant paddles reach to chop me, suck me too. I cheat them just. Christ I can't go where he's gone. Through sudden clearer spume I glimpse Jamie's fair head like a sea anemone, deeper, deeper, open eyes like marbles, sinking amidst bubbles. And those other eyes next to them. Jamie's mouth open, the other mouth open too, but smiling, water gushing through as they both sink.

During the nightmare days which followed, Barbara didn't seem to understand that Jamie was dead, insisting that he was injured, lying somewhere near the pier, or swept ashore on the headland. She searched and searched.

Derek kept muttering over and over 'Peccavi, Peccavi', which no-one understood. He wouldn't go near the beach.

The local newspaper account was similar to 1933. Though the style was racy modern, the grammar was inferior. It told the same story, except that no mutilated parts of Jamie had come ashore, nor did they ever.

But the report ended identically:

> They didn't know how they would cope with Geoffrey's death. Certainly they could never bear to have another child even if it were possible.

To Derek the misprint of the name was no surprise.

Barbara decided against telling Derek of her Chimaera fantasy. She burned, after one reading, the letter of sympathy from Hazel Roe, which arrived while Derek was in Dearborn Hospital in the weeks following their return to Swallowfield.

It proved that Stuart was not Derek's child. He had been play-acting about his age at Osborne. It had been his ninth birthday. She had been wrong. Was she also tragically wrong in not believing Derek?

It was fact that Derek's unknown brother Geoffrey had been drowned in identical circumstances in 1933. Fact that Jamie and Geoffrey were both ten. Vile fact that her disturbed husband was wanted for indecent exposure. But she couldn't accept most of Derek's horrible story. It was all just terrible coincidence.

She set about tidying up. It consisted of removing everything of Jamie's from immediate sight. She knew it was an artificial remedy. Everything in life was assessable by logic: she'd had a son; she'd loved him; now she no longer had a son. There could be no more Jamies.

She looked at the holiday slides only once. She had not been able to resist having them developed, the last part of a logical sequence. They were odd. Jamie had moved in each one, for there was a double image every time. She would not ask herself how a blurring could produce apparent difference in clothing, for that would have been to half believe Derek.

She burned the lot, and locked all other photographs of Jamie away in the dark attic. Except one for her locket. Logic finally failed her.

Barbara had been right about Derek's salary. They continued

it during his breakdown. But it was a year before he could enter the cathedral.

The man in the Sandown Gardens incident was never traced. Miss Strand's murder remained unsolved. Barbara returned *Highways* to the library. She didn't burn it as Derek had begged.

On the Friday after Jamie's death, the hotel manager telephoned tactfully. Would they care to collect a few items ...? There was an exercise book.

Derek and Barbara had moved out on the Monday to a nearby guest house, and to separate rooms. To enter the hotel was impossible for Barbara, who went down to the beach one last time, to find Jamie and bring him home from the sea.

Derek entered the hotel with difficulty, and climbed the stairs slowly. Jamie's room was unbearable, but he felt compelled to enter it. Awaiting the next guest, it was clinically tidy. Nothing of his Jamie remained. Except for an old thick exercise book by the bed. 'James Henderson, 1973,' it said.

Derek hesitated, then managed to open it. There was no heading. The first page began:

'This is written in a big diary, but it is a letter to you. It's so you'll know all about me when you come to me. It's in my best writing. Mother and Father. Sometimes I really hate them....

When he had read it through, Derek shuffled in slow motion to their room. The Children's David Copperfield still stood on the shelf. They had taken the railway signal downstairs already. He looked through the open window. A tiny Barbara was down under the pier, pacing, searching. The tide had gone, the pier end was empty: there was no steamer, no reflection.

But the bright new mirror gleamed above the dressing table. Derek managed eventually to look into it, and saw but himself. From a long way off, perhaps from Swallowfield, came 'Peccavi', on sonorous viols. But there were voices mingled with them and with the sound of the sea:

> When David heard that Absolom was slain, he went
> up to his chamber over the gate, and thus he said...

There was a momentary pause forty years long, matching his own emptiness. The echo waited in Swallowfield Cathedral.

The rooks waited to fly in the Precincts. Seaweed floated round the pier. A lift of wind fingered the unkempt grass on the bank, and on a plain mound in St. John's churchyard. And then the high haunting of Saville's voice:

'... O my son, Absolom, would God I had died for thee' caused the mask to split into hot tears.